Mystery
at
Lovelace
Manor

BOOKS BY CLARE CHASE

Mystery at Lovelace Manor

CLARE CHASE

Bookouture

Published by Bookouture in 2022

An imprint of Storyfire Ltd.
Carmelite House
50 Victoria Embankment
London EC4Y 0DZ

www.bookouture.com

ISBN: 978-1-80314-201-2
eBook ISBN: 978-1-80314-202-9

For Doreen, with love

PROLOGUE
LOVELACE, SUNDAY 15 MAY

It was a warm May afternoon and crowds were spilling over the grounds of Lovelace Manor. Its annual festival had played out there for hundreds of years, ever since a long-dead lord of the manor had thrown his gardens open to mark the occasion of his marriage. The Lovelaces had plenty of money in those days; the entire hamlet had come along, eager to eat, drink and be merry.

The initial event had repeated, marking anniversaries, then morphing into a yearly ritual, celebrating spring in all its glory.

The event was no longer free of charge. The manor's current owner, Diana Pickford-Jones, felt exhausted as she looked at the hordes who'd bought tickets. Lovelace Sunday was crucial. They made more money that day than any other, and heaven knew the manor needed it. She dashed from stall to stall, checking on arrangements. The scene blurred in front of her. Only the festival's special event that year was in sharp focus: a balloon launch to commemorate an airman who'd lived at the manor. She straightened her shoulders, trying to release the tension which pulled across her back as she thought of it.

But for others near her, the magic of Lovelace Sunday was still working. A regular, who'd attended since he was a child, felt sick with anticipation. On the surface the occasion was a bit of fun, but he knew the legends: that Lovelace Sunday made you lucky in love. The occasion coincided with spring. It symbolised fertility, birth, regrowth, and promise, wrapped in ancient rites and myths. His hopes had been pinned on this day for months. He'd made up his mind to propose to his girlfriend when the festival was in full swing. She must say yes, surely, on Lovelace Sunday? And if she did, it would give them luck for life.

He was pleased the weather was auspicious: warm and sunny with clear blue skies. Frothy cow parsley danced amongst the long grass in the wilder corners of the manor grounds. Birds were nesting in the climbers that smothered the garden's mellow stone walls.

Mentally, he rehearsed his offer of marriage, tweaking it for the twentieth time.

Across the grass, a first-time visitor wandered the grounds. She felt as though she'd walked into another world. All around her, men and women wore leafy green masks, danced and rang bells, weaving in and out of the shrubs and trees. There was a lot of laughing, some teasing, and a certain amount of kissing. She felt a tingle of excitement and giggled as she joined the rest, slipping through an ancient arched gateway, ribbons streaming from her hair. Her heart beat faster; she was caught up in the moment. She watched the man in front of her, sporting a top hat adorned with green and purple feathers. He wasn't the only one. Everyone looked strange, attractive – exotic.

There was a hint of magic that was thrilling yet eerie.

But like most visitors, she wasn't only there for the ancient traditions. She knew the TV historian, Cammie Harrington, was on site. Cammie had been staying close by for weeks now – there to delve into the past, researching a documentary about two former Lovelace residents – Louisa and Seth Pickford. The papers were full of her; she always attracted attention. She wasn't the sort to sit poring over old manuscripts in isolation. She relished adventure – involved herself in the past as actively as she could. Her plan to recreate the Lovelace aeronaut's flight had been the talk of the hamlet for weeks. Just last night they'd discussed it in the pub. Now, the visitor's feelings of anticipation met with reality. A hot-air balloon sat in an open field to one side of the majestic but crumbling old house. She had watched it fill and rise as the burner did its work. As it took shape, her stomach fluttered. She couldn't wait to see Cammie take off.

She glanced at her watch. The time was getting near. Some of the revellers continued to dance and flirt, but she made her way towards the field and the balloon. Her tingling sense of excitement increased as the crowds flowed round her, all moving in one direction.

Cammie was already there, clambering into the balloon's basket, her eyes glimmering, excited. She'd bucked the trend and come in a suit and top hat, rejecting the ribbons and flowers. All around her people were calling out, asking questions, verifying details, nodding, gesturing. The air seemed to prickle with expectation.

A helper who'd joined Cammie briefly climbed back out of the basket, leaving her alone. She looked happy with that: confident, in control. Not like the owner of Lovelace Manor, who stood nearby – she looked strained, though that was understandable. The health and safety paperwork must have been a nightmare.

'Ladies and gents!' A man spoke through a loud hailer, so that everyone hushed. 'It's almost time for lift-off!'

But at that moment, a tall blond man dashed up to the balloon's basket. 'I'm coming with you!'

The watcher held her breath. Was Cammie's adventure going to be a romantic one, as well as daring? It was like a film.

There was a mischievous look in Cammie's eye. 'Oh you are, are you? Don't you ever give up?'

She laughed, but the owner of Lovelace Manor shouted something about insurance. It would be miserable to spoil their fun, but it was all right. No one was taking any notice. Lovelace's gardener offered the blond man a leg up. Everyone was whooping, calling out: 'Yes! Yes! Go on! Go on!'

And before the owner could get near, the balloon lifted off the ground, its burner roaring, bright and fierce. It was awe-inspiring – the sheer force of it. Next to her, a man in a top hat grinned at her expression and she grinned back.

She remembered that moment, looking back. It marked the end of before.

And then there was afterwards. Trying to take in what had happened and unscramble her memories, caught in a fog of horror.

People had been all over the place. Some close at hand, some scattered in the grounds. It was hard to tell who was where, or even who was who, as most people wore masks.

But the images would never leave her. The balloon on its ascent, still low over the gorse bushes. Someone in the crowd shooting a streamer cannon into the air. The multicoloured ribbons of paper reaching Cammie and her passenger in a frac-tion of a second. The sight of them landing somewhere between the basket and the balloon. Cammie, startled by the unexpected event, but returning her attention to the gorse below. Her blond companion's gaze following the streamers.

And a second later, the man jumped. It all happened so quickly. She hadn't been able to grasp what was unfolding.

Without the man's weight, the craft had shot up, gaining altitude so quickly. A second later, she realised the basket was on fire.

The balloon was high. Far too high for Cammie to jump safely. But the basket was engulfed in flames and smoke, and at last Cammie had jumped. She remembered the sickening jolt as she'd landed.

There was one final image, etched on her memory: the balloon deflating, a moment after Cammie had leaped clear. In seconds, it and the remains of the basket crashed to earth as well.

1

TWO DAYS EARLIER

Eve Mallow was one of a gaggle of volunteers following Diana Pickford-Jones around the grounds of her grand old moated house, Lovelace Manor. It was three miles from Eve's home village of Saxford St Peter, and was one of the oldest continually inhabited houses in England, a rambling place which dated back to medieval times. It had been added to over the years, and the 'new' wing was Tudor. Eve found it fascinating: it told a story of all the generations who'd made their mark on the place. But no one had done much to it over the last century – there'd been no money to spare. It was the reason the volunteers were there.

They were helping to prepare for Lovelace Sunday, a key fundraising date on the manor's calendar. Saxford St Peter's vicar was distantly related to Diana Pickford-Jones and had put out a rallying call for helpers. Eve hadn't needed asking twice. She'd been meaning to visit the manor – it looked so atmospheric whenever she drove past – and she was meeting a new collection of people into the bargain. So far, as well as Diana and the volunteers, Eve had been introduced to Diana's half-brother, Sebastian Pickford. He'd been brought up at the manor and was still a frequent visitor, when he took time out from his modelling career. Eve was also getting to know this year's special guest, the TV historian Cammie Harrington.

Eve was an obituary writer by trade, and people-watching was one of her favourite pastimes. Nothing was more fascinating than working out what made someone tick. Normally, she had to rely on the testimony of surviving friends and relatives, of course. The chance to volunteer at Lovelace was a special treat; everyone she was interested in was alive.

She was especially curious about Diana and Sebastian. The half-siblings were in such an unusual situation: Diana was the current owner, responsible for the manor that had belonged to their father, battling to make enough money to keep it going. But Sebastian would inherit in the fullness of time; he'd end up benefiting from her hard work. Diana was seventy, harried and worried-looking, Sebastian thirty, very aware of his good looks and social standing. They might have been close – Diana was old enough to be his mum, and had been around throughout his childhood – but Eve could imagine resentment building up, if she did all the work.

Cammie Harrington piqued her interest too. Not because she was a celebrity especially, but because of her daredevil reputation. The newspapers described her as an adrenaline junkie. She was renowned for re-enacting dramatic exploits, and Lovelace Sunday would be no different, what with her balloon ride. She got her hands dirty too – she was there with the volunteers. She'd been helping with everything from litter picking to scrubbing grubby stonework. Eve admired her for it.

The balloon launch wasn't part of the standard format. The annual occasion was centuries old, but these days it was famously associated with the love story the manor was known for – that of Diana and Sebastian's great-grandparents, Louisa Lovelace and Seth Pickford. The aeronaut who'd lived at the manor pre-dated them by two generations and no one had bothered celebrating him until now. He'd been a keen amateur but never achieved any world firsts.

Diana was retelling the love story as she showed them the grounds.

'It was at the end of the nineteenth century that the daughter of the house, Louisa, fell madly in love with a dark and handsome man called Seth Pickford. Unfortunately, they were star-crossed lovers. Seth was the family's gardener and certainly not the match Louisa's father had in mind.' Diana's brow was furrowed, as though she was finding it difficult to concentrate. She must have told the tale countless times before. 'Pa Lovelace watched his daughter like a hawk. Her mother, Cecily, was dead, so all his attention was on Louisa, especially as she was an only child. One sniff of the relationship would have meant the sack for Seth. He and Louisa had to court in secret in the manor's walled garden.' She gestured ahead of them. 'We'll visit it presently.

'Louisa was young and passionate. She was only sixteen when she eloped. She and Seth used the hubbub of that year's Lovelace Sunday to escape. It delayed the discovery of their flight. That's how the event became associated with their love affair.

'Louisa's father was devastated but also furious. He felt rejected. Louisa and Seth lived hand-to-mouth, constantly looking over their shoulders for Lovelace servants who might come after them. But in fact, the old man cut his losses and removed Louisa from his will.' This was met with much tutting and sighing. 'The manor was already destined to go to a cousin as the closest male heir, but Louisa would have been a wealthy woman, if it weren't for her elopement.

'But the story has a happy ending,' Diana continued. 'The cousin was a romantic who was already rich, and he gifted the manor to Louisa and Seth when he inherited it in 1899.' Someone clapped their hands together. 'The rest is history; the couple lived happily ever after, and the manor passed to Pickford offspring.

'Everyone loves a real-life fairy tale. It became legendary, giving rise to a popular folk ballad and even a play.'

As well as volunteering, Eve was helping directly with the fundraising, thanks to her second job. To support her uncertain freelance journalism, she worked part-time in Saxford St Peter's teashop, Monty's. Viv, the creative genius behind the place, had brought her in to bring order to the operation. Aside from people-watching, organising was one of Eve's favourite pastimes; she'd quickly discovered that Viv was allergic to it.

Three months earlier, a long-term volunteer had found an old bun recipe in the manor kitchens and someone had suggested bringing Viv onboard to bake batches to sell on the day. She'd insisted on adding some secret ingredients to improve the taste ('I'm not putting my name to them otherwise.'), and Diana had given in. Viv's version was a heck of a lot nicer.

But this year, it was Cammie's balloon ride that would really draw in the visitors. Advance ticket sales were excellent.

Diana had moved on to talk about the balloon launch now, as she guided them through the grounds, following the route Louisa had reputedly taken when she'd eloped with Seth. 'We're expecting a lot of press, of course.' She looked straight ahead, her jaw taut.

That would be down to Cammie. Both the balloon ride and her planned documentary about Louisa and Seth were attracting attention.

At that moment, Saxford St Peter's storekeeper Moira Squires stepped forward. Eve and Viv exchanged a quick glance.

'Here we go,' Viv said, under her breath.

Diana continued to stride ahead, but Moira turned to Cammie. 'Getting the press interested is such a coup. We're ever so grateful to you.'

'Anyone would think she lived here,' Viv muttered. 'Talk about acting lady of the manor.'

In fact, Moira had stepped into the breach as chief volunteer just a week earlier. A woman called Irene Marston, who'd fulfilled the role for more than a decade, was out of action due to a sprained ankle. She and Moira were old buddies, and Moira had been quick to spot the chance to become kingpin for a couple of weeks. ('It's the least I can do at a time of crisis,' she'd said. 'You know me, Eve. I don't like to push myself forward, but if help's needed...') Her sister was minding the store in her absence.

Moira was still beaming her gratitude at Cammie, all gracious patronage. It made Eve squirm, but the historian seemed to take it in her stride. Her sleek chestnut hair shone in the afternoon sunshine. 'I wanted to give something back. Diana and Peter looked after me like one of their own when I stayed here last.'

Peter Pickford-Jones was Diana's late husband. The struggle to look after the manor must have been all the greater since he'd died two months earlier; the grief would be so raw.

As for Cammie's previous stay, the Suffolk papers had been full of it in the run-up to her current visit. She'd lodged at the manor five years earlier while she filmed a documentary about Suffolk's smuggling history. (There had been sword fights on the beach and a daring bareback ride across country.) The manor was open to paying guests; any way to make money was embraced. But for her current stay, Cammie had opted to lodge separately. Viv's brother was renting her a place called Lavender Cottage in the hamlet of Lovelace-by-Sax. He owned the stables in Saxford St Peter, and dabbled in property.

Cammie's choice of accommodation made Eve curious. She imagined Diana would have hosted her for free, under the circumstances. But perhaps she wanted her own space, or somewhere with mod cons.

Cammie turned to Diana suddenly. 'I really appreciated it, you know: the way you looked after me.' She was rubbing her wrist.

The message mattered to her, Eve reckoned.

It was a moment before Diana spoke. 'I do know. I didn't realise quite how much at the time but now I do.' She held the historian's gaze for a moment but before Eve could wonder at her odd words, Sebastian Pickford broke the silence in a stage whisper.

'Give something back? For pity's sake, a balloon flight's got nothing to do with my great-grandparents. Lovelace Sunday's all about Louisa and Seth Pickford these days, but now apparently it's a celebration of the brilliant Cammie Harrington instead.'

He was at the back of the group as they walked across the lawn, Cammie and Diana at the front, but Eve was in no doubt Cammie would have heard. She wasn't the only one. A young woman with long red-gold hair dropped back to speak to him, her hand on his arm, her voice low.

'Cammie's really very nice you know, Seb. I've spent a lot of time showing her round the house and she's so friendly.'

'And she could make a difference to Lovelace's fortunes,' an elderly volunteer said. Her tone was hushed too, but a lot harsher. 'You should be grateful. After all, it's your inheritance, as you keep reminding everyone.'

Sebastian turned to the older woman and smiled. 'Of course, you're right. I was forgetting myself.'

The woman still looked stiff and severe.

'Please forgive me.' He stepped forward, hanging his head, his tone sincere, his look utterly contrite. 'I must have got out of bed on the wrong side, though it's no excuse.'

There was a pause, but then the older woman nodded, her face softening a little.

As he turned away, he indulged in a private eye roll. Eve

didn't think anyone else had seen. A moment later, he was smiling down at the redhead. 'As for you,' he patted her hand, 'you make me the best I can be.'

Nice line. Eve wondered if he'd read it in a dating manual.

The younger woman entwined her fingers with his and gazed into his eyes.

A second later he'd half turned so he could address both his critics. He grinned sheepishly, then said in an undertone, 'You must admit though, Cammie is a little bit irritating, isn't she?' His look was conspiratorial.

The older woman's lips twitched as the younger one flipped him on the arm. But it was a playful flip. He'd won them both over.

Eve assumed the redhead was a girlfriend. Sebastian didn't deserve her. She'd seen him chat up one of the younger volunteers earlier, his deep brown eyes on hers, a smile playing round his lips. Eve wouldn't trust him as far as she could throw him, and he looked quite heavy.

As for his outburst about Cammie, the elderly volunteer was right, it made no sense. Eve had heard him boast about inheriting the manor mid-flirt. He had every reason to be glad Cammie was there, boosting visitor numbers. It made Eve wonder if something had happened between them on her previous visit.

Perhaps that was why she'd chosen to lodge elsewhere.

2

Diana Pickford-Jones had ignored her half-brother's remarks. It was one way of dealing with his rudeness, though in her place, Eve would have shown him up to the best of her ability.

'For visitors, the key areas of the grounds are the gateway over there,' she pointed at an arched opening, 'and of course the walled garden.

'Louisa, Seth and Seth's half-brother Edwin – another servant – left the manor for good via the gateway. Edwin had to go too, of course. He'd have been thrown out otherwise, because of his brother's actions. But they stuck together and looked after each other. People like to walk through the archway for luck, and first-time visitors will probably ask you for directions.' She walked up to the archway and pointed to its surround. 'You can see how smooth the stone is here. A result of year upon year of people touching it for good luck.'

She walked back towards the volunteers. Her eyes were on Cammie for a second, but then she focused on the wider crowd. 'And everyone will want to walk through the walled garden, so we try to keep people moving. Come and have a look.'

They filed after her, through another gateway.

The walled garden was idyllic. Sun shone through the dripping golden flowers of laburnum trees, recently in bloom, framing Eve's view. Beyond, a sea of purple alliums contrasted the yellow. Pathways wove between the flowers and shrubs, their gravel dappled with sunlight.

'It's peaceful now, but it won't be come Sunday.' Diana sounded rather grim. 'Our gardener, Josh Standish, has been working day and night, with wonderful results as you can see.' She nodded an acknowledgement to a swarthy man with dark eyes and deep brown hair who stood leaning on a fork. He'd been interrupted by their entrance; Eve had a feeling he resented it.

'Oh my word,' Viv muttered, her eyes on him. 'Moody, yes, but a bit of all right, don't you think?'

'I'd like some of you to stay here and check for litter,' Diana said, relieving Eve of the need to reply. 'We have visitors in most days, and they shed tissues like cats shed fur. But we're closed tomorrow for final preparations. A quick check then should finish the job.' She counted out a group which included Eve, Viv and Cammie.

'Sebastian, perhaps you could take a group over to the kitchen gardens and check the situation there.' She turned to Moira. 'And you'll stay here while I deal with the home covert, will you?'

The storekeeper nodded and stood up straighter, like a child who'd been made pencil monitor.

Diana walked out of the garden with a handful of volunteers.

Moments after she'd left, Sebastian went with his team, which included the redhead. Moira peered after him, frowning. 'You know, Eve, I think Diana made a mistake, letting him include the pretty young lady he was flirting with in his group.'

'The red-haired woman?' Eve said. Maybe they weren't a couple yet, after all.

The storekeeper shook her head. 'No, the brunette with the unsuitable top.' Her lips pursed.

It had to be the young volunteer he'd been flirting with earlier. Eve might have known.

'The red-haired lady is actually his girlfriend,' Moira went on. 'Irene says she's a treasure. But unfortunately, Sebastian has a wandering eye.' She tutted. 'Sapphire's sure to notice sooner or later. Irene's worried she'll get fed up and leave him.'

Eve exchanged a glance with Viv. It sounded like just what Sebastian deserved. 'I suppose these things happen.'

Moira nodded. 'But Irene says Sapphire's a valuable asset to the manor. Did you know she's custodian of Millingford Hall? She knows all about historical buildings and how to turn a profit and she's giving her advice for free. I promised Irene I'd do my best to keep her on side. Of course,' she sighed a little, 'young men will sow their wild oats.'

Eve felt her temperature rise. Moira's opinions were out of the ark. And the girlfriend's welfare should come first. The thought of her being groomed so she could sacrifice herself for Lovelace's future left a nasty taste in the mouth.

'You'd think Sebastian would be straining every sinew to make the manor pay too, if he's down to inherit.'

Moira nodded. 'But from what I've heard, he sees it as Diana's affair while she still owns the place. Of course, it's understandable. He's ever so busy with his modelling. Have you seen his work? Irene showed me his photograph in *Vogue*. A most handsome young man, I must say.'

Eve was a believer in handsome is as handsome does.

'He looked ever so dashing,' Moira went on, her eyes dewy. 'Irene says advertisers always make the most of his heritage. Seth Pickford was such a romantic hero.'

It sounded as though he owed his career to the legend. *How irritating*. If he was in *Vogue*, he must make a good living from Lovelace without doing anything to rescue it. Poor Diana.

Eve turned to start work, scanning the borders and path for litter. It wasn't long before she'd found three receipts, two tissues and the lid of a biro.

She was distracted by an eager volunteer who'd appeared in front of Moira. 'I just found this.'

It was a smart black jacket.

'Oh, thanks ever so much!' Moira took it and the volunteer beamed. Eve was surprised Moira hadn't patted him on the back. 'Now, where did you find it?'

'Hanging on the arm of a bench. It was half hidden behind a rose bush.'

Moira examined the garment. 'This is real leather.' Eve glimpsed a designer label. 'Someone will be missing it.' She fished in the pockets. 'Now what's this? Some sort of ID – a membership card. *Leonora's.* I wonder what that is?' She frowned. Moira hated not knowing anything.

Eve was stooping to pick up a sweet wrapper, but she glanced up out of curiosity. The card looked swanky – gold and embossed.

'Pamela Graves.' Moira frowned. 'I'm surprised she hasn't called us to ask about it. Still, I suppose we can manage to trace her through this Leonora's place if nothing else.'

But Josh Standish was at her side and held out his hand for the jacket. 'I'll take care of it. It's no trouble.'

His tone and expression had softened. Moira simpered and Eve cringed.

'What a blessing that Diana has you in charge of security as well as the grounds,' the storekeeper said.

'I was born to it. My dad handled it too, until the day he died.'

Eve wondered if he'd worked into old age, or if his death had been untimely. As for Josh, his inheritance must involve long hours and responsibility. Eve hadn't seen any other gardeners on site.

'How does he cope?' she asked Moira, as Josh walked away. 'There's plenty of garden to be getting on with, without finding time to sit in front of a bank of security monitors. Although I haven't seen any cameras around...'

The storekeeper leaned in and lowered her voice. 'There's no money for them, according to Irene.' She shook her head. 'Diana's lucky to have her volunteering so willingly. It's very gracious of her, but of course, her husband was well off. She busies herself with committees and charities.'

'Is it me,' Viv said, as Moira retreated and they got back to work, 'or are we surrounded by weirdos?'

'Hush! We're going to have to work on your whispering skills.'

'Ha-de-ha. Seriously though. And I'm not just talking about Moira, though if I hear her say "Irene says" one more time I may have to gnaw my own arm off. But Diana, for instance. She's wound up so tight I think she might snap. She barely seems with us half the time. And the gardener might be good-looking, but he's scary.'

Eve nodded. 'Fair point. There's something odd about the dynamic between Diana and Cammie, too,' she glanced over her shoulder to check the historian was out of earshot, 'and as for Sebastian...'

'I'd so love to take him down a peg or two.'

'Same.'

By the time they'd checked the flowerbeds for litter, Diana Pickford-Jones had reappeared. 'Perhaps it's time for a break.'

'Of course.' Moira was at her side in an instant like a faithful spaniel. 'Now,' she turned to the group of volunteers, 'who'd like to slip up to the manor and fetch the tea things?'

Eve waited for her to add 'spit spot!', like Mary Poppins.

. . .

Five minutes later, Eve crossed the driveway that spanned the moat. She was ahead of the other volunteers, bound for the kitchen where she'd been told she'd find trays of soft drinks. She paused to peer down into the water. It looked deep and dark.

'Anything could be lurking down there,' said Viv, who'd caught her up. 'Perhaps they've got a Lovelace monster.'

Eve laughed. 'Maybe.' But as she spoke, she glanced up at the crenellated turrets of the gatehouse, and thought how forbidding they looked. They might not have any monsters here, but there was a heck of a lot of history. A place didn't exist for as long as Lovelace without drama and turmoil in its past.

As they entered the manor, the quiet, dark interior seemed to engulf them.

'It's this way, I think.' Eve found herself whispering as they made their way along a panelled corridor.

It was as they neared their goal that they heard voices.

'Someone left their jacket in the walled garden.' That was Cammie. She must have left the group sooner than Eve and slipped back indoors. 'I thought maybe you were up to your old tricks, using this place to charm your way into some young woman's knickers.'

Eve pulled up short and Viv followed suit, bumping into her and raising an eyebrow.

'I do wish you wouldn't talk like that when my girlfriend's visiting.' That was Sebastian's upper-class drawl. 'I'm not the lothario I was back when you lodged here. I've only got eyes for Sapphire now.'

'Oh yeah, right. That poor woman.' Eve could hear the shake in Cammie's voice. Anger, barely controlled.

'In any case, can you imagine me using the garden to woo my dates? Josh would beat me to a pulp. He's so damned precious about it.'

Eve could imagine the gardener being territorial.

'So you're telling me you've grown up? Forgive me if I don't buy the personality change. And your flirting's the least of your sins. Sebastian, I know what you did. I only understood the truth the last time I visited.'

There was a long pause.

'Your actions required the worst, most despicable sort of guile. I don't know how you could. Does Diana know what you did? Does Sapphire? You appal me.'

'I have absolutely no idea what you're talking about.'

But his confident drawl had morphed into something less certain, his pitch rising a notch. A moment later, Eve heard the kitchen door creak, and footsteps approaching.

She indicated a doorway and Viv followed her through so they could peer from a safe distance. They avoided Sebastian by seconds. He was muttering to himself, anger robbing his face of his usual good looks.

'Interfering witch. If only the moat had a ducking stool. I'd take great pleasure in watching you drown.'

3

The following day, Eve arrived early at Lovelace Manor and parked her Mini Clubman in the front drive. She'd been preoccupied with Sebastian and Cammie's row overnight, thinking of it each time she woke. By six, she'd given up on sleep. Diana had made it clear the volunteers were welcome as soon as they could get there. There was plenty to do before the following day. Moira had said it was all right for Eve to bring her dachshund, Gus. She'd spoken as though she was doing Eve a special favour...

Eve met Gus's soulful brown eyes as she released him from his travel harness. 'You'll have to stay home tomorrow though.'

He gave her a mournful look.

'It's for your own good, buddy.' He'd get overexcited, and she couldn't watch him properly when she was on bun detail.

From where she stood, Eve could see Josh Standish's cottage – a small, squat building of worn brick with lattice windows. It was as though time had stood still. Eve didn't imagine it had been brought up to date any more than the manor had. The house must go with the job; his role and his home life connected, 24/7.

Eve spent her first hour at Lovelace continuing the litter check, this time in the woods. It was peaceful and cool under the trees, birdsong the only sound. But by the time she'd covered all the paths the air was warming and voices floated towards her on the gentle breeze.

Cammie Harrington was standing by the bridge over the moat. She looked the picture of health, her hair glossy, cheeks rosy, and was downing a Lascelles smoothie – a posh sort stocked by an upmarket health-food store in town. Cammie was in the habit of bringing her breakfast to the manor too – muesli in a plastic pot. She paid attention to her nutrition.

Eve shifted focus and turned to Viv, who was putting up their bun stall.

'Need a hand?'

Viv shook her head. 'All done. Moira's asked if I can help clean the loos next.'

'Ugh. Bad luck. Still, if you make a good job of it, she might give you a sticker.'

Viv stuck out her tongue and marched off towards the house.

'Ah, Eve.' Moira was bearing down on her. 'Perhaps you could help Raven prepare.'

'Raven?'

Moira indicated a young woman with straight jet-black hair that reached well below her shoulders. She looked elven in her floating ankle-length dress, like something out of *The Lord of the Rings*. 'Raven Allerton. She's a professional storyteller. Irene says her association with Lovelace goes way back.' The storekeeper lowered her voice to a whisper and said, 'I under-stand she performs in a bell tent,' as though it was rather embarrassing. She seemed to have forgotten the time she'd worked under canvas herself, telling fortunes at the local fete. But perhaps she thought it didn't count if it was in aid of charity.

'It'll need putting up and decorating with all her bits and pieces,' Moira added.

Eve walked over to Raven and introduced herself.

'Thank you for the offer,' the woman said, standing straight and regal. 'There's a lot to do, but it all feels worth it when the children arrive. I like to take them away from their everyday lives. Make them forget.'

Before long, Eve and Raven had the tent up. Eve had to make an effort to focus on the guy ropes and pegs. She found Raven distracting: light on her bare feet, she seemed to flutter from place to place. Eve wondered if she always moved like that, or if she was in character. Her hammered silver rings (several on her fingers, and one on a toe) caught the light. She wore a delicate floral armlet too.

'I like to have the doors to the tent wide open,' Raven said, as she tied them back. 'I can't bear rules. I want the children to come and go as they please. Join in if they like. Heckle, cheer. It's so important for them to be heard.'

Eve would have had reservations about the heckling, but each to their own.

'Here' – Raven handed Eve a half-moon of sleigh bells – 'I'm going to strew these around. There are some musical elements to the stories – a bit of audience participation.' She grinned. 'Have a go now if you like. I hate the way adults feel too shy to join in. We should all be able to express ourselves.' She took a flute from an indigo velvet bag and started to play.

They were surrounded by volunteers. Not only was Eve expected to let rip and sound her bells, she was required to do it at just the right moment, so it blended with Raven's tune. She gave the bells a hesitant shake. She was perfectly happy to march into a roomful of strangers and chat, but unselfconscious bell-ringing was beyond her.

Raven paused and laughed. 'You don't need to worry. There aren't many adults who can just let go.'

Her words stung, and Eve's resolve strengthened as Raven continued to play her strange and haunting tune. At last, she developed a way of tapping the bells gently so that they didn't fight with the flute.

A couple of children – offspring of volunteers – had migrated to the tent and sat down. They stared up at Raven and she managed to twinkle at them, her eyes smiling as she played on. When Saxford's vicar, Jim Thackeray, passed through, he patted Eve on the back, then grinned and did a little dance.

'You're an excellent influence, Eve,' he said, peering at her from under his bushy white eyebrows. 'I shall whistle as I work today.' Then he lowered his voice. 'Do you think Diana's all right? She seems very preoccupied.'

Eve nodded. 'I thought that too. But it must be hard, coping without Peter for the first time.' As her distant cousin, the vicar knew all about Diana's circumstances.

He frowned, his eyes far away now. 'Poor woman. Perhaps that's it.'

After he'd moved on, Raven stopped playing.

'Come back soon,' she said to the children at her feet. 'It'll be story time at eleven.' She wore no watch and her long dress lacked pockets for a mobile. Instead, she glanced up at the sun.

Really?

She stowed her flute in its bag and turned to Eve. 'It's been a few years since I've performed at Lovelace Sunday, but the volunteers like it if I do a practice run the day before. The kids here with their parents are usually after entertainment.' She shook her head. 'At least they get the weekend free. I hate the thought of them stuck in the classroom, week in, week out, when it's so glorious out here.' She lifted her arms to the sky and put her head back, staring into the blue. 'Our learning's narrow. We miss so much.'

'I suppose children can run around after school, though.'

Eve agreed that spending time outdoors was crucial, but there was a balance to be struck.

Raven waved a hand. 'Ugh. In between all that pointless homework. Do you have children?'

'Adult twins.'

'Here in England?'

'That's right.' The question was understandable. She still had her American accent. She'd been born and brought up in Seattle, swapping the laid-back city for frenetic London as a student. She'd stayed on to marry and raise her family. Her toad of an ex, Ian, had walked out but she never regretted their marriage for an instant. The twins meant everything to her. 'What about you?'

'Oh no!' She laughed. 'I love children, but I wouldn't want to be tied down.' She didn't look old enough, anyway.

Already a collection of children was trooping back to the bell tent, ready for the story Raven had promised, though it was only ten to eleven. But Eve was distracted. Raven's voice had risen a little as she'd talked about her desire to remain a free spirit. *Curious...*

As Eve glanced around, she saw the gardener, Josh Standish, had appeared. He was standing close to the moat, not far from the bell tent, talking to Cammie Harrington. Something told Eve one or other of them had been meant to hear Raven's words.

'My, you're all so keen.' The storyteller's bright blue eyes were on the young children at her feet. 'You want me to start already?'

There were cheers.

'But what about the other children? I told everyone eleven!' She was laughing. 'All right, all right then.' Another glance at the sky. 'It is very nearly eleven now. Why don't you get comfy? This isn't school. You don't have to sit up straight. Stretch out if you want to.'

Some of the older ones sprawled elaborately and a toddler stuck his bottom in the air, all to laughter from Raven.

A moment later, she sat down cross-legged and began her tale. It was of witches and goblins and a shade more frightening than Eve would have expected for the age group of her audience, but it certainly had them spellbound. Eve counted seven open mouths. All gazes were fixed on Raven.

Until there was a loud splash from outside the tent.

With the flaps wide open, they had a good view of what was going on. Eve wasn't immune – she turned to look just as the children had. She saw a pile of clothes where Cammie had been standing, and Josh Standish looking down into the moat.

'Can you reach the bottom?' he called.

'Not yet! It must be deep.'

'Best keep to the surface. Safer that way.' Cammie had all his attention.

A boy of about four had left the storytelling tent and was on his way to investigate. Three more children were standing or half standing, their eyes turned towards the garden and the splashing from the moat.

'Children!' Raven's tinkling laugh rang out. 'There's more story to come.'

But even the ones left in the tent were getting restless now.

Raven played a short refrain on her flute, but it wasn't enough to focus their attention. Witnessing her failed attempt left Eve feeling awkward. She was worried about the smaller children getting close to the moat, too. She scrambled to her feet just as Josh realised he'd got company and turned to head them off.

'Back to the tent!' His face was stern.

As Eve approached him to collect the children, she looked down into the water. Cammie had disappeared. She felt her stomach knot. 'Could she have got into trouble?'

Josh turned to look and at that moment, the historian's head appeared above the water.

'What happened?' Josh's voice was sharp and anxious.

Cammie laughed. 'I just dived down to see if I could touch the bottom. And I could.'

The gardener's face was taut. 'Best not do that in front of the kids. Maybe you should come out.'

'You're such a stick-in-the-mud! But, oh hell. You have a point. I'll go and swim around the other side, so I'm out of sight.'

She ploughed off, moving swiftly through the water.

'I should keep an eye on her.' Josh left Eve with the escaped children.

He looked genuinely anxious. Of course, Moira had said he was responsible for security. Perhaps that covered health and safety too.

Raven had joined Eve and taken the hand of the lead escapee. She kept a close eye on those still in the tent, Eve noticed.

Uncertainly, the group allowed themselves to be guided back inside.

The spell had been broken though. The children were laughing, talking about Cammie and her swim. One of the toddlers was saying 'splash' over and over again, increasing the volume each time. Eve looked at Raven to try to share a laugh, but her focus was entirely on her capricious audience. Eve could see the anger in her eyes.

'Children,' Raven said, after a moment. 'I've got something to show you.'

She turned her back and was busy at the rear of the tent. 'Who wants to see first?'

One of the older more biddable girls had followed her, leaning in close to find out what Raven had.

'Close your eyes. I want it to be a surprise.'

The girl did as she was told and Raven put her own hand over the girl's and opened it, dropping something into her palm.

In a second, the girl screamed, flinging her arm down, her fingers outstretched, body shuddering.

Eve saw a large black spider dart across the tent floor, its thick legs scurrying. Raven must have noticed it earlier when they'd been setting up.

There was a collective gasp from the children. Several of them, including the girl, were in tears.

'Oh my goodness, don't you like nature?' Raven's smile told Eve her stunt had had the desired effect. 'Here, look – there's no need to be frightened.'

Eve watched as the storyteller leaped lightly after the hairy black spider and picked it up again. For a second, she held it and looked at the children. Almost all of them cowered.

At last, she blew the spider a kiss and put it out of the tent.

Rushing back, she lifted the girl who'd screamed onto her hip. 'I thought you'd like to say hello to it.' She pouted. 'Poor spider.'

Eve found her duplicity chilling. If Raven was that keen on spiders, why risk that one's life by putting it into unsuspecting hands? The girl might easily have squashed it in her fright.

'Why don't you come and sit back down, and we'll start a new story?' Raven said. 'Stay close to me and if there are any more spiders, I'll put them out for you. How's that?'

The girl clung on to Raven and nodded. Several of the others were holding on to the folds of her long dress, their eyes wide.

Within moments, she had them all quiet again, hanging on her words once more. She told them a story of a worldly adventuress who came to visit a peaceful manor in a quiet hamlet. The adventuress upset everyone, poking her nose into their business, stealing their friends and lovers, hogging the limelight. Until one day the manor's staff and inhabitants saw her for what she was and hounded her off their land, pelting her with rotten tomatoes.

Eve had worried the ending would be a lot more sinister. But the rotten tomatoes had the children laughing, just when Eve had feared tears again.

The children wouldn't work it out, but the story was transparently about Cammie. Eve was certain Raven was fantasising about a worse punishment for her than rotten tomatoes too. Was this seriously just because Cammie had robbed her of her audience?

And what about the lengths she'd gone to in order to get it back?

4

Eve caught up with Viv at lunchtime. Diana Pickford-Jones had laid on sandwiches and fruit. The volunteers filed into the kitchen to fetch trayfuls and carry them into the grounds.

'How were the loos?' Eve asked, after she and her friend had filled paper plates and found a patch of shade to sit in.

'Not as bad as I'd thought.' Viv picked up a triangle of cheese, tomato and chutney. 'Truth to tell, I don't think visitor numbers are that high normally, so they manage to stay on top of the cleaning.'

'When you say "they"?'

'I gather Diana does them, with the help of the mysterious Irene, when she's not laid up with a sprained ankle.'

'Heck.' The set-up really was precarious. 'Diana's seventy – she might wish she could retire. She must have been working hard for a long time. And as for Irene, I guess the "chief volunteer" role isn't all glamour.'

Viv grinned. 'You said it. But from what I hear, she made the manor her mission ten years back when her husband died. She brought him as a visitor when he was ill, apparently. Looking after him meant dropping her other interests, so she was desperate for a focus when she lost him. Moira says the husband left her a lot of money. She hasn't had to work.'

'Just as well.' It was clear there was no money to pay an employee at the manor. The grand title of chief volunteer was all Diana could offer. Eve was torn between sympathy and feeling it was exploitation. Her mind drifted irritably back to Diana's half-brother. 'Sebastian doesn't seem to do much, even when he's here. I'm surprised Diana doesn't put her foot down if he's due to inherit.'

'Me too. From what I can gather his only contribution is to charm the guests when he happens to be around. I overheard him claim he's upped visitor numbers, but a handful of his conquests won't turn the place around.'

It must be frustrating for Diana, seeing him get so much attention in the modelling world as Seth Pickford's descendent while she struggled to keep the manor afloat.

'How's your morning been?' Viv asked.

Eve told her about the storytelling session.

Viv's mouth formed an O. 'I can't believe she behaved like that.'

'She certainly didn't like Cammie stealing her limelight. Or Josh trailing after her.'

'I've got relevant gossip there.'

Eve raised an eyebrow.

'Raven skipped the last four Lovelace Sundays, but before that, she and Josh were an item. It only lasted six months, but it sounds as though it was intense.'

'I can't imagine it being anything else if Josh was involved.'

'I hear you. Those brooding eyes...'

'Concentrate, Vivien.'

'Yes, well, anyway, the same person who told me about them reckons Josh has been trailing round after Cammie ever since she turned up. I stumbled across them earlier,' Viv went on. 'He was watching her every move. I'd say he's smitten.'

'If Raven skipped the last few Lovelace Sundays because of Josh, the break-up must have hit her hard. Seeing him and Cammie together can't be easy. But all the same, she was cruel and manipulative with the kids.'

Viv shuddered. 'She sounds like a dangerous character.'

'Floaty on the surface, but vicious underneath. And needy.'

After they'd finished their lunch, Eve and Viv went to join the other volunteers by the bridge. Diana Pickford-Jones was there, ready to dish out the afternoon's instructions. She waited for more people to report for duty, her jaw tight, the shadows under her eyes dark.

Cammie arrived almost immediately, accompanied by a tall, well-built blond man with sculpted cheekbones.

'So how *is* it going? Really?' He was addressing Cammie.

The historian raised an eyebrow. 'I've told you before, I'm not commenting on my research. You can wait and watch the documentary like everyone else!' She was laughing, but shot him a sidelong glance at the same time, a knowing look in her eye.

'You're a hard woman. If you don't watch out, I'll sneak round to your cottage and go through your papers!' The blond guy was grinning.

'Ha! No point. You won't find anything. And my conclusions are all up here.' Cammie tapped her head.

He raised an eyebrow. 'Can you at least tell us if you'll be able to raise Lovelace's profile?'

Diana Pickford-Jones went very still. She wasn't the only one listening for an answer. Her layabout half-brother and Josh the gardener's eyes were on Cammie too.

'Oh yes,' the historian said. 'I can *definitely* promise that. And that's all I'm saying. A documentary loses its punch if everyone knows the content beforehand.'

A moment later, Sebastian's girlfriend Sapphire took her leave.

'I'm so sorry I can't stay on for tomorrow. This wretched event at Millingford Hall is badly timed.'

Sebastian leaned in to kiss her and stroked her arm as she gazed up at him. His look excluded everyone else, as though she was the only woman in the world. But the moment she'd turned towards the driveway, he was winking at the volunteer he'd been targeting previously. Eve felt her heart beat faster, anger bubbling up inside her.

Cammie took one look at Sebastian's antics, then ploughed past him and jogged to catch up with Sapphire. He looked untroubled, though his gaze flicked briefly in her direction.

It was Moira who trotted after her. 'Cammie, can I ask for your help?'

But Eve didn't think Cammie was going to be deflected. 'Don't worry, Moira. I just want a quick word with Sapphire.'

The storekeeper returned to Eve's side, shaking her head. 'I feel I shall have failed Irene if the word is about Sebastian.' She stood biting her lip as the pair talked.

Cammie's frown was intense, and a moment later Sapphire turned to look at Sebastian, but he had the situation covered. He'd distanced himself from the woman he'd been flirting with and was chatting to a male volunteer. Cammie shook her head and gave Sapphire a quick hug.

'She's not going to believe Cammie, is she?' Viv said despondently.

'I'm afraid not.'

Eve spent most of the afternoon fixing laminated signs to posts. As she went to fetch another, she caught sight of Raven. She'd abandoned her storytelling and was pursuing a man with short dark hair and horn-rimmed glasses. The man overtook Eve, moving at pace.

'I'm sorry, Raven,' he said. 'I haven't got time to talk today. I need to speak to Cammie Harrington about our interview. There are some details I have to finalise.'

The storyteller trod lightly after him, her dress trailing in the grass. 'You know the producer. The station promised me an answer months ago. We're talking local radio. It's not as though I'm asking for a slot on the World Service.'

'Sorry, Raven,' the man said again, more irritably this time. 'I'll get it in the neck if I don't get the Cammie interview sorted. It's a big win for us – you must see it takes priority.'

Eve watched Raven's fists clench as she hurried on past. Half a minute later she flung her hands down to her sides in a gesture of despair as the man from the radio station reached Cammie.

Eve and the other volunteers worked hard into the evening, lingering over slices of pizza followed by toasted marshmallows as the sky turned dusky. In the distance, Eve saw the tall blond man with the sculpted cheekbones again. What was he up to, sneaking into the woods? They'd already agreed to call it a night. Curiosity got the better of her and she stood, ostensibly to fetch a cup of squash from the drinks table. Once she was level with it, she could see the path the blond man had taken, and there beyond him was Diana Pickford-Jones. She must have joined him using a more obscure route. She glanced left and right, as though to check they were alone. Eve looked down quickly. Was Diana trying to keep tabs on Cammie's progress with her research? Had she put the blond man up to asking her, because Cammie was being cagey? But if so, she'd heard the result. Cammie had told him nothing. So why meet now, and in secret?

'You're taking your time.' Viv had joined her at the drinks table. 'Raven's being weird again, by the way.' She jerked her head towards the manor.

Close to the bridge over the moat, Cammie stood talking to Josh Standish. To their right, a little further from the water,

Raven was staring at them. Eve could see her side-on. She'd drawn herself up tall, her gaze fixed on Cammie's back. Cammie and Josh talked on, oblivious.

As Eve watched, Raven clutched her armlet and twisted it, muttering under her breath. Eve didn't believe in magic, but the effect was still chilling. She was pretty sure Cammie was being cursed.

5

Elizabeth's Cottage, Eve's seventeenth-century home in Saxford St Peter, provided a cocooning effect that evening. The house was cool and calm, with a thatched roof, thick walls, and beams that curved over Eve's head as she lay in bed. She always felt like they were protecting arms, arched over her.

But despite all that, Eve couldn't entirely switch off. Thoughts of the tensions at Lovelace Manor swirled in her head. It was clear that Raven hated Cammie. Eve wondered what had triggered it. Raven was highly strung; she could imagine her blaming others for her troubles. Could Cammie have been instrumental in her break-up with Josh Standish? But it didn't seem likely. The historian had moved back to London after her previous stay at Lovelace. There was no hint that she and Josh had kept in touch. But Raven might still be jealous now. And of course, Cammie was getting a lot of attention from other quarters; the man from the radio station had brushed Raven aside as he looked for the historian. Eve imagined she'd been incensed. She'd seen how much Raven hated being ignored.

And Cammie in her turn was livid with Sebastian Pickford.

She'd clearly met him on her previous visit, and not been impressed. Then a recent realisation had left her almost speechless with anger. What could explain her words in Lovelace's kitchen? *I know what you did. Your actions required the worst, most despicable sort of guile.*

No wonder Cammie had spoken to Sapphire about him. The sight of his flirting must have tipped her over the edge.

After Eve's uneasy mind had pored over that scene, it flitted to the sight of Diana Pickford-Jones, exhausted and distracted, meeting secretly with the mysterious blond man with the sculpted cheekbones, and Irene, the absent chief volunteer, using the manor to blot out her grief and loneliness. Going about her role with an intensity born of desperation, perhaps. Happy to let Sebastian get away with murder so long as it didn't affect Lovelace's future.

Eve must have dropped off at that point. She didn't remember anything more until she woke in a cold sweat at three in the morning, her heart pounding. She thought she'd heard footfalls outside her bedroom window, down in Haunted Lane. According to legend, they were echoes from long ago. Back in 1720, a hue and cry had been sent to scour the village for a poor servant boy who'd stolen a loaf of bread to feed his starving siblings. Legend had it the mob had chased him like a pack of ravening wolves, desperate for blood. If caught, he'd have faced the gallows – all for trying to protect his family in the most desperate circumstances. Elizabeth, who'd lived in Eve's cottage back then, had taken the boy in and hidden him in a tiny chamber under her floorboards. Periodically, Eve was overtaken by the terror the boy must have felt. The hue and cry had searched the house. One sneeze, one creak, would have given him away. And he must have feared Elizabeth would buckle under the pressure of their fierce questioning. But she'd stood her ground and at last the men had left. Later that night, Elizabeth had rowed the boy across the River Sax, allowing him to escape. He'd found new work and sent money home to help his siblings. Elizabeth's grandson had renamed the cottage in her memory and she was celebrated in the village to this day.

Eve loved living in her house – her story was inspiring – but hearing echoes of the hue and cry was said to signify danger. As she got up and parted the curtains, she heard Gus whining outside her bedroom door and went to let him in.

'There's nothing there,' she said. Dreaming up the ghostly echoes made perfect sense. She'd gone to bed ill at ease, thoughts of hatred and rivalry filling her head.

But that doesn't explain Gus's wakefulness, a tiny internal voice said.

She shook her head. Maybe Gus had heard the floorboards creak as she got out of bed. That would make sense.

But it took her a long time to sleep again.

6

Eve had been right to leave Gus at home. Although she'd heard huge numbers were expected, she hadn't been able to imagine the reality of Lovelace Sunday. The noise and hubbub was everywhere. It felt chaotic too, with almost everyone in disguise. The manor grounds were a sea of Louisa Lovelaces with flowers and ribbons in their hair. They wore long flowing dresses and delicate masquerade ball-style masks.

To her discomfort, Eve was no exception. When she'd first heard about the tradition of dressing up she'd found some Venetian masks online. Although she'd still feel like a jerk wearing one, they were at least well-made and attractive. But Viv had been horrified at buying something commercial and had nagged her into making her own.

'So much prettier,' her friend said now, looking at the wonky bit of card Eve had managed to fix in place using elastic.

'I hate it.'

'You can't see that you made it from a cardboard box. You look beautiful. The green sets off your brown eyes perfectly.'

'Hmm.' Viv looked spectacular – both mask and hair green

– though she wasn't the only one. Lots of visitors had used temporary dye for the day.

'Laughable,' Viv said. 'If you're going to go green, do it like you mean it.'

It was just as hard to identify the men striding through the manor grounds. Many of them were in top hats decorated with green and purple feathers. Some had dyed their beards to match and they wore green masks too.

Eve and Viv's stall was busy. Someone had suggested the Lovelace buns might bring luck and they'd had queues ever since. They'd been taking it in turns to sneak off and explore.

When Eve got her break, everything was in full swing. The queues to get into the walled garden were long and the one to move through the archway snaked around stalls selling circus equipment, silver jewellery and crystals. Raven ought to be pleased. She had crowds of children in her storytelling tent, spilling out onto the grass.

As Eve wandered round the moat, she could see Cammie's hot-air balloon, not yet inflated, standing in a neighbouring field. It had been delivered early that morning. She glanced at her watch. Four hours until lift off. The dream of the night before played uneasily in her mind.

At that moment she heard a splash. Peering into the water, she realised Cammie was swimming again. Her hair was wet; Eve had the impression she'd just come up for air. The historian raised a hand when she realised she'd been spotted.

'Waving not drowning.' She laughed. 'I thought I'd take a quick dip while everyone's busy.'

'Good idea.' If Eve had a balloon ride ahead of her, she'd be making notes about procedures, or checking her equipment or something. That and feeling sick.

Eve had strolled on, past stalls selling hand-painted stones and tealight holders, when she caught movement out of the corner of her eye. She turned to see Cammie emerge from the moat. She was looking left and right quickly, her hands clutched to her body. A second later she'd grabbed a towel, holding it awkwardly, pulled about her with one hand. She managed to crouch on the bank, so she was almost out of sight, and appeared moments later, clothed, a frown on her face, the towel held to her front. Glancing around again, she made off across the grass.

What was she up to? Eve felt twitchy, watching her make for the manor's exit. She was due back at the bun stall in five minutes, but on instinct, she followed Cammie between the stalls. No one would notice her nosiness; she blended with the crowds, weaving between them to keep up. At last, Cammie left through the main gate. Maybe she was nipping home – back to the house she'd rented from Viv's brother. Eve wasn't the only person to notice her go. She spotted Sebastian, who was chatting up a woman dressed as a fairy. (Did fairies normally wear fishnets?) He was masked like most people, but hatless, so his bronze wavy hair gave him away. He glanced at Cammie as she passed and followed her with his eyes as she left the grounds. Eve also spotted a tall well-built man in a top hat staring after her. Eve thought it was the guy she'd been chatting with the day before – the one with the sculpted cheekbones who'd pressed her for details of her research, and met secretly with Diana Pickford-Jones. And lastly, Eve saw Josh Standish, policing the entrance of the walled garden. He had a hand on the shoulder of someone going in, but he raised his eyes as Cammie dashed out.

At last, Eve returned to the bun stall and switched focus to serving the customers.

An hour later, Diana Pickford-Jones appeared at Eve's side. 'No one seems to know where Cammie is.' Her voice was tense, shoulders up. She took a shaky breath and Eve was convinced she was close to tears. It must be a huge responsibility dealing with Lovelace Sunday, especially with so much riding on its success.

Eve was about to explain she'd seen Cammie leave when the historian reappeared, close to the bun stall, hair dry, eyes sparkling. She'd opted to wear the same costume as most of the men: a dark suit, black feathered top hat and green mask.

'I suppose I'd better take a look at the balloon!' she said as she passed the stall.

Diana looked after her, her hands clutched together, twisting.

7

During Eve's early afternoon break, she went to look at the dancing. Diana had kept an area clear for the purpose and a small band was playing folk music.

It was like a game, trying to see who she could recognise in their costumes. Jim Thackeray, Saxford St Peter's vicar, was obvious. No one else would career around the dance floor in that abandoned way. He was partnered with Moira, who was blushing like mad under her mask. Her dour husband Paul stood with his back to the spectacle. You'd never get him on a dance floor.

Eve could see her neighbours from Haunted Lane, Sylvia and Daphne. Sylvia's plait was flying as she swung round, laughing.

As the fiddlers stopped their playing, the vicar slumped into a chair to one side of the dancers, roaring with laughter, and Moira spotted Eve.

'Ah, Eve dear. There's someone I'd like you to meet.' She cast her eyes over the crowds, then dashed to a portly man with the most incredible ears. Eve guessed he might be around twenty years her senior. A moment later, Moira had put her arm through his and was leading him to Eve's side. 'Eve, this is Harold Bromley. I've been thinking for ages that you'd get along. Harold is a funeral director, so you'll have lots in common.'

Seriously? Eve tried to quell a sour look. She wrote about life, not death.

'May I have the pleasure of the next dance?' Harold said, as the music began again.

'Um, of course.' There wasn't much else she could say.

The Lovelace folk song floated through the air. Eve had only learned the legend of Louisa and Seth recently, but Viv had assured her the tune was familiar to people in Suffolk and beyond. It was a shame the legend wasn't enough to make the manor financially viable.

Harold spent the dance telling her about the last three funerals he'd arranged, and what he had planned for himself when the time came.

'I love considering the details.' His eyes were sparkling. 'It's nice to have control over everything. Perhaps you'd like to come and visit the funeral parlour? It's like a second home to me and I'd love to show you round. Any day, any time. Just let me know when's convenient.'

Eve hesitated. It was difficult to say 'never' tactfully.

'In fact,' Harold filled the pause, 'you might like to discuss your own arrangements while you're there. We could have a look at some caskets over a glass of wine? And then I could take you out for a bite to eat perhaps?' he added hastily.

Eve wasn't sure if she was being offered a date or a sales pitch.

'What's all this?' said a voice at her shoulder. A masked man in a top hat was grinning down at her. 'Going on a date with someone else?'

Harold blushed. 'Oh. Oh dear me, I *am* sorry. I understood from Moira... but I can see she was mistaken. I certainly didn't mean to...' A second later he bustled off, dashing between the dancers.

The masked man took Eve's hand and she followed him to the woods, just next to the field. A second later, he was leaning in to kiss her as the music, which now seemed magical, played on.

She kissed him back, but then remembered herself.

'Robin! I can't believe you just did that in public.'

'It's too tempting. Especially when someone was about to whisk you away.'

'I was just working on my exit strategy.'

'I sensed that. I thought I might be able to help.'

She grinned. 'Much appreciated.' But then worry struck. 'Though Moira will be asking questions when she hears back from Harold. Half the village will know someone saw him off.'

It was a problem. Robin was Eve's secret lover. It wasn't for any of the usual reasons, but because he had a secret of his own. One that could endanger his life if it got out. These days, he was Saxford St Peter's reclusive gardener, but he'd once been Robert Kelly, a police detective in London. Uncovering a network of corrupt officers and their criminal contacts had forced him to take a new identity. Under his assumed name, he'd made a career of his hobby, though he still helped the police covertly. If the villagers knew he and Eve were in a relationship they'd pummel her for information about his past. He'd been in Saxford for over a decade now, but it was still a cause for speculation. Eve would have to lie, and lie convincingly, to protect him. She'd decided it was too big a risk, so they kept their relationship on the down-low. In the village, only the vicar knew the truth about his background, and just he, Eve's neighbours and Viv knew about their secret meetings.

'This is your first time at Lovelace Sunday, isn't it?'

She nodded.

'It'll be full of people asking each other out. You could explain me away as a stranger who decided to try their luck.'

'If I do, she'll probably tell Harold it's back on.'

Robin frowned. 'Maybe I could be a new boyfriend from out of town?' He bent to kiss her again. 'I'm not sure it has to be this way, Eve. We could take a risk—'

He still had her in his arms and the effect was powerful. She ached to be with him properly. What had begun as a liking had unfurled inside her, developing into physical desire and now, though she tried to damp it down, into love.

She hadn't told him. Hadn't dared. And she didn't dare agree to relaxing their secrecy either. What if his old enemies found him because of her? She took a deep breath. 'Don't worry. I'll explain you away somehow.'

He laughed, but then his eyes turned serious as he took her hand and kissed it. It was such an old-fashioned gesture. It made her think of Seth Pickford wooing Louisa Lovelace. How did Robin look so good in a green mask?

After another flurry of activity at the bun stall, an announcement went round via loud hailer that it was time to assemble for the balloon launch.

Eve and Viv put a cover over the buns and turned to walk towards the field.

'I'd love to go up in a balloon,' Viv said.

'I'd hate it. How could you be certain where you'd land? You can't plan properly with something like that.'

Viv rolled her eyes. 'Don't you ever let go?'

'Certainly not.'

Not everyone was rushing towards the balloon. Eve could see some couples were too involved in each other to pay any attention, and there were children scampering around in all directions, despite their parents' attempts to corral them. But most people were making their way in that direction – even

Raven. Eve had wondered if she'd stay in her tent, given her feelings towards Cammie.

By the time Eve and Viv reached the edge of the balloon field, Cammie was in the basket and some kind of helper was climbing out. Cammie looked excited, high almost. Eve thought again of the press's description of her: an adrenaline junkie. Everyone was shouting, calling out questions and instructions.

'Ladies and gents!' Silence fell at the announcement. 'It's almost time for lift-off!'

But then suddenly, a tall man ran through the crowd towards the balloon. His top hat fell off as he went, but he ignored it.

Without it, Eve could see him better. It was the blond man with the sculpted cheeks from the day before. The one who'd asked Cammie about her research and sneaked off to talk to Diana privately.

He approached the balloon, calling out: 'I'm coming with you!'

Eve could see the flash of Cammie's smile. 'Oh, you are, are you? Don't you ever give up?' She was laughing.

Diana rushed towards the balloon now, one hand to her head. She was shouting something about insurance.

But the crowd was with the blond man, and Cammie seemed happy to have him aboard. A chant of: 'Yes! Yes! Go on! Go on!' started up.

Josh Standish was giving the blond man a leg up and Diana fell back, white-faced.

Moments later, the balloon was airborne. Eve was struck by the fierce flame from the burner. Cammie was busy, making everything shipshape as her companion waved and grinned at the crowds. The craft was low over some gorse bushes as it left the field, the masses following it, determined to keep it in close sight. Cammie joined the man now, waving too.

At that moment, someone from amongst the Lovelace

crowds shot a streamer cannon into the air, making Eve jump.
Its contents went high and fell into the balloon, coming down
around the shoulders of Cammie and the blond man.

He looked into the basket, and seemed to shrink back,
distracted, whereas Cammie's gaze was outside the balloon,
fixed on the ground below.

For a moment, Eve couldn't see what the blond guy was up
to. A fraction of a second later, she watched in utter confusion
as he leaped over the side of the craft. They weren't high up and
the thick vegetation cushioned the landing blow. Eve caught
movement and knew he was all right, but Cammie wasn't.

The balloon shot up as soon as he jumped, his weight light-
ening the load. Eve saw Cammie leaning over the basket's edge,
a look of horror on her face, one of the streamers still over her
shoulder. And then, behind her, Eve saw smoke.

The basket was on fire.

'Oh no, oh no, oh no,' Viv whispered, over and over again.

It was far too high to risk a jump now. Seconds passed. Eve
guessed Cammie must be trying to control the craft and extin-
guish the flames, but it was taking too long. The black smoke
billowed out.

At last, Cammie did jump. It seemed like the only option,
Eve guessed. She landed with a sickening bump on the grass
and lay still.

A second later, the balloon deflated. It and the badly
burned basket landed nearby.

The press were on site of course. The radio journalist from
the day before and a local TV crew too. And multiple people
from the papers. Eve's stomach twisted as she watched their
clamour. All the cameras were pointed at Cammie's body and
the wreckage.

8

Eve stood shaking in the field, her arms covered in goosebumps. First aiders pushed their way past camera operators and journalists, reaching Cammie first, but there was no help for her. She lay unprotected from the glare of the media and onlookers, who had their cameras out too. A moment later they reached the blond man.

It wasn't long before they were joined by paramedics. They rushed to Cammie's side too, but shook their heads in turn. Moments later they erected a screen around her body, but it was far too late to stop the horrific photos that would end up online.

And then the police came, marching across the grass. Eve could see Detective Sergeant Greg Boles. He happened to be married to Robin's cousin and was the only member of the local force who knew his past.

Greg used the loud hailer to call everyone to order.

'Ladies and gentlemen, please remain in the field and form three separate queues at the tables my colleagues are putting out. I'm sorry for your distress, but we'll need to take your details before you leave in case we have to follow up. It's not yet clear what led to this tragic event. We'll be with you as soon as we can. I'd also ask the person or persons who fired the streamer cannon to come to my table. You can jump the queue. You're not in any trouble, but we need to speak with you.'

Could the streamers have led to the fire? Maybe they'd caught in the burner, and allowed the flames to spread, but Eve couldn't imagine the thin strips burning for more than a moment.

Greg moved to one side, taking a seat at the first table.

'Oh no.' Viv's voice was shaky. 'Palmer's here. That's all we need.'

Eve and Detective Inspector Nigel Palmer had history. She could see him bearing down on her now. Despite his seniority, he often spoke to her in person – mainly to make sure she remembered her place.

'Ah, Ms Mallow,' he said as he reached her. 'I thought it might save time if I talk to you before you start playing amateur detective. We've no reason to think the incident today was anything other than a tragic accident. The forensics team will check, but *if* there's anything to investigate – which I doubt – we won't need your assistance. Have I made myself clear?'

'Abundantly, Inspector.' Eve tried to relax her shoulders and steady her breathing. 'Though I hope to write Cammie Harrington's obituary.' It was horrible to state it so bluntly, so soon after her death, but Eve was determined to get the work. Cammie had been a fascinating livewire. Eve needed to pay tribute to her. And if she'd been deliberately killed, Eve wanted to know why. She had inside information – it would be wholly wrong not to use it. 'I'll be interviewing her contacts as usual if I get the commission. I presume you'd like me to tell you if I stumble across vital evidence?'

It was perfectly possible. She'd be talking to the exact same people as the police if Cammie's death turned out to be murder.

'I'd like you to stop interfering, Ms Mallow. There's a difference between "stumbling across" and ferreting, as I'm sure you're aware.'

He turned on his heel and made a beeline for Diana Pick-ford-Jones.

'He's such a numpty,' Viv said. 'Do you think it was murder?'

'If so, I don't know how it was done. I don't imagine it's easy to sabotage a hot-air balloon, and it was only here since this morning. But the place has been milling with people, and I've already come across two who might have wanted Cammie dead.'

'Sebastian and Raven?' Viv said, as they moved over to the shortest queue.

Eve nodded. 'Cammie knew a dark secret of Sebastian's and he was aware of the fact. She asked if Diana or his girlfriend knew what he'd done. Her words kept coming back to me last night. "Your actions required the worst, most despicable sort of guile." Whatever it was, I'd say he had a lot to lose if his secret got out. And yesterday, just before Sapphire left, Cammie took her to one side. I'd guess she was warning her about Sebastian's flirting, rather than passing on the secret, whatever that is. So he might have decided to kill her before she took the next step. As for Raven, I'd say her hatred for Cammie is deep-seated, though I'm not sure why.' Eve took a long breath, her heart still on over-drive. 'The accident could be a coincidence, but I'm not convinced.'

After they'd given their names and contact details to a police officer, they went to pack up their stall. It felt so weird, being surrounded by people in their crazy costumes, flowers and ribbons, when the day had turned so dark. Eve couldn't wait to get out of her floating dress.

As she shook and folded the tablecloths they'd used, she spotted Robin, lurking in the trees. He'd removed his mask. No one was wearing them any more.

Eve slipped off to meet him and he took her hand, drawing her to him.

'I haven't heard anything yet,' he said, 'but I can tell you more once Greg's been in touch.'

Greg found DI Palmer's laziness and close-minded attitude almost as trying as Eve did. It meant he'd taken to secretly chewing over cases with Robin as a like-minded outsider. It had benefited Eve in the past. She'd written the obituaries of several murder victims, and inside information had helped keep her safe.

'Thanks, I'll wait to hear.'

He squeezed her hand and she felt herself start to shake again as visions of the fire filled her head. Greg's information couldn't come soon enough.

9

That evening at Elizabeth's Cottage, Eve changed into jeans and a T-shirt, then sat down at the kitchen table and wrote a pitch to *Icon* magazine for Cammie Harrington's obituary. Her next of kin would know of her death already. News and social media sites were full of photographs. It would be the worst possible way to find out.

'I can't imagine what they're going through,' Eve said to Gus, reaching down to stroke his head. Images of the crash and wreckage spooled through her mind. To be faced with that reality...

The online reports named the blond man who'd jumped from the balloon as Ralph Roscoe. There were photographs of him, square-jawed, his fringe flopping over his eyes, tears on his cheeks.

I CAN'T BELIEVE I JUMPED, the headline said. I BLAME MYSELF FOR CAMMIE'S DEATH, another announced. He was her ex from university days apparently. They'd fallen out of touch, but as he was staying locally, he'd been keen to volunteer and see his old friend strut her stuff. He'd made a lot of money a while back, launching a tech company, and was now a business angel, lending cash to start-ups in return for a share of their profits.

I decided it would be a lark to join Cammie for her flight, he was quoted as saying. *We used to be in the university skydiving club together. I thought the balloon ride would be like reliving old times. I feel terrible, but I jumped on instinct. The streamers shot into the basket and made me look down and I spotted the fire. I think I shouted as I scrambled over the side – I wanted to warn Cammie, but I was on autopilot. And by the time I'd jumped it was too late. The balloon rose so fast. I saw her struggling to reach the cord to pull the parachute vent open and bring the balloon down, but the fire was fierce, and she didn't manage it.*

Eve tried to imagine the scene. Did he really not have time to stop and think? To suggest they jump together? It hadn't been long before the fire took hold, but Eve still judged he could have waited longer. In which case, had he been so terrified that he'd made a terrible mistake, or was his move more knowing? If it was murder, his opportunity was second to none. He could have damaged the fuel line while he was onboard, ignited the escaping gas and leaped out.

The press were making much of the streamer cannon. Did outsize party popper contribute to fatal balloon crash? No one had admitted to letting it off and there were no eyewitnesses. Everyone's attention had been on the balloon. The streamers had certainly been a distraction, but Eve couldn't see them causing the fire on their own.

Another familiar face in the press coverage was the technician Eve had seen clambering out of the balloon's basket, minutes before Cammie and Ralph Roscoe got airborne. He said he'd been trying to perform final safety checks but Cammie had laughed and ushered him off the craft. She said she'd done them herself and he knew she was qualified. When she called him a fusspot he'd joined in the laughter and left her to it. Josh Standish had heard the exchange as well.

'Maybe Cammie missed something,' Eve said to Gus. 'I had her down as impulsive. She certainly wasn't the sort to worry over details and she was as brave as they come. Maybe she checked the equipment before it was transported to the manor, and something came loose. If there was a fuel leak, and one of the streamers caught fire, even for a moment, that might explain it. The spark could have ignited the gas.'

There'd been a fire extinguisher on board apparently; the flames must have spread too quickly for Cammie to bring them under control.

Eve felt a chill creep through her. Life turned on a dime sometimes. Was that what this was? Just a case of appalling bad luck? Despite the tensions at the manor, it was still possible.

Eve turned her attention to Cammie's life next. She wanted to get the basics straight in her head. The historian had been thirty-six when she'd died, according to her Wikipedia page. Her TV career had begun by chance over ten years earlier. After finishing her PhD, she'd been interviewed for a documentary and the programme makers had spotted her talent for delivering compelling content. She was happy to get her hands dirty and attractive to watch too, with her bright sparkling eyes and glossy chestnut hair. In that first TV appearance, she'd acted the part of a sixteenth-century lord of the manor, re-enacting a sword fight. There was an interview with the show's producer on YouTube. He said he'd never met anyone so fearless and charismatic.

It seemed to run in the family. Cammie's father had been a racing driver. He'd been killed on the track five and a half years earlier. It would have been shortly before Cammie's previous visit to Lovelace. It made Eve think of her words to Diana on

Friday. *I wanted to give something back*, she'd said about her current visit. *Diana and Peter looked after me like one of their own*. Eve wondered if Peter had been like a replacement father, so soon after she'd lost hers. Now he'd died too, just eight weeks ago. Eve understood Cammie had kept in touch with the family; she'd probably been grieving his loss. Eve was curious about her relations with Diana. The older woman didn't *seem* motherly, or at least, not these days. She was too tense, distracted and brittle. Maybe she wished someone would mother her for a change.

As for Cammie's real mother, she was still living. She was a big-shot entrepreneur in London – the owner of a craft ale company, one of the trendiest brands around. Eve would need to request an interview to ask about Cammie's formative years. She'd been an only child, but there was a university friend who cropped up in various photographs too. Eve noted her name as another useful contact.

After that, Eve checked Cammie's Instagram account and Facebook profile. The pictures said plenty about her as a person: shots of her galloping on that horse, skydiving, doing a stunt on a trapeze, swimming the Channel. But there was nothing to shed more light on her connections at Lovelace. Scrolling back five years, she only found formal, posed pictures. There was one of the manor. A man who must be Peter stood in the foreground, arm-in-arm with Diana, next to the bridge over the moat. They were smiling broadly. In the caption, Cammie thanked them for having her while she researched the smuggling documentary. Eve got up and paced the room. She'd need a lot more to understand the relationships involved.

Sitting down again, she drafted emails to the historian's mother and the long-standing friend, to send the following day. She wanted to give them time to absorb the awful news, and she'd wait to hear back from *Icon* first.

In any case, it was Cammie's Suffolk connections who'd be

top of her list of interviewees. She couldn't shift their behaviour from her mind. Diana's half-brother Sebastian Pickford, and the storyteller Raven Allerton. And now Ralph Roscoe, who'd leaped to earth and left Cammie to die.

10

———

Eve nipped into the village store the following morning for a pint of milk. Moira peered at her eagerly from behind the counter.

'Ah, Eve. I can hardly believe what happened to poor dear Cammie. She was so full of life. Of course, I've told Diana I'll make myself available as often as she needs me, even though Lovelace Sunday's over. I'm sure she'll want plenty of support.'

And Moira would be dying to know what was going on.

'I suppose it'll be a while before Irene's back on her feet,' Eve said.

The storekeeper nodded eagerly. 'I was there when the doctor visited, and he made her promise to rest for another two weeks. She can get about slowly on a walking frame, but it's no good for anything but the shortest of journeys.' She shook her head and sighed. 'It's shocking that the person who fired those streamers hasn't come forward. Still, I gather the police think the crash was a tragic accident.'

Eve had read that news too. A technical team had scoured the balloon wreckage. Everything was badly damaged by the fire, but their conclusions matched Eve's thoughts the day before: if the streamers were significant at all, they'd ignited some leaking gas by accident. The idea of someone compromising the fuel line then banking on the streamers acting as a fuse was simply too far-fetched, and Eve had dismissed it. Whoever shot the streamers was probably too ashamed to come forward. Eve felt a twinge of sympathy. They could never have predicted the terrible fallout.

So, maybe the crash *had* happened by chance. If Eve hadn't heard Sebastian Pickford wish Cammie dead, she wouldn't have murder on her mind.

'Incidentally,' Moira said breathlessly, as she took Eve's milk, 'who was the gentlemen who saw Harold off at the dance?' She raised an eyebrow. 'You are a dark horse, Eve. I had no idea you were seeing someone. Harold was ever so embarrassed, poor man. And it's such a shame, I really thought you'd make a good match.'

Their suggested first date popped into Eve's head. To think that she'd missed out on choosing her own funeral casket, followed by dinner. 'It's early days. I don't want to say too much in case it doesn't go anywhere.'

Moira sighed. 'Of course. But if you make it official, everyone in the village will be so pleased. We've all been thinking what a lonely life you lead. And if not' – her eyes twinkled – 'then I know Harold will be waiting in the wings. You two have such a lot in common, working in the death industry.'

Later that morning, Eve bumped into Viv's brother Simon on the village green. He greeted her with a hug, making her glance anxiously towards the village store. Not long ago, Moira had suspected him and Eve of having an affair. Given Simon was engaged to be married, it was a development Eve could have done without.

'How are you?' Eve realised he'd be having a hard time, as

Cammie's landlord. 'It must be difficult, liaising with Cammie's mother and sorting out the house. Have the police been in?'

Simon sighed. 'Just briefly, but they've decided the balloon crash was an accident now. They told me I was free to go in from this morning. I've got a cleaner there from the letting agency today. I wanted to tidy the place before Cammie's mother comes to pick up her stuff.' He bit his lip. 'It looked so lived in when I let the constable in. Heartbreaking to see a mug still on the side by the sink, and her bed unmade.' He shook his head. 'It's crazy, I know. Nothing can make it less awful for her family, but—'

Eve put a hand on his arm. 'I understand. And I think you're right. It was thoughtful of you.'

He took a deep breath and forced a grin. 'Thanks. I haven't spoken to the mother yet, just left a message. She wasn't taking calls – she must be devastated.'

'Did you meet Cammie in person when she arranged the rental?'

'Fleetingly. I popped over to show her the house. Truth to tell, I was keen to meet her as she was a celeb.' He blushed. 'She was so down to earth. And delighted with the cottage, even though it's such a small place. She said Diana had offered to have her at the manor, but she wanted her own space.'

Once again, Eve wondered if that was down to Sebastian.

'Are you writing her obituary?' Simon's bright eyes met hers. 'I'm going to give the cottage a once-over after it's been cleaned. Come along if you like. Would it help to see her things – get an impression of her style?'

Eve's pulse quickened. It felt like an invasion of privacy, but she was curious. The cottage had only been Cammie's temporary home, but you could tell a lot from a person's belongings. It was a shame she hadn't seen it before the cleaner made their mark.

'I'd love to. Thank you.'

. . .

Eve met Simon by the village green at one, ready for the drive to Lovelace-by-Sax. From the window of Monty's, Viv watched them go. She looked like a disappointed dog, left behind by its owner.

Simon parked in a lane just off what passed as the main road through the hamlet. They got out to the sound of birds rustling in the hawthorn hedgerow, which was festooned with white blossom. The sun was warm. In the distance, Eve could see the chimneys of the manor. The field beyond, where Cammie had died, filled her head.

They rounded the corner towards Lavender Cottage. There was a sit-up-and-beg bicycle propped against the side wall.

'That's odd,' Simon said. 'The agency said the cleaner would be done by midday. They normally run to time.'

He bent to retrieve a key from under a plant pot in the front garden.

Eve shook her head. 'I can't believe you leave a key lying around like that, after everything I've said.'

He looked sheepish. 'I got fed up with being called out when the tenants forget theirs. And it's convenient when I misplace mine, too...'

'So put a key box up!'

'I know, I know,' Simon replied, holding his hands up in a mea culpa gesture. He was about to put the key into the lock, but then hesitated. 'If the cleaner's still on site, maybe I should knock. Who knows what they're up to!'

He rapped on the door and they waited. After a moment, he turned to Eve with a frown and she pressed her face to the sash window.

As the dim scene inside came into focus, she felt the air go out of her lungs.

She must have made a noise. Simon leaped to her side. 'Are you all right?'

She gestured through the window. A woman was lying on the sofa in the shadows. One part of Eve's mind said she must have fallen asleep, tired after her morning's work, but another was already dismissing the idea. The position of her body wasn't right for that.

'Something's wrong,' she said, turning to Simon, who snapped out of his trance and rushed to the door. He fumbled with the key and finally managed to turn it.

In a moment they were by the woman's side. Her eyes were open. Glassy. A sheen on her forehead, her iron-grey hair damp at the roots.

Eve put a hand to her neck and Simon caught her eye as she shook her head. 'No pulse.'

'Oh my goodness.' Simon had his phone out. 'This is terrible. Could her heart have given out? I'll call an ambulance.'

Eve manoeuvred the woman and tried to remember her first aid. It was so clear in her head when she wasn't in a panic. Was it a rescue breath first? She tried and then started doing chest compressions, but even as she worked, she knew it was no good.

As soon as Simon had hung up he swapped places with her but after another minute or two his eyes met Eve's. 'It's too late, isn't it?'

Eve nodded. 'I think so.'

Close by, on a coffee table, sat a small bottle of fruit smoothie, empty, its lid lying next to it. Eve recognised the brand. It was Lascelles, the same sort Cammie always brought to Lovelace Manor. She crouched down to peer at it, then stood and put a hand on Simon's arm. 'Look at this.'

She pointed. It looked like a tiny manufacturing defect in the plastic bottle. So small you might miss it, if you weren't already on edge.

Simon was peering at the bottle now too. Neither of them touched it.

'It could be nothing,' Eve said. 'But it's the same brand Cammie drank. I'm wondering if it came from her fridge. If someone pierced the bottle and doctored the drink they could have used a tiny blob of glue or wax to seal the breach and cover their tracks.'

Simon blinked, his face pale.

Her eyes met his. 'I'm wondering if someone rigged the balloon crash after all. Perhaps they had a back-up plan, and this poor woman was their accidental victim.'

11

Even if the cleaner's death was natural, Eve knew the police would come soon after the paramedics did. They were called after any sudden, unexplained death. They'd have to agree to release the body.

'You can make yourself scarce if you like,' Simon said. 'It's bound to get back to Palmer if you stick around to be interviewed, and I don't think anyone saw us come in.'

It was tempting, but so was hanging around to look at Cammie's rental in what little time they had left. If her accident was murder, and her killer had recklessly caused the death of a second woman, Eve was duty-bound to use her knowledge to try to unmask them.

The police never saw a victim's private interactions, that was the trouble. Whereas she'd seen Sebastian and Raven, spouting hatred. She could tell the authorities what she knew, but she only had partial information. She had no idea what pain she might cause by revealing that Sebastian had a dark secret. Cammie's words told her it was serious. What might it do to his half-sister if it came out? How could Eve possibly know whether bringing it to light was the right thing to do? Diana seemed distracted and on edge – stressed and miserable. If Sebastian's secret was irrelevant, Eve might hurt her for no reason. She needed to investigate herself, so she could be sure.

'Thanks, but I'll stay.' It was better to be upfront anyway.

Eve knew she mustn't contaminate the scene, but she and Simon were already standing in the middle of it. She guessed looking couldn't hurt. She cast her eyes over the living room. It had a desk at the window facing the lane, with shelves to its right, then a dining area and dresser, and at the back, a pair of sofas and the coffee table. Eve turned again towards the cleaner. 'It feels awful not even to know her name.'

'I know,' Simon replied.

Eve sensed the poor woman had barely got started on her morning's work. There were still plenty of belongings strewn about the place. Boots sticking out from under a side table, a fleece dangling off a chair, ready to drop to the floor, and a plate with crumbs on it sitting on a shelf. Cammie hadn't been a tidy person, but her papers were neatly arranged. Maybe that signified what mattered to her.

Eve scanned the shelves for anything personal, but of course, most of what was there probably came with the house. Simon followed her gaze.

'I'm sorry.' She turned to him. 'It feels callous to be looking around while we wait. It's just that – well, if it does turn out to be murder, it might be my only chance.'

'I understand. I'd rather you looked.'

'Do you know if any of the trinkets here belonged to Cammie? I'm guessing you bought most of them to furnish the cottage?'

Simon went slightly pink. 'I have to confess, I didn't kit it out myself. Polly took over. She's very into interior design.'

Polly was Simon's fiancée; their wedding was in under a month. Eve ought to have spotted her hand at work. In fairness, she'd managed to switch off her passion for overpriced city style and choose items that were right for a country hideaway. Eve found herself wishing Polly was there, which was a rare emotion. In fact, she was away for work, so they couldn't rely on her help.

'There's an inventory,' Simon said. 'That should give us the answers we need.'

'Wait a moment, what's that up there?' She'd almost missed the object, half hidden behind a book. It was a silver cup with two handles, tarnished and dented, with pens in it. It sat on a high shelf and definitely didn't match Polly's scheme. It was distressed, but genuinely so, rather than cleverly designed to look that way. And silver didn't match the cottage's vibe in any case.

Simon frowned. 'It does look out of place. Feel free to take some photos if you like. I can't bear the thought of someone taking that poor woman's life in my house.'

'Thanks.' Eve reached for her phone and held it up to get a better shot. She took one of Cammie's desk too, with its pen pot, laptop and neat stacks of paper, then photographed the rest of the room and the smoothie bottle.

The cleaner had left the back door open off the kitchen; Eve could feel the breeze as she wandered to the doorway. The worktops there were tidy. Everything spick and span. Eve guessed she'd started in there, then stopped for a break and spotted the smoothie in the fridge – destined to be thrown out unless someone drank it. She'd have thought it was a waste. Eve would have too. Of course, she couldn't be sure. The cleaner *could* have brought the drink with her, but it would be a heck of a coincidence.

She turned to look into the garden. 'That's odd.'

Simon appeared at her side. 'What?'

'There's a chewing gum wrapper out there.' She put her head on one side. 'I can't see Cammie littering. It's not as though the kitchen bin's far away.' And she couldn't imagine a professional cleaner leaving it there either.

And then another oddity caught her eye. There was a scorch mark on one of the flagstones on the garden path.

'You're looking at the burn mark?' Simon said.

She nodded. 'And look down here.' She pointed to a couple of cigarette ends next to the back wall of the house. 'Cammie didn't smoke and the poor cleaner doesn't smell like a smoker either. I'm wondering about bored teens. Chewing gum, setting off firecrackers, something like that.' She frowned. 'But why come here?'

It wasn't the only puzzle. If Eve was right, and the smoothie had been poisoned in case the balloon accident failed, why hadn't the killer removed it from the house when their original plan succeeded? It would have been easy to get in, thanks to Simon's sloppy security. Surely they'd want to cover their tracks? Without the smoothie, Cammie's death would have been written off as bad luck. Unless she'd had two killers after her, which didn't seem likely.

But Eve had no chance to consider the matter further. The paramedics were at the door.

12

Soon after the paramedics arrived at Lavender Cottage, police officers descended as predicted: a bright-eyed, dark-haired young man of around thirty and a lively blonde-haired woman. As always, Eve felt grateful not to be dealing with Palmer, but Simon was right. Word would get back.

The officers called the letting agency and established that the cleaner was a woman named Stella Hilling. Eve's heart contracted as she overheard someone telling the police her next of kin was an elderly mother. The thought of them breaking the news was unbearable. A moment later, the female officer had her doctor's number from her HR file. One call later and it was established that Stella had been in good health. That and the fact that she'd drunk Cammie's favoured brand of smoothie was enough to make them call the coroner to put the wheels in motion for an investigation.

Once Eve had given her statement, she left Simon in the thick of it and took the bus home.

It was a relief to be back at Elizabeth's Cottage. Gus welcomed her with some balletic skipping. Cuddling him was comforting. A moment later, she called Robin to update him.

He promised more news as soon as DS Greg Boles supplied it and she hung up and checked her messages. *Icon* had accepted her pitch to write Cammie's obituary. It was time to get to work.

She sent off the emails she'd drafted to the historian's mother and her old university friend, Phoebe Richmond. Phoebe ought to be especially useful for the murder investigation: she, Cammie and Ralph Roscoe had been students together.

After that, she set about contacting Diana Pickford-Jones and through her, Sebastian. She already had Diana's details, thanks to the volunteering she'd done. Sebastian was of special interest, of course, given his antagonistic relationship with Cammie. Eve asked them if they knew where Ralph Roscoe was staying, and put in a request to Diana for Josh Standish's email address. A quick google provided Raven Allerton's contact details – she had her own website. Eve made a mental note to explore it properly later. The absent chief volunteer, Irene, crossed her mind as well. She'd ask Moira if she was up to being quizzed. As an old timer, she must have met Cammie during her previous visit.

It was only after the flurry of activity that the shock of Stella Hilling's death engulfed her, falling like a thick, suffocating blanket. She'd managed to block it out as she dealt with practicalities. Now she felt sick.

'I think we should go and talk to Jim Thackeray, Gus.' If it came out that Cammie was murdered it would put a lot of strain on Diana. Jim would want to support her – as a relative and in his professional capacity too. He might like to know the latest.

Gus had jumped up at the vicar's name. They got along well. Despite having to reach down from a great height, Jim was generous on the tummy-tickling front. He welcomed animals to his Sunday services and seemed to quietly applaud Gus's 'singing', despite his unorthodox style.

And Eve knew he'd be a useful person to talk to. He'd have

lots of insights into life at Lovelace Manor, and Eve had plenty
of questions. If Cammie *had* been killed, she was sure her
Suffolk connections were key. Only a local would have chosen
to murder her at Lovelace Sunday, rather than finding a simpler,
more convenient way. Talking to an insider about the manor's
residents would be crucial. She wanted to understand the legal
set-up. Was it set in stone that the manor would go to Sebastian
after Diana's death? What control did Diana have over her half-
brother's future? If Cammie had given away his secret, could
she have disinherited him?

Eve slipped Gus's leash on, fumbling for the ring it went
through as he skipped sideways on the doormat. The day was
warm again, there was no need for a cardigan over her fitted
daisy-print dress. As she walked down Haunted Lane and
crossed the village green towards the vicarage, she tried to focus
on the sun on her back. To one side, the parent and toddler
group was having song time outdoors. The heavenly day and
the singing bumped up hard against the vivid memory of
Lavender Cottage. Poor Stella Hilling. And her mother. Eve
breathed in deeply to control her emotions.

She found Jim at home in the vicarage next door to the
imposing church, its tower impressive against the blue sky.

'Eve! And Gus! How lovely to see you. How are you feeling
after yesterday?' He was looking up at Eve, having crouched to
make a fuss of her dachshund. He shook his head sadly. 'I still
can't take in what happened. Cammie was so full of life. You'd
like to talk? What about a stroll around the ruins of the old
church?' He knew Gus preferred that to sitting in his study.
Standing up, he took his keys from a hook in the hallway and
secured the front door after him.

'That would be wonderful, thank you.' She held off sharing
her news until they were close to the old church – near the also-
quite-ancient 'new' one. As they reached the low lengths of
crumbling wall, she turned to face the vicar. 'I'm afraid there's

more bad news.' She explained about her and Simon's discovery of Stella Hilling's body. Across the lane on the green, she could hear faint strains of 'Head, Shoulders, Knees and Toes'.

The vicar put his hand to his mouth. 'The poor woman.' He paused a moment, his eyes shocked and serious under his bushy white eyebrows. 'You think it's too much of a coincidence?'

'I'm afraid it might be.'

He nodded. 'I'm glad you told me. I'll be ready to step in if Diana needs some moral support.' He gave her a knowing look. 'And perhaps you'd like to ask me about the set-up at Lovelace Manor?' His brow furrowed further and she wondered what he was thinking. Did he worry his cousin or her half-brother might have been involved in Cammie's death? He was a perceptive man. If there were signs to pick up, he'd probably spotted them.

'That would be useful. Did you meet Cammie when she first visited Lovelace Manor?' She wanted the background. What was happening back then? How had she got on with Sebastian? Had there already been tensions?

'I went to lunch with them once during the six months she was there.' Jim pinched the bridge of his nose and closed his eyes for a moment. 'I can still picture them all in that dark dining room of theirs. Peter, Diana's late husband, was on genial form. A couple of pre-lunch sherries, I seem to remember, and Diana was motherly towards Cammie. I thought it might irritate her – she seemed so independent – but in fact, I had the impression she was enjoying it. Sebastian was there too. It was before his modelling career took off.'

He gave Eve an apologetic look. 'It's not done for vicars to tell tales.'

Eve smiled. It was time for her to do some speculating out loud. She thought it through. Cammie had been a little older than Sebastian, well known, vivacious and beautiful. She met Jim's eye. 'Not to speak ill of Diana's half-brother, but I suspect he turned on the charm and fully expected to have his attentions welcomed.'

'You got to know him quite well over the last week, I imagine.'

Bingo. 'I'm assuming he hasn't changed over the last five years.'

Jim just smiled.

'And knowing Cammie,' she felt her way again, 'I'd guess his approach didn't appeal. If it was early days, and she didn't know him well, I imagine she was polite – charming but firm.'

'You got to know her too, I see.'

'Not well enough, I'm afraid. I had the impression there were tensions between her and Sebastian, though. From what you haven't quite said,' she smiled at him, 'it sounds as though she bruised his ego.' She imagined Sebastian was the sort to hold a grudge.

Jim had bent to fuss Gus again. 'I couldn't possibly comment, obviously.'

Eve could hear the amusement in his voice. This was a well-worn dance between them. His response confirmed he agreed with her, and his opinion was worth a lot.

So Sebastian probably felt humiliated by Cammie, and it looked like she'd become a threat as well. 'It's interesting that Diana was motherly. Cammie said she and Peter treated her like one of their own. She sounded sentimental, but these days, Diana seemed rather offhand.'

The vicar frowned. 'It might be a result of losing Peter. He was ill for a while before he died but I never knew the exact details. I've had very little contact with them for the last couple of years.' He sighed. 'It was disconcerting, to be distanced like that, but she turned down all offers of help.'

'You were close, previously?'

He chuckled. 'This is going to sound very un-vicarly, but I had the most tremendous crush on her when I was twelve. She's five years older than me and at seventeen she seemed the epitome of sophistication. She loved riding and the freedom of roaming the countryside.' His eyes became sad and he shook his head. 'That was before she had the weight of responsibility for Lovelace resting on her shoulders.' He turned to Eve. 'The crush faded of course, as these things do. I did marry. When I was just twenty-five. No children, of course, or you'd have met them.'

Eve held her breath. She'd had absolutely no idea. For her money, that meant no one in the village knew.

'Maria died soon after her fortieth birthday, falling off a horse. She broke her neck.' His eyes glistened. 'It's relevant because Diana supported me through it. She spent hours just sitting with me. Please don't tell anyone. You're the first person in Saxford I've told. It changes the way people look at you. I found that in my previous parish. They try to match-make, assume you want someone else, pity you. Whereas Diana was quiet and matter-of-fact. She let me feel my feelings and was simply there for me.'

'I understand. I won't tell. But I'm sorry.'

He nodded and took a handkerchief from his pocket. 'Thank you.' A moment later he shook himself. 'Back to business. Yes, I'm very fond of Diana and I'd have said she regarded me as a firm friend, but something made her pull back when things got tough.' He bit his lip and Eve sensed he felt guilty about it. As though it was his failing. 'It's not uncommon,' he added firmly. 'Many people find it easier to give help than accept it. I attended last year's Lovelace Sunday but I barely saw her, she was so busy. As for Peter, I only glimpsed him through a window. He was in a wheelchair. It was sad to see him looking so frail. Sebastian came down for the event as usual, with a glamorous woman on his arm. Another model, I think.'

'He seems very proud of Lovelace.' Eve imagined it gave him a certain cachet, run-down though it was. The thought set irritation fizzing in her chest. 'I gather he often refers to it as his inheritance. I wasn't sure if that was literally true.' She glanced at him. 'Sorry, it's a bit of a personal question.'

'I trust your motives.' Jim put his hand on an old stone buttress as he moved through the ruins, a world-weary smile on his face. 'In fact, it's not a given. Diana's father left it to her, and for forty years, she was an only child. It never seemed likely she'd have to share it. So when Sebastian came along – a product of a second marriage – he decided it would be unfair to withdraw the bequest, though the manor normally went to the eldest son by tradition. Instead, he rewrote the will, offering two alternatives. Either the house should go to Sebastian on Diana's death, or – if Diana found the burden of keeping the place too much – she could opt to sell and split the proceeds with Sebastian, fifty-fifty. Peter had been trying to talk her into selling and I sympathised. It ate up all the hours God sent them. He was an academic, so the house wasn't his only concern. There's never been enough money.'

Eve had come across a lot of unusual bequests during her career. Interviewees sometimes told her about them, usually because they were furious. Eve applauded Diana's father for not going with tradition. It would have been horrible to pull the carpet from under her feet like that and sons and daughters ought to be treated equally anyway. But Sebastian might feel resentful, given his character. Did he fantasise about what might have been? The manor could already have been his. She doubted that he focused on the responsibilities that went with it: the endless need to cover the upkeep. It looked as though Diana dealt with all that.

'What did Diana think about Peter's suggestion? Did she ever consider selling up?' Eve could imagine the temptation. If it were her, she'd find a business plan that worked or move on. But of course, the will had put Diana in a tricky position. If she sold, she effectively halved Sebastian's inheritance. He might not be a nice man, but he was her half-brother. Would she feel able to do that?

Perhaps not in the ordinary way, but she might have, if Cammie had revealed Sebastian's secret. He'd had a lot to lose.

'When I saw her after Peter's death,' Jim said, 'she seemed determined to sell, after years of rejecting the idea. On the rare occasions we'd talked about it before, she'd felt it was her duty to keep it in the family.'

It was ironic that she'd finally seen her husband's point of view but it made sense. Suddenly she was faced with sole responsibility.

'It seems to me that Lovelace requires absolute dedication,' Jim said, 'and that it wears people out. Josh Standish – the gardener – his father's a case in point. He lived in the same cottage as Josh does, and died while working.'

'You think the job caused it?'

'I don't imagine it helped. I think managing the manor has affected Diana too, over the years.' His eyes were sad. 'She was fierce as a young adult. Now, I think she's too exhausted to do anything more than claw her way through the days.'

'Sebastian must have been upset at Diana's decision to sell. And what about people like Irene Marston?' The absent chief volunteer sounded deeply invested in the place.

'She and the residents of Lovelace-by-Sax all felt the same way. The prospect of developers getting their hands on Lovelace Manor gave rise to a collective howl.'

'Poor Diana.' She must have felt trapped. 'So she had another change of heart?'

'That's right.' Jim frowned. 'Within a week or so she'd thought of contacting Cammie in case she could help. Irene was delighted about that, and Diana seemed almost feverish about it. Desperate for her to come.'

Like a drowning swimmer clinging to some passing driftwood, perhaps. Unless there had been another, more sinister reason...

'But Sebastian wasn't keen,' the vicar went on. 'Even though he ought to have been moving heaven and earth to secure the manor's future.' He lifted his hands helplessly. 'His behaviour gives me the most uncharitable thoughts.' His eyes were on the River Sax, which ran to one side of St Peter's and the old ruins, curving round the main village. 'But Cammie had kept up with Diana and Peter, so she was an obvious person to turn to. She visited when Peter was dying; she knew how difficult things were. She probably knew more than I did.' The last sentence came out on a sigh. 'So anyway, when Diana wrote to her, she agreed to come and research a documentary about Lovelace's history. She made it a priority – dropped everything and arrived within a month.' His eyes met hers. 'If her death was murder, do you suspect Sebastian?'

Eve hesitated. 'I think Cammie knew he was keeping a secret. A damaging one.'

'Ah.'

'If Diana didn't know already, or if Sebastian's girlfriend was unaware, Cammie might have posed a threat to him. It's hard to know, without discovering what he's hiding.'

'I understand, and I'm afraid I can't help. If Diana knows or suspects, she's never told me.'

'Perhaps she's in the dark. She and Sebastian don't seem close.' Diana might have mothered Cammie at one point, but Eve never saw her act that way towards her half-brother, despite the age gap.

The vicar nodded. 'No, that's right. Their father died sixteen years ago, when Sebastian was fourteen. He was already at boarding school by then, and although his mother, Christine, was a sweet woman, she wasn't business-minded. Managing Lovelace fell solely to Diana then, and even before that she'd done the lion's share. It didn't leave much time for big sistering. Besides, Christine doted on Sebastian.'

It figured. He struck her as spoiled. 'There wasn't much room for anyone else?'

He nodded.

'What happened to Christine? And what about Diana's mother?'

Jim's eyes were sad. 'Diana's mum died of leukaemia when Diana was thirty-eight, and Christine was killed in a car accident just after Cammie's previous visit. Sebastian took himself off to London at that point. The modelling work fell into his lap by all accounts.'

Eve could imagine Diana struggling to feel pleased for him. He'd been cosseted his entire life while she'd battled to preserve their family home.

13

Back at Elizabeth's Cottage, Eve mulled over what she'd learned as she dished up Gus's supper. It certainly sounded as though Cammie had had the power to make or break Sebastian's future at Lovelace, and Diana's desperation to get her on site was interesting. Whatever their relationship in the past, Diana hadn't been motherly towards her on this latest visit, and Cammie hadn't wanted to stay at the manor.

For a second, Eve thought of Diana rushing towards the balloon just before it launched – trying to persuade Ralph Roscoe not to join Cammie because the insurance didn't cover it. Was she just anxious about the legalities? Or had she planned the balloon crash, and was she horrified that he might be a victim too?

But Diana had no obvious motive; her recent offhand attitude might be down to stress.

Ralph seemed a more likely suspect, for opportunity at least. She checked her emails. No reply from Diana yet, with or without his contact details.

She called Robin to tell him the latest.

'Greg's suggested a late beer this evening. Shall we meet for

breakfast tomorrow? What about a picnic by the beach beyond Watcher's Wood? It's normally quiet there.'

'Sounds great.' Eve liked being out with Robin. Meeting in secret at home was all very well, but walking along the beach made her happy. She could almost imagine they were a normal couple.

By the time she hung up, she'd had a text from Viv, demanding a meetup and news. She must have spoken to Simon. They were close, unlike Diana and Sebastian. Eve texted back to agree to dinner at the Cross Keys, then sat down to go through the photos she'd taken at Lavender Cottage.

She'd almost forgotten about the battered silver cup until she came across the picture of it, high on the shelves in Cammie's temporary home.

She zoomed in to examine the photo in detail. Gradually, an engraved inscription revealed itself.

To Louisa and Seth Pickford on the anniversary of their marriage
With love from their cousin and friend, J.M.L.
14th May 1899

Eve felt her scalp tingle – 1899 was the date when the cousin who'd inherited Lovelace Manor had gifted it to Louisa and Seth. J.M.L. Was that him? His support must have meant so much. And he'd had the money to give them this precious keepsake too.

Cammie had hidden it in plain sight. Did Diana or Sebastian know she'd got it? She couldn't imagine them lending it to her. Why would they? Eve guessed the historian had found it and kept quiet about the fact. Perhaps she wanted to present the results of her research in one go: a grand reveal. She'd certainly been tight-lipped about the details of her progress when Ralph asked.

But how had the precious item got so battered? And where

had Cammie found it? Eve doubted she'd take something from the manor house. That would count as stealing, not discovering.

It was one more puzzle to add to her list.

Viv had her last forkful of crab and asparagus risotto halfway to her mouth. They were sitting in the back garden of the Cross Keys, looking out towards the River Sax. Gus had been playing with Hetty – the co-landlord Toby's schnauzer – but was settled under their table now.

Eve had already given Viv her updates.

'So what's next?'

'Lots of interviews and research. I want to take a closer look at Raven's website for a start.'

'Find it now and I'll look too.'

Eve had just called it up on her phone when her friend sounded the alarm.

'Uh-oh! Jo, at your six o'clock.'

'You've been watching those action movies again.' Eve picked up her phone and tucked it into her bag. Really, there was something slightly shaming about two grown women acting like a pair of schoolkids, caught playing on their phones by a teacher. But Jo, the pub's superb cook, didn't approve of technology at mealtimes, and she was a formidable character.

'That was amazing,' Viv said, as Jo collected their plates. She often visited the tables personally to make sure people were concentrating on her food.

Jo smiled, as Eve echoed Viv's words. Her sea trout and samphire linguine had been phenomenal. No argument there.

When the cook retreated, Viv leaned forward. 'All clear. Let's see Raven's website then. You mustn't miss out on my insights.'

'Perish the thought.' Eve took one last glance over her shoulder and reached for her phone again.

The site's home page had a picture of Raven surrounded by children. Someone had done something to the photo so that their faces glowed as though each one was lit by candlelight. It was subtle, but it made them look completely engaged, as though they'd turned towards the sun.

Raven was gesticulating, her eyes dancing.

Viv shuddered. 'I still can't believe what she did with that spider. You'd never guess it from that photograph, would you? She looks like a sort of Arthurian Mary Poppins.'

Under the photo, Raven set out her stall:

Available for children's and adults' parties, weddings and funerals.

'I ought to tell Harold Bromley about her,' Eve said.

'You're keen to see him again, then?'

Eve gave her a withering look. 'Joking apart, it's an interesting idea, to have a storyteller at a funeral. I guess she must do a sort of oral obituary.'

Raven's list continued:

Village fetes, stately homes, schools and playgroups. Attract new visitors to your venue or event!

Eve looked at the page on fees. 'Diana must have paid her a flat fee and banked on her bringing in extra visitors. I can imagine it working, so long as the parents didn't look at her methods too closely. The kids were loving her again by the end of the session I saw.'

'I wonder if that girl mentioned the spider to her mum and dad.'

'If she did, I have a feeling they'd imagine it was all a misunderstanding. Unless I'd seen it with my own eyes, I wouldn't have realised how cunning she was. And how ruthless.'

The tab on past events was interesting. Up until five years ago, she'd been a regular feature at Lovelace but then, as Eve had already heard, there'd been a gap. But Eve hadn't realised quite how much of her work she'd dropped by severing her links with the manor. The number of events went right down. She'd bigged up her other bookings, but there was no disguising it.

Eve pointed out the numbers. 'I can't believe she sacrificed that much income over the break-up with Josh Standish. There must have been something else.'

'A falling-out with the family?'

'Could be... or maybe,' Eve paused, thinking of the timing, 'with Peter specifically. Perhaps that's why she's back now. Because he's dead.'

Viv frowned. 'That's a thought. You should write it down. Let's see the "About Me" section. I love looking at what people say about themselves.'

Eve scanned the text.

Raven's unconventional mother wanted her dark-haired daughter to be as free as a bird, hence her given name. Raven's father abandoned them when Raven was six months old, after which the pair travelled extensively. Raven's mother eked out a living singing ballads in country inns and taking odd jobs. Raven was never in one school for long, but it taught her independence, and a love of meeting new people. It's this that allows her to bond with her audiences, young and old.

Yeah, right. All the same, it sounded as though she'd had it tough. Just the thought of that lifestyle left a knot in Eve's stomach. She'd always felt a strong anchor fixing her to home. Leaving familiar friends and places was hard.

But maybe Raven's experiences had left her more prepared to abandon her work at Lovelace. Out of pride perhaps, or spite or even principle. She was used to uncertainty.

When she was old enough, Raven joined her mother on stage. They sang at festivals, and increasingly, organisers booked Raven to give storytelling sessions too. Raven's mother is still travelling, but Raven has paused for now in Suffolk, with its wide skies and rich history. But who knows when she might be off again!

The last bit sounded like embroidery. Raven had been in the area for years. It looked as though she'd settled. That probably hadn't been easy either. She'd been giving something up all over again.

An email notification popped up on Eve's phone. She scanned her messages. 'I'll get to dig deeper with Raven soon. She's agreed to see me on Wednesday. And Cammie's university friend, Phoebe Richmond, is coming to Suffolk tomorrow. She wants to be on the spot by the sound of it. She's asked to meet in the grounds of Lovelace Manor. I don't think she can believe what's happened.'

Viv shuddered. 'It'll be hard, going back there.'

'But worth it.' If Cammie had been killed, returning to the site might reveal something. And Phoebe Richmond could be a very useful interviewee. 'I'm hoping Cammie was the sort to confide in her closest friend. If anyone picked up on clues about the way the wind was blowing, it's likely to have been her.'

14

Eve and Gus met Robin on the beach beyond Watcher's Wood at eight the following morning. Robin had arrived by bike, along with warm croissants, Gruyère cheese and a flask of coffee.

'Special treat,' he said, after kissing her hello. 'I took a detour via the bakers at Wessingham. It's not as though we get to do this very often.'

He laid out a tartan rug under the trees that bordered the beach and they sat down.

'I can't think of anything nicer.' Eve pulled the early strawberries she'd brought from her bag. It had been on the tip of her tongue to say, *I think I love you.* It would be a light-hearted, casual way to say what she actually felt. The desire to announce the fact had been welling up inside her for some time now, but it was tricky. It would be a quick way to ruin a romantic breakfast if he didn't feel the same.

Even this early in the morning it was warm enough to sit without a coat. The sky was blue and the North Sea as calm as it got.

Robin poured them each a coffee and Eve stretched back, imagining for a moment that they were there just for pleasure.

She took the knife Robin passed her, cut open her croissant and added a slice of the cheese. 'What news?' She sensed he'd been hesitating, unwilling to break the spell.

He sighed. 'I'm afraid you were right. The smoothie was poisoned – injected through the tiny hole in the plastic you spotted, then resealed with a minuscule quantity of transparent glue.'

Even though she'd expected it, hearing the harsh reality made Eve's heart sink. 'Are the police treating the balloon crash as murder now?'

He nodded. 'They're linking one to the other, just like you did.'

'And what about the poison? Does that tell us anything?'

He sipped his coffee. 'I'm afraid not. It was ethylene glycol. These days, products that contain it usually have a bitterant added for safety but that wasn't the case a few years back. Anyone could have had it lying around in their garage.'

'Is there any way of telling when the poisoned bottle was put into Cammie's fridge?'

Robin shook his head as he prepared his croissant. 'With the spare key hidden in the front garden, people could have been in and out all week.'

'I had words with Simon about that.'

He gave a flicker of a smile. 'People round here are far too trusting. But logic says it must have been planted on Lovelace Sunday. Assuming it's just one killer we're dealing with.'

Eve knew that made sense. 'Because if they'd put it there any sooner, Cammie might have drunk it before the balloon launch. They wanted to try to engineer the crash first, in the hope they'd pass her murder off as an accident. But if they failed, they were desperate enough to resort to poison, which was almost certain to lead to a police investigation.'

'Exactly.'

Eve shivered. 'And Cammie normally drank her smoothie at

Lovelace Manor. If she'd taken it there on Monday, ready to carry on her research, she'd probably have thrown the bottle away in some shared bin, amongst rubbish left over from the event. The police might never have discovered how it was administered.'

'It's possible.' Robin took a mouthful of his croissant.

Eve took a deep breath and bit into hers too. It was bound to help her think. She stared out to sea and concentrated. 'It wouldn't have been hard for any of the key players to nip over to Lavender Cottage and plant it on Lovelace Sunday,' she said at last. 'It was so chaotic, and it's a very short journey. Cammie went back there herself in fact, just after she'd been for a swim in the moat.' In her mind's eye, she could still see the historian, weaving through the crowds. 'Several people saw her go: Sebastian, who was in the middle of chatting up a woman dressed as a fairy, and Josh Standish and Ralph Roscoe too.'

Robin glanced at a note on his phone. 'The police have asked for everyone's movements that day. Officially, Standish was in charge of the walled garden, Pickford was supposed to be guiding visitors,' his eyes met Eve's, 'though from what you say, he was focusing on one-to-one sessions. And Roscoe was just a visitor, though he'd volunteered in the run-up; he had the most free time, but Greg agrees with you. Any of them could have managed it.'

Eve nodded. 'Raven had gaps between storytelling sessions too – she'd have found it just as easy. And all Cammie's connections at Lovelace knew what brand of smoothie she drank. She brought her breakfast with her each morning: that drink and some muesli. Even I know her habits.'

'So then we come to why the killer left the smoothie in the fridge, rather than removing it. Unless we have two killers.'

'She had more than one enemy, but for two people to decide to murder her at the same time seems unlikely. As for removing the smoothie, I wonder if it might have been kids that stopped the killer getting inside.' She'd already told Robin about the gum wrapper, cigarettes and scorch mark she'd noticed in the garden. 'If they hung out there on Sunday evening, they might have frightened them off. Tammy comes from Lovelace-by-Sax.' She was one of the regular helpers at Monty's. 'She might know the local youths well enough to guess who's been there. But it still seems weird. Why hang out there? I suppose ghoulishness might explain it, but it looks like they hung around. You wouldn't think the place would hold their attention for that long.' She ate some more croissant. She was appreciating it now: the salty tang of the cheese in the slightly sweet pastry.

Robin gave a dry laugh. 'Things could have got a whole load more exciting if they'd gone into the garden shed.'

'Excuse me?'

'The police found a container with cocaine in it in the pannier of Cammie's hire bike.'

'That's a surprise. I wouldn't have had her down as a drug user. She seemed very fit when she was ploughing round the moat.'

He nodded. 'I take your point. The container was covered in her prints, and the police have found traces of coke around the house, but the killer could have organised that. They nipped in to plant the smoothie, after all. Anything in the kitchen might have her prints on it.'

'What does Palmer think?' Eve hardly dared ask.

'He's convinced the drugs and the murder are related, and that a "London connection" of hers is responsible.'

'I can imagine him seizing on that idea. He'd never focus on Diana and Sebastian. They might be strapped for cash, but they're part of an old, influential family.'

'I'm afraid you're right, and it's worse than you know. Their father and the Chief Constable's dad were friends.'

'Ah.' That was that then. It would be down to Eve to investigate the half-siblings.

'But Palmer's got his eye on Ralph Roscoe. He's staying locally, but he's normally London based, and an ex-boyfriend was always going to attract attention, even if he hadn't been in the balloon.'

Eve nodded. 'His opportunity's certainly clear, though I don't have a motive for him. The method put him at risk too, but he's brave, by all accounts. But as far as London connections go, Sebastian spends plenty of time down there according to Jim Thackeray. And I overheard him wishing Cammie dead on Friday.'

'But if Sebastian – or any of the others – are guilty, they must have managed the accident from the ground. Palmer can't imagine how they'd have done that.'

'I hate to agree with him, but I can't either. Is there any evidence that the key players know about ballooning?'

'No, but it's nothing you couldn't look up online.'

Eve took a sustaining swig of coffee. 'I suspect Palmer's being a bit narrow-minded, assuming the cocaine points to London.' She put her cup down. 'I took some photos at Lavender Cottage by the way.' Robin raised an eyebrow. 'Just while Simon and I waited for the police. I didn't touch anything.'

He winced. 'Okay.'

'I'll send them to you, but this one's particularly interesting.' She showed him the loving cup, presented to Louisa and Seth Pickford after they took up residence at Lovelace Manor. 'It's probably unrelated to the murder, but I suspect Cammie found it while she was researching her documentary. My bet is that Diana and Sebastian never knew she had it.'

'Any ideas where she got it?'

Eve had been mulling it over. 'She swam in the moat, the day she died. It was after that that she dashed off home. And thinking back, she looked furtive. She pulled her towel around her rather awkwardly. Now I'm wondering if she was hiding something underneath it.'

'You think the cup might have been in the moat?'

Eve nodded. 'I've no idea why. Maybe it fell from a window or something.' Though it was quite battered. If it had simply landed in the water and sunk, Eve doubted that would be the case. 'It wasn't the first time Cammie had explored the moat either. I heard her tell Josh she'd managed to touch the bottom on Saturday.'

'I'll alert Greg, in case it's relevant.'

'So where does all this leave us? Palmer's focused on Ralph Roscoe or some other mythical London connection of Cammie's?'

'That's right.'

'Is Raven Allerton on his list?' Eve had already told Robin about her behaviour.

'She's not even crossed his radar.'

There was plenty for Eve to do then.

Together, she and Robin discussed the suspects and Eve prepared a list on her phone. They'd even included Irene for completeness's sake, though they both agreed she was out of it, thanks to her ankle injury.

Key players, thoughts and queries

Sebastian Pickford – Cammie clearly knew something damaging about him. Even before that he hated her. Made a play for her five years ago and was rejected.

Raven Allerton – jealous of Cammie (professionally, and possibly over Josh Standish). Not enough of a motive in itself, but appeared to really hate her. Why? More information needed.

Ralph Roscoe – best opportunity to engineer the balloon crash but no obvious motive. Is it coincidence that he managed to jump so quickly and survived? And is it significant that he was seen sneaking off to talk to Diana about something?

Diana Pickford-Jones – no obvious motive. Tried to stop Ralph from joining Cammie. Did she know something? Was super keen to have Cammie to stay. Jim Thackeray described her as 'feverish' about it. Was motherly towards Cammie when she lodged at the manor previously, but seemed distant and distracted this time.

Josh Standish – no obvious motive. Used to date Raven Allerton, so possible love triangle, though no proof there was anything between him and Cammie. However, kept a close eye on her when she was swimming etc. Has to be kept on the list.

Sapphire Colby – no obvious motive and wasn't on site on Lovelace Sunday. Seems to have got on well with Cammie and they had a shared interest: securing Lovelace's future.

Irene Marston – no obvious motive and ankle injury. Injury is genuine, confirmed by Moira who saw her doctor visit. Impractical to walk without a frame. Wasn't in a position to clamber in and out of the balloon and plant anything, even if she'd managed to sneak on site during Lovelace Sunday.

They'd just finished when Diana Pickford-Jones's email popped into Eve's inbox. She and Sebastian were free to talk on Thursday morning. She claimed not to have Ralph Roscoe's contact details, despite their secret meetup.

As Eve kissed Robin goodbye and began her walk back to Saxford, she felt overwhelmed with the task ahead. Whatever happened, she must reach Cammie's old boyfriend. But next on her list was the meetup with Phoebe Richmond, her old university contact, over at the manor. She wanted to know which of the key players at Lovelace Phoebe was aware of. Who had Cammie talked about and what secrets had she shared? And what had Cammie and Ralph Roscoe's relationship been like, back in the day?

15

Eve and Phoebe Richmond were standing inside a dark, oak-panelled room upstairs at Lovelace Manor. Phoebe seemed to want to retrace Cammie's steps – a way of coming to terms with her friend's death perhaps. When they'd arrived, Eve had spotted Moira. True to her word, she must have wangled more time off from the village store. She was taking a small tour party over the bridge and through the manor's main entrance. Eve asked if Phoebe would like to join them. She was keen to get the interview underway, but Cammie's friend was still in a state of shock. Giving her some processing time might help the conversation in the long run.

Eve tried to focus her thoughts on the interview ahead, but her mind was preoccupied. Stella Hilling's death had made the news that morning, now it was known to be murder. The write-up had referred to her voluntary work at the local primary school, where she'd listened to children read twice a week. Eve couldn't stop thinking about the uncomprehending kids who'd want to know where she was, and their tears when they realised she'd never be back.

It meant it was a relief when Moira restarted her commentary, though that only lasted a moment. Her words made Eve squirm.

'This is one of my favourite rooms to sit in.' Moira smiled at the visitors. 'The house shows signs of wear and tear of course, and the money you're contributing today will help restore this precious place. That said, I find the scuffed floorboards and threadbare patches add character. I've always felt comfortable here.' You'd think she'd been volunteering for years, if not living there.

'In the glass case to your left, you can see a formal photograph of Louisa and Seth Pickford. They posed for it later in life, here at the manor, where they lived out their days. But I find the sketches in the cabinet by the door most charming. We found them fifteen years ago, under a loose floorboard in what was once the young Louisa's bedroom. It's my favourite discovery. They're signed by her, as you can see. She sketched herself and Seth together.'

We found? Seriously? Moira hadn't even been volunteering then. Eve watched the admiration in the visitors' eyes. One of the drawings showed the young lovers' heads close together, framed with a border of flowers.

'It must date back to when she and Seth were courting in secret,' Moira said. 'I think we can assume the picture represented her dreams.'

One of the tour party sighed sentimentally and reached for her husband's hand.

Eve watched Phoebe Richmond. She was wearing a floating sleeveless navy dress that almost reached her ankles, and flat navy sandals with large buckles. Clouds of dark hair hid her face as she peered into the glass case. Eve wasn't sure she was seeing what was in front of her, though she was staring at a plaque which told Louisa and Seth's love story.

As Eve looked up, she realised Moira was on her way over

to them. Phoebe was pulled out of her reverie as the storekeeper held out a hand.

'You must be Cammie's university friend,' she said, her expression sympathetic. 'I heard you were coming to visit us today.'

Eve had been in touch with Diana to let her know. She must have told Moira.

'I'm so sorry for your loss.' Moira put a hand on Phoebe's shoulder.

Phoebe blinked. 'And you must be Diana. Cammie spoke so fondly of you. I know how much she loved it when she came to stay last time.'

Moira went pink, but Eve could tell it was down to pleasure, not embarrassment.

'Actually, I'm Moira, Diana's right-hand woman at Lovelace.' She glanced at Eve, who raised an eyebrow. 'Just at present, of course. Diana would love to have seen you, but she's got all sorts of appointments today. Insurance, police and so on.'

'I understand.' Phoebe stepped back. 'I'll write to her.'

When the tour had finished, Eve led Phoebe down a long dingy corridor, and back into the light. Another sunny May day. It was a stark contrast to the gloom inside and made Eve blink.

'I should have realised that wasn't Diana,' Phoebe said as she crossed the bridge at Eve's side. 'The woman looked too young, come to think of it. Cammie sent me photographs of the family when she stayed here last, but that was five years ago. I thought maybe she'd dyed her hair.'

'I should have explained who she was on the way in.' They'd been dashing to catch up.

Phoebe gave a sad smile. 'Could you show me the field where the accident happened? It doesn't feel real.'

'Of course.' Eve led Phoebe around the side of the house and over a lawn towards the crash site. As they went, the sight of the balloon filled her mind: Ralph Roscoe jumping, then the craft lifting, faster than she'd ever have predicted. And then the fire.

Phoebe was walking as though in a trance, her eyes on the scene ahead. 'You were here? Please tell me what you saw.'

So Eve went through the tale again. How Ralph had looked down inside the balloon, and apparently seen the fire just as it started. How he'd panicked. How Cammie had jumped too in the end, left with no option.

Phoebe put her hands over her face.

'I'm so sorry.'

'Don't be. I asked you. And it must be horrible to relive it.' She turned to Eve. 'I looked you up before I came here.'

A woman after Eve's own heart. She always researched ahead too.

'I read about the other obituaries you've written of murder victims, and how you've helped the police with their enquiries. If you're gathering information this time, I'd like to help.'

'Thank you. It happens naturally. People sometimes tell me more than they would the police. I try not to break anyone's confidence, but if it's crucial information I pass it on. Sometimes bits of the puzzle come together unexpectedly.'

Phoebe nodded, her dark hair falling forward. 'Maybe you could show me the rest of the grounds as we talk?'

'Of course.' Eve led the way towards the woods. In the distance, by the walled garden, she saw Josh Standish, weeding a flowerbed. He'd been staring after them but looked down when Eve caught him at it. Thoughts of Cammie's death made Eve think of his own bereavement. His father had died while working at Lovelace. Jim Thackeray's words came back to her. *It seems to me that Lovelace requires absolute dedication, and that it wears people out.* What must it be like for Josh, toiling away at a job that had taken his father's life? That might be how he viewed it. And yet here he was, displaying absolute loyalty.

She turned to Phoebe. 'So you and Cammie met at university?'

'That's right. We both read history at Cambridge and had the same terrifying supervisor. We were chalk and cheese really, but he brought out the same reaction in us: the desire to run straight off after a supervision and let off nervous energy. Lark around, laugh, blot out the latest cutting remarks.'

Eve knew they'd both got firsts. 'Did Cammie work hard?'

Phoebe smiled and wiped her eyes, which had been welling up. 'Not always, to be honest, which made our supervisor irate. Whereas I never stopped trying to please the cantankerous old misery. We both came in for equal amounts of criticism.'

'That sounds faintly annoying.'

She grinned now. 'It was. I used to stay up half the night poring over some theory, whereas Cammie was up late adventuring. I felt I deserved more slack.'

Eve smiled back. 'I can imagine. How do you mean, adventuring?'

'There's a secret society at Cambridge which scales the university buildings. Very dangerous and definitely forbidden. I knew she was one of the members. She was in the skydiving and gliding clubs too, whereas I've always liked museums and the cinema. But we sparked off each other. Found the other intriguing, I suppose, because we were so different.' As they walked under a majestic beech tree, with its tassel-like catkins, she turned to face Eve. 'I could hardly believe the report about the cocaine the police found. Cammie was into thrills, but not that sort. I'm sure I'd have known. She didn't hold back.'

'Do you know if any of her contacts used cocaine?'

'Down in London, maybe. But out of the people who were here when she died, I'm not sure. Ralph Roscoe's the only one I know. I think he might have used it when we were students. I don't know about these days.' She glanced over her shoulder quickly. 'There's Sebastian Pickford, I suppose.'

'You've met him?'

She shook her head. 'No, but Cammie mentioned him. Back when she stayed five years ago she said he'd made a play for her but she wasn't keen. She told me he was arrogant and selfish. Didn't pull his weight at the manor. And then more recently, she messaged me about him. She stayed in Suffolk a couple of months or so ago. It was just a weekend trip, I think – before anyone came up with the documentary idea. She said Sebastian was the most despicable person she'd ever met.' She sighed. 'She wasn't very coherent when she messaged and she was never a drinker, so I put it down to upset. Peter Pickford-Jones was terribly ill by that point too, so I don't imagine the atmosphere was great. I texted back in case she wanted to chat, but she said she was going to bed. She promised to tell me about it when we met.'

'But she never did?' Eve could hear the regret in Phoebe's voice.

'No. She was always busy. We both were. Term ended for Easter and I was trying to crack on with some research while my timetable was clear. And she was finishing a documentary, by which time I was lecturing again. And now suddenly it's all too late. Anything we left unsaid is lost for ever.' She took a hand-kerchief from her pocket. 'It's unbelievable. I'm sorry. I've moved away from the point. Sebastian did something that upset Cammie badly, but as for the cocaine, I've no idea really. Though he wouldn't be the first model to party too hard.

'I've got some photographs Cammie took on her visit here five years back, if you'd like copies. I'll WhatsApp them to you.' Phoebe took out her phone. 'Although she hated Sebastian, she said Diana and Peter were lovely.' She shook her head. 'But she always sounded sad when she talked about Diana.'

That was curious. 'Thank you. I'd like to ask you about Ralph too. Do you know him well?'

'We used to see quite a lot of each other at uni, but mainly because he was dating Cammie. I've barely seen him since then.' Her tone was neutral.

'You don't have his current contact details?'

She shook her head. 'I'm afraid not.'

'He and Cammie seemed to talk quite a lot in the run-up to her death.' Eve remembered Ralph asking her about her research. 'And she looked – I don't know, excited, when he dashed over to join her in the balloon. What was their relationship like at university?'

'Passionate. Cammie was always on a high, but while it lasted, that was even more extreme. I still saw plenty of her when they dated; she talked about him ceaselessly. She was gloriously happy.'

'But it ended.'

'Abruptly. He was a year ahead of her and he'd just done his finals. One minute they were celebrating like crazy, staying up all night at a college ball, punting on the river, skydiving together, and the next, it was all over.'

'What happened?'

'I don't know. If it weren't for that, I'd say we had no secrets. I didn't get to see her for a week after the split. She wasn't shut in her room crying or anything. She went off on a trip to Derbyshire with a caving group she belonged to, and when she came back it was as though she'd closed the door on Ralph.'

If she'd blocked it out, maybe he'd left her, though break-ups could be emotional, whoever's decision it was.

'She said they were never going to be a permanent couple,' Phoebe added.

'And more recently?'

'She mentioned him several times in her latest messages. I wondered if their relationship was rekindling.'

'Were you nervous for her?'

'A little, but there wasn't much I could say.'

'I saw Cammie chat to Josh Standish, the gardener here, too. Did she mention him?'

Phoebe frowned. 'Not at all.'

So maybe there was no flirtation then. Eve remembered the gardener watching Cammie as she swam. It was still possible he'd fallen for her, but she wasn't interested. If he was jealous, he could have decided to kill because of it. If so, he probably wouldn't have minded Ralph joining the flight, but it seemed far-fetched. His feelings would have to be way out of kilter. And as with most of the suspects, how would he have ignited the leaking gas from the ground?

16

Over lunch, Phoebe gave Eve lots of useful information that would work well in her obituary: tales of a close friendship, shared fun and happy student days.

After that, Eve just had time to nip back to Elizabeth's Cottage, snatch a look at the photos Phoebe had sent on Whats-App, and walk Gus before her afternoon shift at Monty's. They were in the shade of Blind Eye Wood when her mobile rang. Simon.

'Eve? Viv mentioned you're trying to get hold of the guy who was up in the balloon with Cammie Harrington?'

A flicker of hope sparked in her chest. 'You don't have his contact details, do you?'

'Nothing as good as that. But I know he's renting from the same agency that handles my cottages. He came to look at one of mine and said it was overpriced, would you believe? A bit of cheek, I thought. Anyway, the agent I deal with let slip he'd opted for another property on their list.'

He gave her their details.

'You're one in a million, Simon. Thank you!'

. . .

She turned up to work her shift at Monty's that afternoon with her mind full of the case. Viv wanted her help in the kitchen, which wasn't a surprise. She'd be after gossip.

But before Eve got to work, she had a word with their student helper, Tammy. The lovely Lars, another regular and Tammy's boyfriend, was serving a group of mums and babies in a window seat. Eve noticed one of them smooth her hair as Lars turned to take her order.

Eve told Tammy about the cigarettes, wrapper and scorch marks she'd seen in the garden of Lavender Cottage. 'I know it's your home territory. I wondered if you could guess which of the local youths might have been hanging out there.'

Tammy rolled her eyes. 'Gum, cigarettes and firecrackers? I'd say it's most likely the Turnham brothers and their crew. They go to my old secondary school and we overlapped by a few years. They're much younger than me, but the moment they arrived they were trouble.'

'D'you think they'd talk to me?'

'Maybe if you bribed them with booze or cash.'

'I've got a nasty feeling that might be unethical.'

Tammy grimaced. 'Sorry. They're not keen on authority. You think they might know something important?'

'It's hard to tell. If it was them, I'm curious to know why they were hanging around an empty house. And most especially, what they might have seen.' From what Tammy said, they might have been tempted to break in and make mischief – or steal something even. If they'd got inside the night Cammie died, that could definitely have prevented the killer from retrieving the poisoned smoothie. 'Never mind. Thanks, Tammy. I'll have a think.'

Viv was standing in the kitchen doorway, drumming her fingers on her arm.

'Sorry, boss.'

'You're needed. Partly to cook summer blondies, but mainly

to pass on your news. Why does Tammy get priority? She's not your second sleuth in command.'

Eve explained what she'd been after as she put on her apron.

'Ugh. How annoying. But surely if we went together, we could get them to talk?'

Eve looked at Viv in her blue hairnet, her vibrant green hair visible underneath. 'If we went dressed like this there's a chance. And you could carry a rolling pin. But seriously? Maybe not. And we might only get one go. I don't want to muck it up. I need to think.'

'All right.' Viv sounded disappointed. 'So what's new? Any more discoveries?'

Eve shared everything Robin had told her, passing it off as gossip. 'And I had an interesting session with Phoebe Richmond too.' She continued her updates as she started to weigh out apricots and white chocolate for the blondies. 'I'd love to know what happened between Cammie and Ralph when they broke up.'

'Think you can find out?'

'I've got an idea that might give me a clue. It was good to see the photos Cammie sent to Phoebe last time she stayed at Lovelace too. They're a lot less formal than the ones she uploaded to Instagram. You can look if you like, once your scones are in the oven. I've got copies on my phone.'

'Once my scones are in the oven? Are you mad? I want to see them now.'

Eve concentrated on heating her chocolate and butter. It was best to set a good example. Having Viv's input was great, but the customers would complain if the food ran out.

'How do I get into your phone?'

Eve sighed and raised an eyebrow. 'You don't without my fingerprint. Oh, all right then, but quickly.' She opened it up and showed Viv the series of pictures Phoebe had sent her.

As Viv stared at them, scrolling through the collection, Eve went back to stirring her mixture, lowering the heat a little.

'Well?' Viv said, returning to her dough at last.

'They show how close she was to Diana and Peter when she stayed in Suffolk five years back, don't you think?' Eve had found it hard to believe the talk of Diana's motherliness until she'd seen them. 'There's real affection there.' Her mind drifted back to one of Diana with her arm round Cammie's shoulders. And several of Peter; he'd had such a fond look in his eye. 'I can't help feeling they were like a second family to her. Her dad had just died; she was probably at a low ebb.'

Viv paused in her dough folding. 'But something's changed since then?'

Eve was whisking eggs, sugar and vanilla together. She turned the speed down. 'Cammie and Diana could be mother and daughter in some of the photos she sent Phoebe. You'd never have made that mistake in the run-up to Lovelace Sunday.'

'True.'

What had happened? Eve wondered as she weighed out her flour. Phoebe's words came back to her. Cammie always looked sad when she talked about Diana. Yet she'd kept in touch with her and Peter – been to visit, in fact, around the time he died.

It must all mean something, but she couldn't work out what.

Back at Elizabeth's Cottage that evening, Eve trawled the internet for details of the caving society Cammie had belonged to. Thankfully, it had its own website, together with the names of past presidents, as well as a picture archive. At last she found a photo featuring Cammie dating back to June of her penultimate year at university. It had to be from the trip she'd joined just after her break-up with Ralph Roscoe. Cammie was grinning in the picture, though why, Eve couldn't imagine. Leaving aside her emotional upset, she was bent double, knee-deep in muddy water, seemingly wedged beneath an overhang of rock. Like her two companions in the picture, she wore a helmet with a head torch and blue coveralls, as well as knee and elbow pads. Eve wouldn't go caving if you paid her.

She noted the name of that year's president, as well as those in the photograph caption, then tried to find them on LinkedIn. It wasn't hard – they were all on the networking website. One was now a banker, one a scientist at a pharmaceutical company and one a lawyer. She sent them requests to connect and messages, explaining that she was writing Cammie's obituary. If they replied, she'd ask about Cammie's interest in caving, but buried amongst her questions she'd slip in the key one. Had Cammie always intended to go on that trip, or did she join at the last minute? If it had been a sudden whim, it suggested the break-up with Ralph had come as a shock, and she'd looked for a last-minute distraction. Whereas if Cammie had left him high and dry, it might add to his motive for killing her.

Whatever the truth, Eve badly wanted to talk to Ralph Roscoe. She thought again of his secret chat with Diana, hidden in the woods at Lovelace Manor. She had a sneaking feeling Diana knew exactly where he was staying. But if so, why was she being so unhelpful? It suggested she had something to hide.

Or maybe she'd asked permission to pass on his details and he'd said no. Thank goodness Simon had come up with the name of the letting agency. It was a start, though if he didn't want to talk then leaving a message wasn't going to help.

She sighed. She'd have to think on her feet, but in the meantime, she needed to prepare for the next day's interviews. She had Raven Allerton first thing. Her goal was to find out why she'd hated Cammie, and if the reason was strong enough to kill for. Eve was curious to know why Raven had stopped performing at Lovelace five years earlier too. If she'd fallen out with Peter, had that been anything to do with Cammie? Eve couldn't imagine why it should have, but the timing would fit.

And after Raven, she'd finally get to meet Irene at the White Lion pub in Lovelace-by-Sax. Moira was going to fetch her from her cottage – she said she was desperate for a change of scenery. Eve wanted to hear what she'd thought of Cammie and any insights she might have into Diana and Sebastian. With her long-standing connection to Lovelace, she might be party to all manner of secrets. It ought to be an interesting day...

17

Raven Allerton's address was 'The Shepherd's Hut, Wessingham Hall, Suffolk'. Eve drove through wooded grounds, following the directions the storyteller had given her.

It wasn't long before she saw the hut ahead. It was tiny but in good condition. She could imagine the people at the hall letting it out to holidaymakers – people who preferred glamping to camping. It would suit Eve down to the ground. For a second she imagined weekending there with Robin, hidden away from the world, under the trees, with just the birds for company. But it might not be so great in winter, with snow on the ground.

Eve parked and walked up to the hut's open doorway to find Raven waiting for her. 'What a pretty place to live,' she said by way of greeting.

'It's similar to the places Ma and I ended up in as I grew up.' Raven stood back so Eve could walk inside. 'We travelled a lot.'

'I read about it on your website.'

She nodded. 'This place is far more done up of course. There's an indoor loo and shower room. The heating's crazily good. Underfloor. I'm used to making do with far less, but it suits me all right. And if the mod cons distance me from nature

I can always get outside. Sleep under the stars, if I want. There's lots of wildlife in the woods. And the rent's a bargain.'

That surprised Eve. The hut would fetch a lot from holiday-makers. It was certainly upmarket, with Quaker-style kitchen units and Lloyd Loom chairs.

'Have a seat. Would you like a coffee?'

'Yes please.' Eve took a place at Raven's table and carried on assessing her home. There was a screen at one end of the room, a double bed just visible beyond, complete with a patchwork quilt. At the other end was a door Eve guessed must lead to the bathroom. Even if the rent was cheap, Eve wondered how she afforded it, after her absence from Lovelace. For a second her mind strayed to the cocaine in Cammie's bike pannier. Might she deal drugs as a sideline? If she wanted to kill Cammie and tarnish her name, she could have planted them there. Or she could have sold her some, even if she'd hated her.

'The old boy who lives at the hall's a sweetie,' Raven said, as though reading Eve's mind. 'Money's not important to him. He doesn't want the bother of short-term rentals. Letting me stay stops the place getting damp. Here.' Raven put their coffees down and joined Eve, sitting on a bench opposite her. 'So, what do you want to know?'

Why did you leave Lovelace when you did? Why did you hate Cammie? The questions circled in Eve's head. 'I'm after insights from people who knew Cammie well. Did you see much of her when she visited Lovelace the first time?'

Raven wrinkled her nose as though Eve had wafted sulphur under it. 'She was hard to avoid. Got her feet under the table very quickly.' Then she sat up straight and sipped her coffee. 'But Peter and Diana treated me well too, of course. Peter said I was like the daughter he'd never had.'

And that might have meant a lot to Raven. According to the 'About' section of her website her father had never been around. Peter had had two women on the spot who were likely vulnerable. Bereaved Cammie and anchorless Raven. Cammie's novelty value might have made Diana and Peter turn their focus on her.

'Did you feel cut out when Cammie arrived?'

'Oh no.' But Raven's jaw was tight. 'It made no difference at first. Diana and Peter were just as nice to me.'

'At first? I'm just trying to get an impression of what Cammie was like.' Eve could see how strong Raven's feelings were, just from her body language.

'Not everyone realised it, but she was ruthless. Callous. Prim. Unsympathetic. We were more alike than she cared to admit, yet she didn't try to understand.'

Eve was torn about what to seize on first. Cammie hadn't struck her as at all prim, but that could wait. 'What didn't she understand?'

There was a long pause. 'The way I'd chosen to live my life.'

'How do you mean?'

The woman's piercing blue eyes met hers. 'Just what I say.'

She was definitely holding back, but her folded arms told Eve she'd need to change tack. 'And you found her prim?'

'Holier than thou. She looked down her nose at the choices I made. It wasn't just me she objected to. She and Sebastian didn't get on. They never did, but something extra must have happened recently. She was shaking with anger after she spoke to him, a couple of days before she died.'

It fitted with what Eve knew, but coming from Raven it seemed like an attempt to change the subject.

'I'm sorry you and Cammie didn't get on. It must have been tense. But it sounds like you had some happy times with Peter, if he thought of you as a daughter. Did he end up thinking of Cammie in much the same way?'

Eve watched Raven's eyes, looking for signs of jealousy. What she saw was spite.

Raven drew herself up tall in her seat. 'Oh, I hardly think so.'

Eve was surprised. Raven sounded pretty definite about it, yet Eve certainly had the impression Peter had bonded with Cammie while she was at Lovelace.

'They didn't get on?'

Raven raised an eyebrow. 'They got on all right. But not in a father–daughter way, if you get my drift.'

Heck. This wasn't what Eve had expected. How much older had Peter been than Cammie? Thirty-five years or thereabouts? 'You're saying they had an affair?'

Raven opened her eyes wide. 'You think she wasn't the sort? He was a kind man in a loving marriage and she snared him. Made him think and act like her.'

It sounded as though Raven had liked Peter as much as she'd hated Cammie.

'You have proof of their relationship?' But Eve guessed not. She bet she'd have used it against Cammie if she had. Threatened to out her to Diana unless she stayed away, perhaps.

'I just knew. I was close enough to see the signs.'

'Your relationship with Peter never strayed into that territory?' Eve had to ask.

'Good grief, no. What do you take me for? As I said, Peter treated me like a daughter.'

Up until around when Cammie had arrived. But something had changed. An estrangement had taken place.

'What made you leave Lovelace?'

'I'd been reliant on my work there for too long. It's my rule never to put down roots.'

Like heck. Eve could imagine Raven going off if Peter started to ignore her in favour of Cammie. She'd seen her reaction when someone stole her audience. But why not come back once Cammie left for London?

'So what made you return to Lovelace now?'

'When I heard Peter had died, it felt like my duty to come back to support Diana.'

Eve didn't think Raven was ruled by duty. 'What about Cammie's relationships with other people at Lovelace? She seemed to get on all right with Josh. They spent a lot of time talking.' It felt mean to goad Raven, but she could be a killer. The police hadn't seen her hatred for Cammie, which left Eve feeling responsible for understanding it.

Raven shrugged. No tight jaw or red cheeks this time. 'You probably know Josh and I went out. And I know about you too: how you pass information to the police.'

Eve had expected as much. Local press coverage meant anyone who googled her would find out. It meant Raven could have guessed the direction her questions would take and prepared for them.

'Josh and I still see a fair amount of each other. As for Cammie, you have to bear in mind that Josh devotes all his waking hours to Lovelace, just like his father before him. It's a mystery to me. You'd think seeing his dad drop dead, after slaving away for next to nothing, would make him want a different job, but he's utterly dedicated. It's not surprising he wanted to know how Cammie was getting on with her research. If she'd managed to help publicise the place, his future would have been more certain.' Her eyes met Eve's. 'It's the same for me. Whatever I thought of her, it was in my interests that she got the job done.' Her eyes were far away for a moment. 'I do wonder if something's going on...'

'What do you mean?'

'I saw Diana and Josh having a private word, a few weeks ago, while I was at Lovelace. I mean, they talk all the time of course, and there are any number of reasons she might want to speak to him alone, but this was odd. She checked over her shoulder before she went into his house. It wasn't just the contents of their talk that was secret. It was her visit too.'

That was interesting. It made her think of Diana's private chat with Ralph Roscoe.

'But as for Cammie and Josh?' Raven shook her head. 'No. Cammie had other fish to fry, in any case. I saw her kissing the guy who went up with her in the balloon. Ralph. They looked pretty involved.'

The rekindling Phoebe had suspected had happened then. 'Did you tell the police about it?'

Raven shrugged. 'They didn't ask. You can pass it on if you think it's relevant.'

She might as well have said she didn't care two hoots about the murder. But wouldn't she have mentioned the kissing to the police if she was guilty? The entanglement would make Ralph an even stronger suspect. He and Cammie had a past after all, and a troubled one at that.

'Do you mind if I use your bathroom before I head off?'

Raven gestured towards the door Eve had seen. 'It's not hard to find.'

As Eve covered the short distance, she reflected on the storyteller's home environment again. She noticed some very old wellington boots to one side of the front door that might date back to childhood. She caught sight of letters inked into them. It made her think of her old school sneakers. Her mum had always initialled them like that too.

She guessed the hut had come furnished. The patchwork quilt on the bed didn't fit Raven's style. But inside the bathroom, the robe on the back of the door looked far more like her. It was vintage green velvet, a bit threadbare at the shoulder and hem. She saw jewellery on a stand too: silver, the sort you'd get on the hippy stalls at Blyworth market.

Eve wouldn't have thought about the wellington boots further, if it hadn't been for the comb she spotted in Raven's bathroom. And she wouldn't have seen *that* if she hadn't been being nosy. It was tucked behind some medicines on a shelf, but it attracted her attention because it was covered in a floral design, and she could just see part of a letter on it. Not an R or an A, but a J. She moved a packet of paracetamol so she could see it better. The letter J was inside a heart. She took a photo and put the paracetamol back.

Whichever way she looked at it, the comb was odd. Floral and sentimental wasn't Raven's style, and it wasn't as though plastic combs were expensive. She couldn't see Raven opting for a second-hand one. The thought gave Eve a momentary shudder.

So why did she have it?

As Raven saw her to the door, Eve managed to take one more surreptitious look at the wellington boots. The glimpse gave her a tiny adrenaline rush. The inked initials were J.B.

18

Eve's mind was full of the interview with Raven as she drove to Lovelace-by-Sax to meet Irene Marston. Had Cammie and Peter really had an affair, or was Raven muckraking? A relationship would be an alternative explanation for the fond look in his eye in the photographs she'd seen, and maybe the sadness when Cammie talked about Diana. That could be down to guilt, especially if they'd started out close. An icy shiver snaked down her spine. Jim said Diana had been feverish in her desire to get Cammie to Lovelace Manor. What if she'd known?

But it might all be rubbish, invented by a vengeful Raven. Eve still didn't know why she'd hated Cammie but it was clear that she had.

The initials on the comb and wellington boots also floated in the back of her mind. Who was J.B.?

Eve was delayed getting to the pub due to a visit to Ralph Roscoe's letting agency. As she'd expected, they wouldn't give out his address, so she'd had to leave a stamped envelope for them to forward. It wasn't ideal, but Eve had caught sight of their out tray before she left. It had given her an idea for after lunch…

The White Lion was a whitewashed sixteenth-century building on the main road leading through the hamlet. It must only be five minutes' walk from the manor, so the landlord probably knew Diana and Sebastian. He was standing at the bar now, talking to a punter, his bald head gleaming in the sunlight that flooded through a sash window, his cheeks rosy, a broad smile on his face.

Eve scanned the pub's interior and spotted Moira, sitting at a window table overlooking the garden. The woman next to her must be Irene. She was thin, alert and bird-like, with bright eyes and grey hair. Behind her was a walking frame.

In a far corner of the bar, Eve spotted Josh Standish too. He was sitting opposite a woman with long dark hair, the colour and lustre of polished mahogany.

A moment later, Eve had reached Moira's table.

'Eve dear, this is Irene.' Moira leaped to her feet.

'I won't stand if you don't mind.' Irene nodded behind her to the walking frame. 'But it's wonderful to be out of the house. I can't wait to leave that thing behind.'

'Thank you for seeing me.' Eve reached to shake her hand. A moment later, she'd taken her and Moira's orders, and was up at the bar.

'We'd all like the fish pie,' she said, 'and two glasses of house white please, plus a St Clements for me. I need to concentrate. I'm writing Cammie Harrington's obituary and I'm here to interview Irene.' Eve could see the landlord and the chief volunteer knew each other. He'd given her a wave when Eve put in her order.

The landlord looked mournful as he reached for a bottle of orange juice and poured it into a glass before topping it up with lemonade. 'That poor woman.' He lowered his voice. 'And to think it looks like murder now.'

'You must have known her, I suppose?'

'Not well, though she came in here with the volunteers. I

see plenty of Diana and Irene of course.' He paused and reached for a bottle of Chardonnay. 'Peter now, he used to be a regular. In here chewing the cud with the locals. It's so small we all know each other. But for the last two years of his life, he was a recluse. Never saw him. Too ill, I heard. Shame. He was the life and soul of the party, once upon a time. I saw more of Cammie last time she visited. She was always on an up – full of her latest exploits.' He'd poured the wine now and handed the glasses over, shaking his head as he presented Eve with the card reader. 'Ah well, there it is. We'll bring your food over.'

Irene thanked Eve as she set the drinks down. 'Did I over-hear Harry talking about Peter?'

Eve nodded as she took a seat.

'It was so terrible, when he was ill. Harrowing to see him in such a reduced state.'

'Did he still play a role in running the manor?'

Irene shook her head. 'Not near the end. I rarely saw him at all. He was unsteady on his feet.' Eve remembered Jim saying he'd been in a wheelchair at Lovelace Sunday last year. It would have been ten months or so before he died. 'But I had to visit the ladies' room during an update meeting with Diana and I heard him. He was calling out and he sounded pitiful.' She leaned forward. 'I can hear him now. *I want Sebastian. He under-stands...* It was very near the end. Poor Diana. It was she who was always fetching and carrying for him, bringing him meals, calling the doctor.'

Moira shook her head sadly.

Eve couldn't help being surprised that anyone would request Sebastian's presence. And he and Peter must have had their disagreements. Jim said Peter had wanted Diana to sell Lovelace.

Eve leaned forward. She sensed Irene wanted to share. People tended to treat her like a confidante, even though she was a journalist. 'It must have been heart-rending to hear that.'

Irene sighed. 'It was. I still wonder what went through Peter's mind during those last days. What do you say when you know you're dying? When it's your last chance to set the record straight? Diana was distraught one day after leaving his room.'

Eve's pulse quickened as Moira took an audible breath and leaned forward. Irene's words brought back Raven's insinuations. Maybe she wasn't lying. If Peter had had an affair with Cammie, the guilt might have got to him in the end. Maybe he'd confessed on his deathbed.

'What do you think it meant, Irene?' Moira said breathlessly.

But the chief volunteer shook her head. 'I don't know. And I'm sorry. It's no use getting maudlin.'

Moira slumped back in her chair. Eve had a feeling it was the withdrawn promise of gossip that was making *her* mournful.

'How's your research for the obituary going?' Irene asked.

'I went to talk to Raven Allerton this morning.' She let the sentence hang. It would be interesting to see if Irene filled the silence. She must know her well, after volunteering for so many years.

Her brow furrowed. She glanced over her shoulder and lowered her voice. 'Josh Standish popped in with some flowers for me just before Cammie died. He was worried about Raven. He said she seemed obsessed with Cammie. He thought she might cancel her event at Lovelace Sunday and turn her back on us all again. The manor is always his first priority, just as it is mine. But everyone else was delighted that Cammie was coming.'

'Except Sebastian,' Eve said.

Irene shook her head. 'Some old disagreement between them, I presume. He should have put it behind him for the sake of the manor. He needs a spot of mothering, that boy.'

Eve thought he could do with a kick in the pants. Beyond

Irene, she saw Josh Standish take the hand of his beautiful companion. Eve doubted they saw the pub around them.

'Diana was thrilled that Cammie agreed to come,' Irene went on. 'She hoped she'd stay at the manor like old times. She did her utmost to persuade her. I think it upset her a little that she chose to rent somewhere instead.'

But why did she push so hard? That was the question. If she'd found out Cammie had slept with Peter she might want her under the manor's roof for all the wrong reasons.

'And what about you?' Eve asked. 'How did you find Cammie as a person?'

Irene took a deep breath. 'She was lively. Gregarious. Easy to get on with. And affectionate. She came to see Peter when he was ill and she agreed to the documentary at almost no notice. I put that down to loyalty to Diana.

'But truth to tell she was competitive too, driven to win. To achieve for her own sake, not just for the manor's. She was secretive about her research. I think she genuinely hoped to help, but she wanted the glory if she found anything new.'

That all rang true. And if she'd had an affair with Peter, she could have rushed to Diana's rescue out of guilt, especially if she'd been genuinely fond of her. Emotions were complicated.

At that moment, a young woman with elbow-length red-gold hair appeared in the pub's doorway. As she turned and scanned the room, Eve recognised her as Sebastian's girlfriend, Sapphire. She rushed over as soon as she'd spotted them.

'Hello, Moira. And Irene – someone said I'd find you in here. So lovely to see you out and about!' She nodded to Eve too. 'What awful times! I can't believe what's happened.' She kissed Irene on both cheeks, then introduced herself to Eve.

'We met, didn't we? You're one of the volunteers?'

'You've a good memory.'

Irene leaned forward. 'Eve's writing poor Cammie's obituary.' Then she turned to Eve. 'Sapphire's been a godsend to us.'

Sapphire blushed and waved a hand. Eve remembered she ran a stately home. She'd know all the headaches Diana Pickford-Jones was facing. Eve wondered if Sebastian would try to keep her onside once he inherited the manor. She might help him bring in enough money to turn the place into a fine country home, written up as a top attraction in the Sunday supplements. She was sure he'd love that. She doubted he'd stay loyal though. How much would Sapphire put up with?

Eve stood to reach her a chair.

'Thank you.' As Sapphire sat down, Josh and his companion walked towards the door and left the pub. Josh nodded to their group as he passed.

'You arrived back today?' Irene seemed excited.

'That's right. I had a few days' leave booked already. It's such a shame I couldn't take Lovelace Sunday off. As soon as I heard what had happened, I wished I was back here to support Seb – and Diana of course. But it must have been horrific to witness the crash.'

'It was awful, wasn't it, Eve?' Moira's eyes were wide. She'd be giving a blow-by-blow account in a minute.

Eve moved to stem the flow; she needed new information. 'How did you and Sebastian meet? It's quite a coincidence that you're both connected with historic houses.'

Sapphire smiled. 'It's not chance really. You know Josh Standish, the gardener at Lovelace, who just left the bar?'

Eve nodded.

'He introduced us. I came to give a talk in Blyworth and Josh was in the audience. After the event, he talked me into a drink. There was I, thinking he was chatting me up, but in fact he brought me here and sat me down with Sebastian. He thought we'd have lots to talk about, and the rest, as they say, is history.' She shook her head. 'Seb's got no head for business of course.' She bit her lip, but Irene gave a wry smile.

Why was Sebastian being rubbish a source of entertainment

for her? Eve spent a moment fantasising about telling him what she thought of him, but let it go.

'I almost felt fate had sent me to him,' Sapphire went on. 'In fact, I accused Josh of match-making to secure Lovelace's future.'

Perhaps that was just what he'd done.

'I know we can make a go of it, as a couple,' Sapphire went on. 'And to run somewhere that's also your home. That's special.' She leaned forward and lowered her voice. 'This isn't official yet, but we've been talking about marriage. He sent me the most beautiful bouquet of flowers the other day, completely out of the blue. The card said "My future is with you."' Her tone was serious. It was Irene who made a 'squee' face and Moira who clasped her hands together.

Eve had to admit, it was a wonderfully romantic gesture. She just hoped Sapphire saw through Sebastian before the big day. 'Wouldn't you be sad to leave your current role?' she asked.

'Not really. My employers aren't... Well, I don't want to be unprofessional, but they aren't easy people. And working in support of my own home, preserving Sebastian's heritage, would be different. A vocation almost.'

Eve nodded. 'Did you get to know Cammie well?' She remembered Sapphire defending her to Sebastian.

'We talked a lot about Lovelace – and about Millingford Hall, where I work. She was interested. And I was excited about the documentary.'

'Would it have made a difference, in your professional opinion?'

Sapphire put her head on one side. 'It would depend on what she came up with. But in all honesty, I'd say only in the short-term. Lovelace needs something more sustainable. But Cammie believed she could turn the place around. And she was kind. It was a shame she and Sebastian didn't get on. I knew I needed to take what they said about each other with a pinch of salt.'

Eve sighed inwardly. If Cammie had warned Sapphire about Sebastian's flirting it clearly hadn't done the trick.

Five minutes later, Eve left the three of them to talk shop and went back to her car. Ten minutes after that, she was back at the letting agency.

'Sorry to bother you again. I didn't leave a set of keys here, did I?'

There was a different woman on the desk this time. She glanced around the front office, then turned to call through to a colleague to check nothing had been handed in.

It was in that moment that Eve managed to peek into the out tray she'd spotted earlier. As she'd hoped, someone had added Ralph Roscoe's address to her envelope. Although another piece of post sat on top, she could read enough to find him.

She wouldn't have to wait for his reply after all.

19

The cottage Ralph Roscoe was renting was a tiny thatched place, tucked away down a back lane in Wessingham. There was no car outside, but Eve refused to give up hope. It could be in the garage she could see, round the back. She knocked, but there was no reply. Sighing, she tried again twice to be sure, then hung around in her car for ten minutes.

What to do? He'd get a letter from her via the letting agents in the morning, most likely. She decided to leave it for now. Writing a second note might make him feel hounded. She could come back easily enough if he didn't reply.

Back at home, Eve found she'd had a response from one of the Cambridge University caving group, saying they were happy to give their memories of Cammie. Eve emailed back with some general questions, but managed to slip in the key one: had Cammie joined the summer trip to Derbyshire at the last minute? Eve claimed she'd heard it was so, and attempted to pass it off as interest in the late historian's impulsive nature.

She spent the rest of the afternoon puzzling over the initials in Raven Allerton's boots and on the garish plastic comb in her bathroom. By the time Viv knocked on her door at six, demanding news, gin, and tonic, in that order, Eve had come to several conclusions.

She filled Viv in on her chat with Raven that morning as she poured their drinks.

'Wow,' Viv said. 'Do you think she's right about Cammie and Peter having an affair?'

Eve re-corked the gin bottle. 'It could fit with Diana's desperation to get her to the manor, if Peter confessed. Irene Marston hinted he might have told Diana something devastating just before he died. But equally, Raven might be lying out of spite.'

'You still don't know why she hated her?'

'No. It's frustrating, but this afternoon I focused on the comb and the wellington boots. They might be irrelevant, but I hate unexplained details.'

'To be fair,' Viv said, 'they could be cast-offs. Maybe a friend or cousin let her have them.'

Eve shrugged. 'For the boots it makes sense, but a cheap plastic comb?' She showed Viv the photograph. 'And there are other possibilities.' She knew Viv must have thought of them too.

'That she's using a false name, and they're hers?'

Eve nodded. 'And if that's the case, I have all sorts of questions. It's not as though Raven's just a stage name. She's turned her into her full-blown identity.' Eve wondered how far the deception went. Was it just the name she'd adopted, because it was more memorable than her birth name? But she'd even detailed her mother's reasons for choosing it on her website.

Viv took the gin and tonic from her. 'You've got that look in your eye. Tell me! You already know more, don't you? You've been tucked away here all afternoon, snuffling your way through the internet no doubt.'

'Say snuffling one more time and there'll be no cashews for you.'

'I meant it as a compliment.' Viv reached behind her and snatched up the bag with an anxious look in her eye. 'I'm right, aren't I?'

'Put the cashews in that blue bowl on the side. I'm not letting you sneak more than your fair share this time.'

Viv saluted and followed Eve into the garden where they sat at the round ironwork table with their drinks.

'You're right. I searched for "Raven Allerton" and I couldn't find any mention of that name before eleven years ago.' It made Eve think of Robin, who'd had to walk out of his former life as Robert Kelly when the network of corrupt police put his life in danger.

'Does she have Facebook?'

Eve nodded. 'As Raven Allerton. A lot of her posts are public and several of them *refer* to her childhood – the version that's on her website – but there are no old photos of her performing alongside her mum at the festivals she mentions. No old photos at all, in fact.'

'Not everyone shares childhood pictures.'

It was true. Eve didn't. 'But for Raven it's a colourful back-story, yet there are none on her website even.'

'She might not have any if she and her mum were short of cash. No camera perhaps?'

'And none from local press archives, or event organisers?'

'So you really think she's not Raven Allerton?'

'I think it's a strong possibility she became her when she was nineteen. And that before that she was the J.B. of the boots. But how much of her life story is true and what J.B. stands for is more of a puzzle.'

Viv wrinkled her nose and sipped her gin and tonic. 'So it's a dead end? What will you do, challenge her on it? You realise she might throw a spider at you?'

Eve remembered Raven muttering what looked like a curse in Cammie's direction. Though she'd cope with either to get at the truth. She didn't believe Raven had secret powers. 'I might, if push comes to shove. But I've got another idea first.'

Her friend raised an eyebrow.

'I found several videos of Raven's storytelling sessions on YouTube. Have a look.' She turned her phone to Viv and set the first one playing.

'She's compelling to listen to, isn't she?' Viv said after it had finished.

It was true. Her eyes were bright as she spoke, her face alive, as though she was caught up in the story, inhabiting the characters, not just a narrator.

The tales were quite short and Eve showed Viv three more.

'I picked those ones specially,' she said when the last had finished. 'Notice anything, or was it just me?'

'She mentions the Golightly Woods in each of the stories. *"Don't go lightly into the Golightly Woods." "Tread lightly if you dare visit the Golightly Woods."* That kind of thing.'

'Exactly. And they crop up way more times than that. I thought she'd made them up at first, because the name lends itself to the stories, but I googled, and they exist. They're down in Essex, bordering a village called Great Foley.'

Viv's eyes were wide. 'You think she's got a connection with them?'

'It's got to be worth finding out. I'm due to interview Diana Pickford-Jones and Sebastian tomorrow morning, but I might head over to Great Foley after that.'

'Good luck! Please report back the moment—'

She was interrupted by Eve's mobile ringing.

'*Eve? It's Tammy. Sorry to bother you at home. You remember I told you about the Turnham brothers' gang?*'

'I do. You thought they might have been hanging around in Cammie Harrington's garden.'

'*That's them. I've got Lars here. He's got an idea about how we might find out more.*'

She put Lars on, and Viv leaned in so close her hair kept tickling Eve's cheek. As she rang off, Viv turned to her.

'You can't say no!'

'It feels wrong.'

'But you're tempted. You stopped drinking your gin the moment Lars told you what was on his mind. You were thinking ahead, anticipating the drive to Lovelace-by-Sax.'

'That was before I understood his plan.' Eve picked up her gin again for good measure.

'Oh you!' Viv took out her mobile and dialled. 'Eve's changed her mind, Lars. She thinks it's a great idea, and I'm coming too.'

Down the line, Eve could hear laughter.

She put her drink down again. 'I shouldn't be involving him in the enquiry.'

Viv grabbed her arm. 'You're taking the whole thing much too seriously. Come along and get changed. That pink dress is far too eye-catching. If spying's on the agenda, you need something nice and dark.'

20

Eve cooked for Viv and by nine o'clock that night, they were in Lovelace-by-Sax, lurking inside Lavender Cottage, having got the back door key from Simon. The police had commandeered the place until that morning, following poor Stella Hilling's death, but all signs of their presence were gone now.

It was starting to get dusky, but although they'd got the lights off, they couldn't risk looking out of the window openly.

'Let's peer from upstairs,' Eve said. From outside, she'd seen that Polly had installed some voluminous luxury curtains up there; they ought to be easy to hide behind. Ideally, she'd like to hear what was going on too, but if they waited in the street, they might muck up Lars's plans. Tammy said the Turnham brothers were a feature of Lovelace-by-Sax most nights, loafing around, stuck for something to do. Their paths had crossed Lars's once before. He'd turned up outside Tammy's house on his motorbike, wearing his leathers, and they'd called him mate and admired the bike. When Tammy had mentioned what Eve was after, Lars had been pretty sure he could get them chatting.

Eve's stomach was in knots about the plan. Her main concern was keeping an eye on Lars and ensuring he didn't get into trouble. Finding out whether the youths had hung out in Cammie's garden had become secondary. If someone had pulled her son into a similar scheme at Lars's age – or indeed any age – she'd have been angry.

Viv was watching Eve's face as they walked into what had been Cammie's bedroom. 'I know what you're thinking, but Lars will be fine. He's only going to chat to some kids! He's older than them, with a lot more life experience.'

Eve wasn't sure about that. 'He's going to try to deceive a gang of juvenile delinquents.'

'Yes, yes.' Viv had set herself to one side of the curtains.

Down below, they saw Lars arrive. He parked his bike diagonally opposite Lavender Cottage outside a house that was in darkness, glanced at his watch as though he was waiting for someone, then took out a cigarette.

Eve happened to know that he didn't smoke. It must be part of the act. A young man was going to smoke what might be his first cigarette because of her.

Viv laughed. 'He's certainly gone to town. He's wasted, waiting tables. He ought to join the police and go undercover.'

'This is definitely exploitation.' Eve was shaking her head.

But at that moment, she stopped talking as five hulking teenagers ambled their way heavily up the lane.

'Tammy said they always meet around nine,' Viv whispered loudly.

Eve glanced at the cottage's old windows, but someone had had them restored. No gaps for the sound to leak out, and they were too far away anyway.

Lars was looking at his phone as he smoked and didn't glance up until the Turnham brothers' crew were almost upon him. At that point he raised his head, gave them an upward nod, and went back to his phone. Eve had to admire his methods. He was remarkably self-assured.

She could see he made the Turnham lot curious. It was the

same at Monty's: heads turned. He was cool and good-looking and he knew it, yet instead of making him arrogant, it made him laugh. The Turnham gang had paused. The bike had got their attention and she imagined there was a bit of hero worship going on. They'd got a quiet Wednesday night in a tiny hamlet with no entertainment. Lars had freedom and a plan they knew nothing about.

They'd stopped to talk to him. He was nodding and offered one of the youths a light.

Eve took a deep breath. They probably weren't even sixteen. She was indirectly aiding and abetting underage smoking.

Lars was patting the bike now and saying something else to one of the lads. Then he shook his head and laughed. She bet one of them had asked if they could try it out. Thank goodness he'd said no.

The chat continued and now it looked as though Lars might be asking the questions. A moment later, he was shaking his head again. Shrugging.

Eve knew his plan. He was going to tell them he was waiting for his girlfriend, but her parents disapproved of him. They might not let her come out. Lars thought they'd probably bond over the control freakery of adults.

'He's going to study psychology when he's finished travelling,' Eve said in a whisper. 'Heck. Tammy will miss him if he goes back to Sweden.'

'Maybe she'll talk him into applying for courses here.'

At that moment, Eve saw Lars point at Lavender Cottage with a questioning shrug of his shoulders. And then they crossed the road. It was impossible to see them, once they were directly under Cammie's bedroom window. Eve had a feeling they might have gone down the passageway at the side of the house.

'Looks as though they're going to show Lars, not just tell

him about it,' Viv said.

'I don't like it. Lars might be an adult, but he's a very young one.'

'He's twenty-four.'

'Exactly. And he's working on my behalf. What if the kids realise he's spying on them? What if they've got something to do with the cocaine that was found in the bike shed?' Eve moved from the window. She'd seen the garden. It was bordered by a hedge, with a field beyond it.

'Where are you going?'

'To get into the field behind the house so I can hear what's going on.'

'Ooh, fun!' Viv trotted after her.

Eve checked the coast was clear, then let them out of the front door. It wasn't ideal, but there were no neighbours in sight, and definitely no sign of Lars and his entourage. She peered down the side passage. It led to a back gate in the hedge that gave access to the garden, but also ran beyond, to the field behind.

She took a deep breath. She wanted to keep an eye on Lars, but walking straight past the garden was a risk. If she made a noise the lads might clam up and leave again without telling him anything. She'd worn plimsolls though, with stealthy manoeuvres in mind. At the last minute she took them off and walked over the gravel in her socks.

Viv gave an exasperated sigh but followed suit.

Eve could still hear her footfalls, but the voices inside the garden didn't falter.

'So you guys seriously believe in ghosts?' That was Lars. He managed to say it in a teasing yet friendly way. As though he knew they didn't really.

The reply was a nonchalant laugh. 'I don't, but Joey does.'

'Yeah, right. Funny.'

Eve and Viv reached the end of the passage and the border

of the field. They went to crouch in the dusty ditch behind the garden, backing onto the crops. They were to one side of where the garden shed stood, with just the hedge between them and the boys.

'But when we saw the shadows in the cottage, we all wondered what was going on. We weren't spooked, but we knew she'd died that day. We saw it – the balloon crash.'

Lars made a noise expressing sorrow and rapt attention in equal measure. 'I wasn't there.'

They all started speaking at once. They loved him all the more now he'd let them take centre stage.

One of them cursed. 'It was horrible. She'd got no chance. We used to walk past here a lot before she died and see her through the window, working.'

'She waved to us once. She was well fit,' one of the others said, before adding sheepishly, 'Feels wrong saying it though.'

'And then you saw the shadows in the cottage the night she died,' Lars said. 'I might have thought it was her ghost.'

'It did look spooky,' one admitted. 'We were watching from the lane, but nothing moved, so we thought we must have imagined it. But then someone came up with the idea of having a closer look.' His laugh was full of bravado. 'Thought we might be able to get inside. Force a window maybe.'

'Only you were chicken!' Another of the lads.

'Was not. I didn't go for it straight away, that's all. It would have been stupid. I needed to size up the options first.'

'Yeah, right. We hung around while he bricked himself.'

'Didn't you get bored waiting?' Lars again, with laughter in his voice. 'But you could sit and smoke I suppose.'

The lads nodded.

'It was boring where I grew up too. Me and my mates used to like setting off firecrackers and stuff,' Lars added. 'Things like that.'

Eve knew they were illegal these days, but people still

managed to buy them.

There was a general murmur of agreement. 'We do too, but we only managed to get them once. We just smoked and waited for Joey to get his act together.'

Lars laughed. 'So what happened?'

'I went for it when I thought the time was right. But when I had a go at shifting the kitchen window, I heard a crash inside and saw a shadow.'

'If you could have seen him jump!'

'I think I made the ghost jump.' There was a moment's clamour before someone shushed the group. 'I know, I know, I don't believe in them. In the end, we reckoned someone had had the same idea as us and broken in for a bet or something. After all, that Cammie was famous. If we'd have thought of it earlier, we might have got there first and nicked a souvenir. I think she'd have wanted us to have one.'

Eve and Viv stayed hidden for some time after Lars made his excuses to the lads. Eve wondered when the heck they'd move and make it possible for her and Viv to go home. Her legs and neck were starting to ache. For what felt like an eternity, sounds of the lads whispering and scuffling came through the hedge, but at last, a mobile rang, one of the youths answered, and within a minute they'd bolted from the garden and back into the lane.

Some time after that, Eve dared to move too. Viv was dragging her by the hand. 'I am so done with surveillance work this evening,' she said, letting go of Eve and wincing as she massaged her back.

Back at Elizabeth's Cottage, Eve and Viv were mobbed by a very overexcited Gus, after which, Eve called Lars to thank him for his help.

'*It's no problem. I enjoyed it. Tammy thinks I should take up acting.'*

After she'd rung off, she updated Robin too, and asked him to tell Greg someone had been inside Lavender Cottage the night Cammie died. He agreed to feed it through as an anonymous tip-off. Eve didn't want the Turnham brothers and their gang interviewed. They'd be sure to think Lars had given their names to the police. And besides, they were useful contacts. They might need to talk to them again.

Viv was in Eve's kitchen when she hung up, making them mugs of hot chocolate. It was cool after dark and crouching in a field stock-still for an hour had left them both shivery.

'It'll help us to concentrate too,' Viv said, bringing the drinks through to Eve's living room and sinking into one of her couches.

'I hope Tammy's neighbours don't gossip about Lars to her parents.'

'I'm sure he'll be able to charm his way out of it.' Viv sipped her drink. 'So, conclusions?'

'Someone was in Lavender Cottage the night Cammie died, but I doubt it was more youths, and they probably used the spare key to get in. I wonder what they wanted. Whoever they were, they're unlikely to be the killer. If they were, they'd have removed the smoothie, safe in the knowledge that their first-preference plan for Cammie's murder had been successful. But they're probably the reason the killer didn't do that. If they came to try, they'd have found the house occupied and the garden full of kids, for part of the evening at least.'

'Makes sense.'

Eve frowned. 'The killer would have had hours to sneak in if they wanted to remove the poisoned drink before dawn, though. Maybe the intruder stayed so long they gave up. It suggests they were after something complicated, not just a souvenir like the boys said.'

The question was, what?

21

The following morning, Eve turned her attention to her interview with Diana and Sebastian. She'd chosen her sky-blue dress with the purple trim for the visit. She sat at the dining table in Elizabeth's Cottage, a blackbird's song drifting in through her open window, and sipped her coffee.

'I've got to tread carefully, Gus,' she said when he pottered in and gazed up at her. 'I need to know if Diana thought Cammie and Peter were lovers, but I'm digging with no proof of my own. Raven might be inventing things.'

Gus shook himself, as though it was all too much for him. *These humans with their crazy shenanigans.*

Eve pursued the theory once again. If Peter had confessed to Diana on his deathbed, or she'd found evidence at that point, then she had a motive for Cammie's murder. Her sudden change of heart about selling the manor and her fervent desire to get Cammie there fitted with that idea. It would explain the emotional distance between her and the historian too. But there was the obvious, innocent explanation as well: that Diana simply wanted Cammie's help. 'I can't confront her outright. It would be awful if the whole thing's a lie – or worse still, that it's true, but Diana never cottoned on.'

She'd have to tiptoe round the subject and see if she touched a nerve. That felt almost as bad, but if she was on the wrong track then her words ought to be water off a duck's back. And if she was right... then her tactics were in a good cause.

But Sebastian was another matter. She fully intended to confront him with what she knew.

It was he who answered the door when Eve hammered on the knocker.

'Come on in.' His eyes were the colour of ginger cake and held Eve's just long enough to make her uncomfortable, after which they showed a flicker of amusement. It got Eve's adrenaline going nicely.

'Diana's in the sitting room.' He took her through a door marked 'No Entry'.

'So this is the part of the house you both live in?'

He nodded. 'Me when I'm down here, Diana all the time.'

He really ought to be contributing to the finances if he got free bed and board whenever he felt like it.

'We each have a suite of rooms to ourselves,' Sebastian went on. 'The kitchen and sitting room, we share. They're smaller than the ones in the main house, but plenty big enough for us both.'

'You keep all the main rooms for show?'

'That's right. Except when we have special events on. We use the large kitchen then if necessary, like in the run-up to Lovelace Sunday.' He stretched and yawned. 'I dream of the day when I can occupy the whole house, like Lovelaces of yore, with no visitors on site. Sapphire thinks it might be possible one day if we make a few changes. Open up a café in the conservatory maybe, and bring more visitors into the gardens. Increase our plant varieties. Josh Standish is on board if we go down that route. So long as his precious walled garden's untouched of course.'

'And what about Diana?'

'Oh yes. She's been full steam ahead with new plans ever since she thought of inviting Cammie down. Thank God she got over her ridiculous notion to sell.'

As he pushed open the door to the sitting room, Eve heard voices.

'And if we made that move, I think we could quadruple your visitor numbers, by which time—'

'Sapphire, for heaven's sake, stop talking.' Diana was standing with her back to some French windows, one clenched hand up to her forehead.

Sebastian raised an eyebrow. 'Sorry, sweetcakes.' He leaned in to give Sapphire a kiss. 'Maybe we need to leave that sort of chat until another time. Diana's not been sleeping.' He paused to hold her gaze, squeezing her arm. He tuned his actions so cleverly when he spoke to her. On the surface, he was every inch the devoted lover.

Diana gave him a sharp look as Sapphire bit her lip and gave Eve a quick, sad smile. She left the room, head down, blushing.

'I heard you pottering about in the kitchen in the middle of the night,' Sebastian said, resting his hand on his half-sister's shoulder for a moment. 'It's no wonder after what's happened. Things will seem very different in a few weeks.'

'Don't baby me, Sebastian.'

He grimaced. 'I'll leave you two to talk.'

There were dark circles under Diana's eyes and her shoulder-length hair was lank. The front portion was pulled back into a ponytail, revealing a pale face.

'Thank you for seeing me,' Eve said. 'I'm so sorry for your loss.'

Diana nodded. 'Shall we sit in the garden?' There was an

area between the house and the moat, just outside the French windows.

'Let's. This is pretty.' The side of the house around the window was covered in wisteria in full bloom. In the compact garden, the first shrub roses were blooming and the air smelled sweet. 'It must be nice to have somewhere private like this, away from the visitors.'

There was a screen up to shield the area from prying eyes across the moat. Just beyond, to the right, there was a gap, and Eve could see the stone wall of the gated gardens and a large greenhouse.

Diana nodded. 'We never make use of the main gardens. They don't feel like ours. This is the one I tend myself; I take a pride in it. Keeping the plants going is soothing.'

'I've heard roses can be tricky.'

'A lot less so than humans.'

'I expect that's true. So Josh Standish manages the rest on his own?' It must be a mammoth task.

'With a few seasonal labourers when he requests them,' she said quickly, but then her shoulders sagged. 'When we can afford it, that is. The work is much too much for him of course, but he insists he can cope.' She sighed. 'I used to wish he'd apply for another position.'

Used to? What had changed, Eve wondered.

'He's a gem,' Diana went on, 'but I worry for him. His father collapsed and died the day of my engagement party. I had no idea he had a weak heart. If the same happened to Josh, I'd never forgive myself. But of course, we couldn't cope without him. Without a gardener I'd have to sell.'

Maybe that would make the choice more straightforward. Once again, Eve sympathised with Diana's desire to let the place go. It was a wonderful, characterful old house, but she must have had a basinful of the headaches involved. Eve could understand her not wanting to listen to Sapphire's big plans at the moment.

Her thoughts were interrupted by the arrival of Sebastian with a jug of iced water and two glasses on a tray.

Eve thanked him. Whatever his failings, she was thirsty and it was another warm day. Diana said nothing and turned away as he put the tray down. The move was pointed. They must have fallen out over something – or she'd finally lost patience with him. Sebastian flashed Eve a smile. For just a second she responded automatically to the warmth in it, but then pulled back. She mustn't let him work her too.

After Sebastian left them, Eve picked up where they'd tailed off. 'Was your worry for Josh one of the reasons you decided to sell up, just after your husband died?'

Diana had been pouring the water but she turned to Eve now and stared at her.

'I heard on the grapevine that you thought you might let the manor go.'

'It's true.' Diana leaned back in her chair and took a sip from her glass, clutching it tightly. 'It was mainly the shock of losing Peter. It made me re-evaluate everything. But I saw sense in under a week. Up until then I'd always been determined to keep the place in the family – that week was a glitch. I pulled myself together and got thinking again about how we might rescue the place. That was when I thought of inviting Cammie here.'

The timing was still interesting. She could have had that brainwave at any stage over the last five years. Why just after Peter's death? Eve wondered again about a deathbed confession.

Diana had seemed almost too tired to speak when Eve arrived, but the tale she'd just told tripped off her tongue. Almost as though she'd rehearsed it. Change of mind first, decision to invite Cammie second. But had it really been that way?

Or had the thought of luring Cammie there made her pull back from the sale?

'You were confident Cammie could make a difference?'

Diana frowned. 'She was good at getting what she wanted. Achieving her goals.'

To Eve, the words sounded loaded, but they didn't prove anything. 'She certainly seemed very charismatic. And of course, TV companies love a pretty face. I imagine she had lots of admirers.' Eve felt mean, trying to get a reaction, but it was better than asking about the possible affair outright.

Diana said nothing but her knuckles were white as she clutched her glass.

'I remember her saying you treated her like a daughter when she stayed with you.'

There was pain and wistfulness in Diana's eyes. 'It was nice to have the company. I thought we were close.' She blinked and Eve realised she was on the verge of tears.

'I'm sorry. You're saying you weren't after all? That she wasn't what you thought?'

Diana shook her head. 'A lot of water's passed under the bridge since that visit.' She sipped her drink and put it down on the table. It was as though the mouthful of iced water had given her strength. She pulled a piece of paper from her pocket and referred to some notes. She told Eve about Cammie's exploits five years earlier: her return to a family supper after the bareback horse riding with oak leaves stuck in her hair, the cut she got from enacting the sword fight, the holes she'd made in her clothes. All great anecdotes for the obituary, but conveyed in a stilted way, like a child standing in front of the class reading out what they'd done in their summer holidays.

Her emotion only started to show when she talked about the dinner Cammie had cooked for them on her last night at the manor. She mostly controlled it, but her breathing changed. She didn't mention Peter.

'Did your late husband mind having a house guest?' Eve watched her closely.

For just a second, Diana met her eye and there was a flash of suspicion there, but then she looked down. 'Peter thrived on company. It made him sparky, brought him alive. I thought what a good thing it was that I'd managed to get Cammie as a paying guest. It was a joy to see him happy.'

When Sebastian came to join them, Diana got up and turned for the house without meeting Eve's eye again.

Her half-brother looked after her, an eyebrow raised. 'She's taken it hard. She was overly fond of Cammie when she came the first time. That sounds harsh, but she seemed to feel Cammie was part of the family.' He turned to Eve and shook his head. 'It's not done to speak ill of the dead, but I imagine you want honesty. I found her rather full of herself. She was the centre of attention the entire time she visited, and she loved it.'

Just as Sebastian had hated it, Eve imagined.

'I knew you didn't like her.'

His eyes met hers. 'Because of what I said about the balloon flight? I couldn't help myself. It was true – she arranged all that for her own entertainment, as part of the Cammie Harrington show, not to big up Lovelace. That was her all over.'

'I didn't mean that. I happened to be on my way to the kitchen to fetch refreshments when you and Cammie were arguing.' *I know what you did.* If she'd overheard Sebastian's secret, she probably wouldn't have challenged him; it would have been too dangerous. But neither of them had put it into words. Eve wasn't a threat to him.

Sebastian frowned, apparently casting his mind back, but after his furious reaction, she suspected the exchange was still fresh in his memory.

'Oh... that,' he said at last, with a lazy wave of his hand. He looked sheepish. 'Look, I'd be grateful if you didn't put it in your obituary, but Cammie and I had a rather passionate fling last time she stayed. What I said was true, she was arrogant, but there was still a spark. We couldn't keep our hands off each other. But' – he bit his lip, yet managed a half-smile – 'I wasn't exclusive. I mean, it's not as though we were seeing each other officially. I never imagined it would be an issue, but Cammie thought differently.' He leaned back in his chair, looking fully relaxed. 'I remember now, the row you're talking about. She asked if Diana or Sapphire knew about the way I'd behaved. The truth is, neither of them do, but it's years back. Diana wouldn't care, and I know Sapphire would understand.' He still looked serious, as though he could convince Eve of his sincerity.

But she knew he was lying. Cammie had said she'd only realised the truth about him last time she'd visited – around two months earlier, by all accounts. It didn't fit with his claim.

'What would I understand?' Eve had seen Sapphire arrive at the French windows a moment before she'd spoken. She'd hesitated before asking, as though she'd like to pretend she hadn't heard.

Sebastian stood up, took her hand and told her the exact same tale he'd told Eve, without missing a beat. 'I just never realised Cammie was taking the fling seriously. And it sounds awful, but my passion for her died when I got to know her properly.' He gazed into Sapphire's eyes. 'I didn't mean to hurt her, but I was young. I didn't know what love was until I met you.'

Eve saw Sapphire's chest rise and fall. 'I feel the same.' She didn't want to believe Sebastian was a toad. She was in love, and happy at the thought of running Lovelace with him, but how would she feel after twenty years of hard grind and putting up with his infidelity? Eve wanted to tell her to run while there was still time, however much she hated her current employers.

Sebastian sat down opposite Eve again and Sapphire took a chair too.

'Did you know Cammie had found the loving cup?' Eve

asked. There was no need to explain further. Its presence in Lavender Cottage had been widely reported.

'No.' Sebastian was frowning now. 'I can't believe she removed it from the manor without telling me or Diana. Some might call it theft.'

'It was a little odd,' Sapphire agreed.

'I assume she wanted to do some sort of grand reveal of the research she'd done, to give it maximum impact.' Eve could understand that, though she could see their point as well.

Sebastian's brow was still furrowed. 'It backs up what I was saying. It was all about her, I'm afraid.'

'Did you know the cup existed?'

He shook his head. 'I can't think why Cammie was so secretive. Yes, it's interesting, but hardly the discovery of the century. The portraits Louisa sketched of herself and Seth were much more exciting. The visitors love them.'

'Still, every little helps, when it comes to publicity,' Sapphire said.

Sebastian gave a hollow laugh. 'True. I must say, I thought Cammie's death might mean we'd be crawling with visitors. People are so ghoulish; death sells better than love. But the cocaine has switched the focus away from us and onto her London friends.' He shook his head. 'It's typical somehow. All about her, once again.'

22

Half an hour later, Eve was with Robin, walking along the estuary towards the sea. The path was relatively lonely, especially on a weekday in term time, so they'd taken the risk. To their left, the Sax sprawled its meandering way towards the coast, curlew sandpipers and dunlins feeding in the shallows. To their right, a reedy ditch separated the path from fields and the village beyond. Gus had dashed ahead, but halted now, his eyes on the reeds, as though in response to a sound. She hoped he didn't explore too thoroughly. Being so low-slung, things got messy very quickly.

'You go first,' Robin said. 'How did it go with Diana and Sebastian?'

Eve filled him in. 'Diana came back to the garden before I left, so I got to talk to them together. It gave me a chance to mention my visit to Raven Allerton. I asked if they'd known her before she started working there, but they denied it and they looked honest. If I'm right, and her real name's not Raven, I don't think they know anything about it.'

Robin nodded.

'The whole interview was frustrating. I know Sebastian was lying. His version of events doesn't fit what I heard, and I'm sure Cammie would never have had a fling with him anyway. The upshot is, I still don't know what his secret is, nor how much of a threat Cammie was.'

'And Diana?'

Eve thought back to her white knuckles and suppressed tears. 'It's clear she adored Peter, and that she was pleased Cammie made him happy at the time. Now, I'd say she's mourning both of them, but in Cammie's case I'd guess it's the loss of their past closeness she's lamenting – and that it died well before Sunday.' The photographs Cammie had shared with Phoebe came back to her. The fond look in Peter's eyes, and the appearance of happy families when Diana was in shot. 'What I saw reinforces Raven's claim that Cammie and Peter had an affair. I got a reaction from Diana, so I'd guess she knows, but I can't prove it. And without cast-iron evidence, I still don't feel I can ask her specifically.' She'd have to think again. 'What news your end?'

'It looks as though you might be right about the loving cup, for what it's worth. The tech team have found traces of mud and reed lodged in the engraved letters and around one of the handles. That would tie in with Cammie fishing it out of the moat.'

'I'd love to know how it got there, and why.'

'It's definitely curious. But there's been a more major development. A half-burned battery's been found at the crash site.'

Eve turned to him. 'What does that mean?'

'The police think it's possible it came down with the balloon debris. They can't get any prints off it, most of it was destroyed, but it could have been part of some kind of improvised device to start the fire.'

Eve took a deep breath. That made all the difference. 'So it's looking more likely that someone on the ground arranged the crash?'

Robin nodded. 'Palmer's still interested in Ralph Roscoe. He blagged his way onto the flight at the last minute and he could have smuggled the device on board. If he'd managed to create a small nick in the fuel line, he'd still need to light the gas. It would have been a lot less obvious than bending down mid-air with a lighter in his hand.'

'True.'

'But he's widening his net now. Someone else could have sneaked into the basket and enabled a slow leak earlier on. It could have gone unnoticed until the device – if there was one – created a spark.'

'Who's he got in mind, as well as Roscoe?'

'Raven Allerton's on his radar now. Interviews have produced several witnesses who saw her and Cammie at logger-heads, both this time and towards the end of Cammie's previous stay too.'

Eve could imagine Raven committing the crime. She'd seemed full of hatred, but in a cold, determined way. Enough to do the planning. Agreeing with Palmer always hurt though. He was such an oaf. 'I hope I'll find out more about Raven this afternoon, with the trip to Great Foley. It's a long shot, but I'd swear I'm on to something. Who else is Palmer looking at?'

'He's still trawling through Cammie's London contacts.' He shook his head. 'Diana and Sebastian haven't made it onto the list.'

It wasn't surprising. Eve's own suspicions were based on whispered conversations, unsubstantiated accusations, and guesses. She needed to work quickly. Find out more.

At that moment Gus dashed back to join them, proudly dropping a sodden tennis ball on the path in front of her. She bent to congratulate him for tidying up lost property.

'The tech team have managed to access Cammie's laptop,'

Robin went on as she stood up. 'There's nothing unexpected. She'd barely made any notes on her research, though there are a number of photos taken at the manor. But just what you'd expect: pictures of the period furniture, the photographs and sketched portraits of Louisa and Seth, the walled garden. I can forward you copies in case anything strikes you. And I've got some shots the police took of Lavender Cottage too. I know you got some of your own, but they had gloves so they could nose around properly.' He grinned and passed her his phone. 'There's a map too, showing where debris from the balloon was found.'

Eve scrolled through the photos. There were pictures of the familiar living room at Lavender Cottage, with Cammie's papers stacked neatly on her desk. The investigators had opened the drawers to reveal a stapler, letter opener, pens and a mouse pad.

The map of the debris showed how far-flung everything was. Bits of basket had ended up strewn around the field. They must have dropped as they'd burned. She was distracted from the diagram by Robin's next words.

'And lastly, the analysis of the cocaine came back. By current standards, it's not very pure. The kind of levels you'd expect in a student stash, rather than that of a richer buyer.'

Eve's gaze rested on a patch of pretty pink cuckooflower, but the blooms went out of focus as her mind drifted. 'And Cammie wasn't short of money. It seems all the more likely it was planted.'

'I agree. It could have been put there to point to a different motive for murder – something less personal.'

That mirrored Eve's thoughts. 'As for the quality, Raven might be in the right income bracket to buy the cheap stuff. Or maybe whoever put it there's a regular user and added a filler themselves, out of meanness or to put the police off the scent.'

'Either of those possibilities would fit. The filler was laundry detergent, so anyone could have made it up.'

So if Eve was right, Cammie's killer knew where to get hold of cocaine. She only wished that got her further.

23

The drive to Great Foley took ninety minutes. It was a fair way to go on a hunch, but Eve couldn't rest until she'd checked it out. She'd managed to leave before twelve, so she could be back in time to give Gus his supper. Her neighbours, Sylvia and Daphne, had offered to walk him mid-afternoon.

As she left the A-road and turned towards the village, Golightly Woods appeared on her left. For a moment, Eve was tempted to pull over and explore. She could see why they'd captured Raven's imagination. The trees were densely packed; they cut out almost all light so that the narrow tracks running through looked menacing. But walking amongst the trees wouldn't solve the mystery.

She drove past large detached whitewashed houses with red-tiled roofs, the sun-dappled road stretching ahead of her, patterned with the silhouettes of leaves. Presently, the houses got smaller and closer together as she entered the village proper. Eve was in a dilemma. She'd got a photograph of Raven. In theory she could just wander round asking people – shop-keepers and the publican maybe – if they recognised her. She was very distinctive. Even if she hadn't visited the area in a while someone would probably remember her.

Unless this entire trip turned out to be a wild goose chase...

But people might not talk. Eve could say she was a friend, but her questions would still look suspicious. If a stranger came to Saxford brandishing a photograph of Viv and asked Eve for information she sure as heck wouldn't give it without getting permission first.

She was mulling the problem as she entered the high street. A moment later she'd pulled over by a post office. An idea was forming.

She went inside and used their photocopier. Thankfully, the clerk at the desk left her to it, simply charging her at the end. She exited the building with twenty pictures of Raven.

Five minutes later she was sitting in a picturesque café-cum-bakery, with cream and turquoise paintwork, enjoying a scone in lieu of lunch. She was ravenous now, and ate with indecent haste. After she'd finished, she went up to pay but bent down at the last minute, close to the counter, beneath the waitress's line of sight. When she righted herself, she was holding one of the pictures of Raven, which she'd slipped from her bag.

'Sorry. I just wanted to pay but then I spotted this on the floor. I don't know if it blew off the counter?'

The woman peered at it. 'No. That's odd. It must belong to one of the customers I suppose. Here, I'll keep it in case they come back.'

There was no sign of recognition in her eyes.

Eve used a similar method in the local bookstore, pub and grocer, emerging with zero information, one paperback, a packet of crisps and an apple. She was looking forward to the book and the snacks, but she'd kick herself if she left Great Foley empty-handed.

She went to an interiors' outlet next, then a dress store and a pet store. She was preparing to ask about guinea pigs as she 'discovered' yet another picture of Raven. The grey-haired man who was serving pushed his glasses hard up the bridge of his nose and leaned over the photo.

At long last, she might be getting somewhere. There was a flicker of recognition in his eyes.

'I can't think what it was doing on the floor,' Eve said. 'It's odd, though. She looks familiar.'

He glanced at her, keenly. 'You're local?'

'Not very, but I used to visit regularly. It's years ago now – maybe more than a decade? But I'm sure I met her. Her name's on the tip of my tongue. Something beginning with J maybe?' *J.B.* What did it stand for, and was this man finally going to tell her?

'I thought I couldn't be mistaken,' he said. 'Julia. Julia Barrington. Used to come in here for hamsters.'

'Yes! I wonder where this photo came from.' Eve didn't dare ask more.

'Maybe they're trying to find her again.' The man shook his head. 'She ran off a long while back now, but why they'd circulate her photo here I don't know. They'd have seen her if she was still local. And I haven't seen the family come into the shop.'

'Oh. That's odd then. I'm sorry; I didn't know she'd run away. How sad.'

'I had her friend in here in tears at the time, asking if I'd seen her. Reckon the au pair was devastated too, though Julia was a proper handful, I could see that. And she wasn't the au pair's responsibility – not by then. She was there to look after the younger brothers. But the family?' The man shrugged and his brow creased. 'Cared more about their dogs and horses than they did about Julia. Now, don't get me wrong – she never wanted for material stuff. Everything money could buy. She only had to ask. But as for love...'

Eve's image of Raven's background shifted. Dogs, horses

and an au pair? And parents that didn't care. 'They lived out beyond the village on the main road, didn't they?' It was risky – a complete guess – but it was where the big houses were.

Eve breathed a sigh of relief as the man nodded. 'That's right. That massive white house with the blue gate and the stables.'

At last, the storekeeper remembered Eve must have been there for a purpose. It was only after taking a leaflet on guinea pig care, and hearing his words of wisdom, that she left again. She felt a twinge of guilt as she told him she'd think it over.

Eve parked on the wide leafy road on her way out of Great Foley, next to the house with the blue gate and the stables. It was vast. The name of the place, Bankside, was on a sign mounted on the wall next to the gate.

She sat in her car for ten minutes, googling. She couldn't bring herself to wait until she got home. She found several Facebook posts mentioning Julia, some from years back, some more recent, all asking if anyone knew where she was. Her parents were mentioned too. Most of the comments echoed those of the pet store owner. *It's no wonder she ran away. I sometimes wonder if Gerard and Paris knew what she looked like.*

She led them a dance though, someone else had commented. *It was no way to treat them.*

It was no way for them to treat her, came the reply.

Gerard and Paris Barrington. What a mouthful. Eve googled them too. They were heavily involved in political fundraising and equestrian events. The articles she read said Gerard was a banker in the city and Paris owned a high-end fashion store in London.

Eve guessed the floral comb she'd found in Raven's bathroom hadn't come from them. Wrong style. Perhaps the best friend the pet-store owner mentioned had bought it for her. And maybe the au pair put her initials in the wellington boots.

As Eve drove back across country she thought of everything she knew.

Raven said Cammie had disapproved of the way she'd 'chosen' to live her life, despite them having a lot in common. She'd found Cammie unforgiving and self-righteous. It sounded as though Cammie had had absentee parents too – a racing driver and the owner of a craft beer company. Was that what Raven had meant? Cammie had enjoyed settling into family life at Lovelace by all accounts. Maybe she'd valued Diana's mothering and Peter's warm welcome, and Raven might have felt the same – for similar reasons. Then Cammie had fallen for Peter, changing the dynamic from comfortable and wholesome to dangerous and precarious.

Had Cammie discovered Raven's true identity? Was that at the heart of their rift? Eve thought of the timing. Maybe Cammie had told Peter, which led to the severing of links between Raven and Lovelace Manor. It would fit. Raven hadn't returned until after Peter was dead.

But would Peter have been that angry at the deception? It seemed extreme to Eve. She could imagine him feeling embarrassed that he'd fallen for Raven's tall stories, but he wasn't the only one. And why had Cammie told him, but kept the secret from the rest of the family? Eve was convinced Diana and Sebastian were unaware.

It would fit if Cammie had been jealous of Raven. She might have used her knowledge as a weapon to remove a rival. But Raven had been dating handsome Josh back then. Eve believed her when she said her relationship with Peter was close, but platonic.

She was pulled out of her thoughts as her mobile rang. She clicked to answer hands-free.

'*Eve? It's Diana Pickford-Jones. Can we meet again, over here at the manor at five? Sebastian and Sapphire have gone out and I think we need to talk.*'

24

Eve glanced at the time. She could make the appointment with Diana on her way home and still be back to feed Gus. She turned off the A12 and made for Lovelace-by-Sax.

It was a beautiful afternoon and Eve had her window down, so all the smells of the countryside wafted into the car. She passed verges thick with cow parsley next to hedgerows of hawthorn in bloom. It was so idyllic, but Eve's stomach was in knots. What was on Diana's mind? She hadn't sounded happy.

At last, Eve turned in at the manor. She parked as near to the house as she could. As she left her car she could see the gardener, Josh Standish, standing close to Diana on the bridge over the moat. He nodded, then turned to leave, making his way back towards his cottage. Eve guessed they'd been talking business; he was clutching some papers.

Diana looked after him pensively, then raised her eyes to meet Eve's. 'Come in.'

No pleasantries. It was clear Diana wasn't pleased with her. Was this about the interview earlier in the day? Eve was sure she'd touched a nerve.

Diana led the way to her study. That spoke of a formal talk. She sat behind her desk and motioned Eve to sit too.

'I decided I'd have to ask you back.' She steepled her hands, elbows on the desk in front of her. 'You know, don't you?'

It was a horrible moment. Eve guessed she was talking about Cammie's affair with Peter, but what if that was all in her head?

'About the affair?' she said at last. 'Yes.' Naming no names was the best solution she could think of. She might be talking about anyone. If she was barking up the wrong tree she could bluff her way out.

Diana got up stiffly and went to pour herself a whisky from a decanter on a side table. She took a large mouthful and swallowed it before sitting back down. 'I knew you must, with all those pointed questions.'

'I didn't want to be specific. I wasn't sure if you were aware.'

Diana took a deep breath, her chest rising and falling. 'I wasn't at the time, of course. Peter told me when he was dying.' She put the glass down heavily on a pile of papers. 'I couldn't forgive Cammie. It wasn't the betrayal – though that hurt. It was what she did to Peter. It ate him up inside. Love for her. Guilt. And he bottled it all up. It made him... more ill. She contributed to his death.'

Eve held her breath and kept quiet. Waiting for more.

'Peter wasn't always faithful, but this' – she clenched her fist and pushed it to her forehead – 'this was different. It meant something. And Cammie came back to visit. Just often enough to keep the flame alive. Even at the last, when Peter was at death's door, she visited. She cried when she left him and hugged me. I took comfort from her. And just after she went, Peter finally told me the truth.' She downed the rest of her whisky in one go. 'He cried too, and I held him. He was so full of regret, but I could see he still loved her.'

Her eyes met Eve's, unblinking. 'I suppose you're

wondering if that's why I changed my mind about selling this place. I saw my chance to get Cammie here – to pass it off as an attempt to rescue Lovelace. But I'd decided Lovelace should stay in the family anyway.' She sighed. 'That being the case, I knew we'd need all the help we could get to increase footfall. Something to put Lovelace back on the map. But I did have a morbid desire to get Cammie here too. If you're thinking I killed her, you're wrong. Yes, I was angry. Violently so. I hoped she'd stay here, under my roof. I wanted to see if she could sit there, facing me at breakfast without crumbling. How could she? I thought I'd confront her. Tell her what I knew but make her fulfil her promise – carry on with the documentary. Live under my nose for weeks on end. I wanted her to feel what she'd done. To live in shame.'

She took a juddering breath. 'But I never even spoke to her about it. Can you believe it? I spent the entire run-up to Lovelace Sunday looking for the right moment. The way to achieve maximum impact. I wanted to make her see what she'd done without breaking down myself. And then someone arranged the crash and I never got the chance. And now she and Peter... she and Peter are together again. And I'm here on my own.'

Eve's heart tightened at her misery, but Diana's feelings were chilling. She felt hatred all right, all mixed up with sorrow and regret. Yet instinct told Eve she wasn't the killer. Cammie's suffering had been over too quickly. Diana had wanted a long, slow revenge.

'I knew I'd have to talk to you about it after this morning,' she carried on. 'I could imagine what you'd write in Cammie's obituary. That she'd had an affair with Peter and that poor Diana who treated her like a daughter never guessed the truth. I can't stop you but—'

'I've got no intention of writing anything like that.'

Diana blinked.

'It's my job to understand Cammie and to tell *Icon*'s readers about her. I'll do my utmost to figure out how her mind worked, her moral code, the positive and negative parts of her character. Understanding her relationship with you and Peter will help me do that, but I'd never go into those sorts of specifics.' Eve's blood ran hot at Diana even suggesting it. She couldn't help herself.

Diana's hand was still tight on her glass as she got up to fetch a second drink, but she only added a finger's worth this time. Her shoulders lowered a fraction as she sat down again.

'I'm sure most people know Peter strayed,' she said, sipping the whisky. 'But no one's ever acknowledged it publicly or said anything to my face. It would be hard if his love affair with Cammie made it into the press. The floodgates would open. People would start gossiping about their suspicions openly.' She leaned back and gazed up at the ceiling for a moment. 'I used to wonder about him and Raven, but he denied that and I believed him.' She shook her head. 'Though he did admit he'd given her presents occasionally. If you dig that up while you're ferreting for information you'd do well not to jump to conclusions.'

Eve never jumped to conclusions. She tried to take a step back. Who wouldn't react like that?

'You'd better go now,' Diana said, standing up. 'I've got to get ready to meet Raven. Some storytelling-trail idea she's had for the woods. It sounds promising if we're going to get this place back on its feet.'

She must know she was clutching at straws. Her tone was weary. Why was she carrying on?

Eve got a rapturous welcome from Gus as she entered Elizabeth's Cottage.

'I know, I know. I was longer than expected.' She crouched down and he lolloped all over her. 'But you got your lovely walk

with Sylvia and Daphne, didn't you? And I, Gus, have got a
whole bunch of news!'

After she'd fed him she checked her emails and double-
clicked on the one that might tell her something. It was from the
member of the University of Cambridge's caving society. He'd
provided lots of useful information but also the answer to her
key question: Cammie *had* joined the summer trip to
Derbyshire at the last minute. It had been a bit awkward and
involved some mucking around with room bookings, but she'd
been so keen that they'd forgiven her.

It added weight to Eve's hunch that it had been Ralph
Roscoe who dumped Cammie back then. It fitted that she'd got
out of Cambridge in a hurry. Buried her feelings. So presumably Ralph hadn't been nurturing a long-term grudge against
her for the last sixteen years. It had never looked that likely, but
until the burned battery was found, he'd seemed streets ahead
of anyone else for opportunity.

After that, she got her supper on the stove, then called
Robin. It took a good five minutes to update him on the trip to
Great Foley, Raven's true background and Diana's revelations.

'*That's some productive afternoon. You must be tired.*'

'I'm looking forward to my supper, but my mind's racing.'

'*I'm not surprised. What do you think?*'

Eve repeated her conclusions about Diana as murderer. 'I'd
say she adored Peter despite it all, and she'd stop at nothing to
avenge anyone who caused him harm. But she'd think death was
too good for them. It was what she said about Raven that really
got me thinking.'

'*About Peter giving her presents?*'

'Exactly. I'd come up with a theory that Cammie told Peter
that Raven was living a lie and he sent her away. She only
returned to Lovelace after he was dead. But although the timing
fitted, it seemed like an extreme reaction on his part.'

'*You think it was to do with the presents?*'

'It would fit, Robin. What if Peter felt sorry for Raven? The story on her website implies she's had a hand-to-mouth existence since she was tiny, and that she's never had a place to call home. Her income from storytelling can't be massive. What if Peter decided to give her some of his earnings? I could imagine it. Raven said he'd told her she was like the daughter he'd never had. She was beautiful and vulnerable. He could have been subbing her for years, for all we know. Or have given her a lump sum to cover some particular expense.'

'That would certainly make it worse, if he found out the truth.'

'Especially if Cammie discovered what I know: that Raven's parents never let her want for cash. She might have rejected their money on principle, and lost access to it once she ran away from home. But if Peter funded her, while Diana scrimped and saved to prop up the manor, I think the truth would have left him feeling duped. She was prepared to accept gifts from him because it didn't offend her pride, but he could ill afford to give them. Whereas her parents must be loaded.' Eve sighed. It was sad to think of Raven inventing a childhood she wished she'd had, though she'd no doubt romanticised the nomadic lifestyle. 'I've no proof, but it would explain Raven being banished from Lovelace. That led to a massive drop in income and the severing of a relationship I suspect Raven really valued.' She thought back to the way the storyteller had spoken of Peter. A kind man. 'If I'm right, Cammie destroyed all that. Raven had a big motive for her murder and I could see her doing it.'

25

'So you think Raven's lonely, and Cammie was probably the same?' Viv said to Eve in Monty's on Friday morning. They were both serving that day, so she was having to glean her updates as they crossed paths en route to the kitchen.

Viv went to fill a teapot from the water boiler and Eve queued up behind her.

'That's how it strikes me.'

'And for suspects you think Raven's top, with Sebastian as runner-up? With Ralph, Diana and Josh still possible but less likely?' She'd filled her teapot and was standing over Eve.

'You don't want that tea to go cold, do you?'

'In this weather? Anyway, the quicker you answer, the faster I'll get back to work.'

Eve started to fill her teapot. 'You've summed it up. Diana ended up hating Cammie, but I don't think the crime fits her character and I haven't found a motive for Ralph or Josh. I thought there might be some kind of love triangle there at first. It sounds like Ralph and Cammie's relationship was kicking off again. But no one I've spoken to thinks Josh was interested and he was in the pub with a dark-haired beauty on Wednesday. I'd guess she's his current girlfriend.'

It was another twenty minutes before they overlapped in the kitchen again. Eve was replenishing a tray of chocolate heart cakes when Viv nabbed her.

'What about the planted cocaine?'

'You could fill the teapot while you quiz me.'

Viv huffed but complied.

'If we take it as read that the killer also planted the drugs, then I guess Sebastian, Ralph and Raven seem most likely. The guys because I can imagine either of them using cocaine for kicks, and Raven if she'd taken to selling it to make some money. I imagine she was short of cash while she was exiled from Lovelace.'

Viv was back to standing over her again. 'That all makes sense.'

'But if it's Sebastian who's got a cocaine habit, I guess Diana or Josh could have pinched some. Josh is in and out, and in charge of security. And cutting it with laundry powder would make sense. It would have reduced the amount they'd have to steal and the chances of Sebastian noticing.' Eve circled round Viv with her tray of cakes. 'I honestly feel like a sheepdog sometimes. The customers, Viv!'

'Spoilsport.'

It was half an hour later that the first ripple of gossip stirred in the teashop. It started as a murmured conversation between a woman sitting by the window and a couple who'd just entered Monty's, setting the bell jangling.

Eve watched as the seated customer leaned over to say something to another woman with a baby at a nearby table. That woman's eyes widened and she bit her lip.

Viv went to serve the newcomers and returned to the counter to fetch their cakes. 'I think there's something going on.

The couple who've just come in drove here through Lovelace-by-Sax. They say the manor's crawling with police again.'

Eve felt goosebumps rise on her arms. 'They don't know anything else?'

Viv shook her head.

Five minutes later, just after Eve had delivered a fresh pot of Darjeeling to a table by the crafts area, she snatched a look at her phone. The *East Anglian Daily Times* had a breaking news item. An 'incident' in Lovelace-by-Sax. Rumours of an unnamed person with gunshot wounds.

As Viv joined her, Eve turned the screen so she could see. Their eyes met. What the heck could have happened?

Eve refreshed her phone each time she got the chance, but the details remained sketchy. Then at half-past eleven, while Eve was taking payment from the woman in the window seat, she saw a car draw up next to the village green.

A man got out of the driver's seat, opened the boot and removed a walking frame, carrying it round to the passenger side. He helped Irene Marston out and walked with her, following her slow progress towards the vicarage.

Eve's stomach twisted as she took the card machine back to the counter. 'It looks as though Irene's come to visit Jim,' she said to Viv. Had something happened to Diana or Sebastian? Either way, Irene might come and let him know. Eve's palms felt clammy. Visions of Jim coming to the door, unsuspecting, filled her head. Imagining his distress made her realise how fond she was of him.

It was around midday when the murmured gossip rose up again in a wave. It was triggered by two new customers, and it flooded the teashop in minutes.

Returning from a table, Viv put her hand on Eve's arm and gripped it, as if to fortify her. 'The woman over there is saying whoever was shot at Lovelace is dead.' It was the first time Eve had heard Viv whisper properly. It seemed as though shock had robbed her voice of its usual energy. 'She says someone saw Sebastian in the driveway with the police, so it can't be him. The woman reckons it's Diana.'

26

It seemed unbelievable. Could Diana really be dead?

Everyone in Monty's was in a state of shock. Eve didn't feel she was functioning properly but she doubted the customers noticed. Her head was full of swirling thoughts of Diana.

Her desire to make Cammie suffer had been chilling, but understandable. Eve was sure she'd adored Peter and then she'd lost him. She was looking for people to blame and Cammie had hurt her deeply. Diana hadn't looked at the situation fairly. It took two to tango, and Peter was far older than Cammie. He should have known better. Diana had seen a young woman seducing an older married man, but you could just as easily turn that on its head: a much older man taking advantage of a grieving young visitor. Or maybe both parties had had their eyes wide open, and had got what they wanted from the relationship.

More thoughts crowded her head: the secret Sebastian had been keeping, and Diana's feelings about the manor, and what a burden it was. Was any of that relevant to her death? Lovelace would be Sebastian's now.

Eve texted Robin in case he hadn't got the news and he texted back, suggesting supper that evening. He might know more by then. She found herself longing to see him – to feel the reassuring comfort of his arms around her.

The entire teashop was still reeling when Viv's brother Simon came in, his brown hair flopping forward as he rushed up to the counter. He put his hands on Eve and Viv's shoulders, gathering them in, sharing in the shock.

'I heard when I stopped at the village shop.' His eyes were wide. 'I hear it's Diana?'

The media still hadn't named the victim, but Eve assumed the rumours were accurate. They'd come from multiple sources now, including a woman whose cousin worked as an administrator at Blyworth police station.

'I was already planning to drop in here before I heard the news.' Simon glanced over his shoulder. 'I think someone's been inside Lavender Cottage again.'

'Really? We were in there on Wednesday night, of course,' Eve reminded him. 'We kept watch from Cammie's old bedroom until we saw Lars meet up with the Turnham brothers and their crew.'

'Yes, but unless you damaged the kitchen window—'

Viv put her hands on her hips. 'Certainly not.'

Suddenly, Eve wondered. She turned to Viv. 'The Turnham gang hung around in the garden after Lars left. They were on the verge of breaking in the night Cammie died, before the "ghost" frightened them off. Maybe they were preparing to have another go. There was an awful lot of whispering before they got that phone call and ran off.'

Simon's face was flushed. 'If I could get my hands on them...'

Eve shook her head. 'They might have done the groundwork, but I don't think they were around long enough to have gone inside.'

'Well, someone did.' Simon's jaw was tight. 'There are several bits and pieces missing. With Polly away, I checked the inventory. And of course, some of Cammie's belongings might have gone too. I suppose the police will have made a list of her things; I gave them details of the cottage's contents so they could single them out. If only Cammie's mother had already been to pick them up.' He closed his eyes for a moment. 'I can't bear to think of the poor woman, dealing with a burglary on top of the loss of her daughter.'

'Have you reported it already?' Eve asked.

Simon nodded. 'The police think it was opportunistic. A thief who knew the house was empty, and that Cammie might have nice things lying around. I suppose that makes sense. It'll be the last thing they'll focus on after the horrific news this morning.'

But Eve wondered. Was it really unrelated to Cammie's murder? She thought of the scene the day after the balloon crash. Cammie's papers, neatly ordered, when everything else was untidy. Maybe the intruder on Sunday night had gone through her notes. Trying to find out about her research? Or for clues about her private life? Maybe this latest break-in was a blind, to disguise what the intruder was really after.

As her thoughts multiplied, Eve saw Irene Marston appear with the young man who'd given her a lift. She manoeuvred slowly past the village green on her walking frame. Eve wondered if Jim had ended up comforting her after she'd told him the news. It would be just like him.

Viv caught Eve's gaze. 'I can manage here if you want to talk to her. Off you go.' She grabbed Eve's arm for a second. 'So long as you report back immediately afterwards of course!'

Eve caught Irene just as the young man unlocked their car. 'Irene. I'm so sorry. Is the news we're hearing true? Diana's really dead?'

The chief volunteer's eyes were wide, and full of tears.

She gave a tight nod and swallowed. 'A visitor found her in the woods this morning. Can you imagine? Josh Standish came straight round to tell me. It's already hitting the news.' She put a hand to her head. 'Poor Diana.'

'She'd been out overnight?' Additional memories returned to her now. Diana had mentioned a meeting with Raven on Thursday evening, sometime after Eve's visit to Lovelace. They were going to discuss a new idea she'd had: a storytelling trail in the woods.

Irene nodded and took a juddering breath. 'That's what Josh said.'

'Sebastian must have been worried when she didn't come home.'

But Irene shook her head. 'They each have several rooms to themselves, and they've never been close. They had such different ideas about Lovelace. Diana had decided not to sell of course, but to her the manor was always a worry, a drain, a burden. Whereas although Sebastian's impractical, he is in love with the place. And now, with Sapphire by his side...'

Sebastian would certainly inherit the place ready to roll. Sapphire had all the right skills to make it work. Eve sensed Irene was already looking to the future. She hadn't been able to disguise the hope in her voice when she mentioned Sapphire.

'So Sebastian had no idea Diana had been gone all night?'

'That's right, from what I've heard.' She shook her head. 'Lovelace has such a magical reputation. A lot of people visit in the hope that some of Louisa and Seth's good fortune will rub off on them. How will they feel now?'

She had a point. After Cammie's death, the press had quickly shifted their attention away from the manor, thanks to the cocaine found in her bike pannier. But this latest murder in the manor grounds was bound to bring it back again.

Irene sighed. 'I know it seems awful to consider it at a time like this, but I've volunteered at Lovelace for so long. It's ingrained to put its future front and centre.'

Eve nodded. 'I understand.' Though in Irene's place, she

was sure she'd still be too poleaxed by the latest death to think ahead.

'But we'll still benefit from poor Cammie's work,' Irene went on. 'And we must celebrate her memory, as well as Diana's. It's so wonderful that she found Louisa and Seth's loving cup. She didn't even hint at it when she came to visit. No wonder she was excited and secretive. Well, we'd better be off.'

She slipped into the passenger seat and Eve closed the door for her as her companion put the walking frame back in the boot.

But as Eve watched them drive off, she dismissed Irene's reasoning. Cammie had certainly looked secretive when she'd dashed off after diving in the moat on Lovelace Sunday. But as an adrenaline junkie, Eve doubted she'd imagined the cup would draw in the crowds. They might allow visitors to touch it for luck perhaps, but it was more of the same. The archway in the gardens was supposed to be lucky. People already touched that.

And besides, Cammie had told Ralph Roscoe she'd be able to raise Lovelace's profile last Saturday, before she'd apparently sneaked off with something from the moat.

There was more to this.

As Eve re-entered the teashop, Viv grabbed her arm. 'Another customer came in while you were talking to Irene.' She pointed to a woman who'd taken a seat by the window. 'The word is the police are looking for Raven Allerton. They think she was the last person to see Diana alive. Apparently, she's nowhere to be found.'

27

Eve texted Robin to make sure Greg Boles was aware of Raven's secret identity. Then, as soon as she'd finished her shift, she went to see Jim Thackeray. Her insides twisted at what he must be going through. Diana had helped him after his wife's death. Today's news would be a huge shock, and it would bring that back too. She needed to focus on him, but thoughts of Raven filled the back of her mind. Had she killed Cammie, then shot Diana to protect her secret? Eve could imagine her doing it, but if Diana knew, why hadn't she gone to the police?

Jim's eyes were bloodshot when he opened the door, but he seemed composed.

'Poor Diana,' he said. 'She suffered, over the years. Too much loss, too much responsibility.' He put a hand to his forehead. 'Eve, if you do get to the bottom of this, I'll be eternally grateful. I wasn't able to support Diana properly when Peter died—'

'It was her decision,' Eve said gently. 'It doesn't sound as though many people saw Peter in his final years.' She remembered the White Lion's landlord saying he'd become a recluse.

Jim nodded. 'But I'm a vicar. I should have been able to find a way.'

That evening, Eve and Gus made their way down the estuary path then cut across, through Blind Eye Wood and into Robin's back garden. Gus had been excitable since she'd told him where they were going, scampering this way and that, pausing for a second, then rushing off again. Eve was glad he was oblivious to the horrendous news. Her mind was full of it, of course, her body taut. She had to get to the bottom of all this; it wouldn't bring the victims back, but it might ease Jim's pain a little.

Inside the cottage, Robin was obliged to make a fuss of Gus, who was ecstatic, but a second later he had Eve in his arms, holding her tight.

The moment extended and once again, Eve was filled with the urge to tell him how she felt: that life was sometimes short, and she loved him. The emotion was so powerful that tears pricked her eyes.

With one last, extra-tight squeeze, Robin let her go. 'I'll dish up our supper, and then we can talk.'

He'd cooked a cheese and wine sauce with Parma ham and mushrooms and mixed it through pasta as Eve uncorked the Viognier she'd brought with her. It was good to do something mundane and mechanical to steady herself.

A moment later they were sitting at the table in Robin's shady kitchen with the back door open, talking in hushed voices. In a house like Robin's, the neighbours were never far away.

'Is the gossip I heard at Monty's right?' Eve asked. 'That Raven can't be found?'

Robin nodded. 'They know she'd asked to meet Diana in the woods – precisely where her body was found. They went to her shepherd's hut but there was no sign of her. Bed hadn't been slept in.'

'What about her things? Had she packed a bag?'

Robin nodded. 'From what Greg says, the basics were gone – no trace of any money, bank cards, anything like that. And her night things, wash kit and toothbrush were all missing. Probably some clothes too. Greg says it's hard to be sure but there were several empty hangers. They're on to Raven's parents now, of course. I doubt she'd run there from what you say, but they're covering the bases. Palmer figures she might change identity again and try to start over.'

Eve sighed. 'To be fair, Raven was high on my list of suspects and if Diana found her out, I can see she'd want to remove the threat. But why wouldn't Diana go to the police?'

Robin shrugged. 'Maybe she wasn't sure of her ground and couldn't quite believe Raven had done it. Raven might have sensed she was suspicious and decided to act immediately, before it was too late.

'The CSIs found her diary in the shepherd's hut and it's full of bile about Cammie. She had a file with press cuttings about her too. It makes her look obsessive.'

Eve could imagine that, if Cammie had robbed her of her place at Lovelace and her close connection with Peter. The diary and the bag she'd packed would convince the police she was guilty, but Eve wasn't a hundred per cent sure. Something was nagging at her, making her pause.

'What about the weapon? Where did it come from?'

'It was an old service revolver which had belonged to Diana's dad, apparently. She shouldn't have kept it of course. She had it locked in a drawer in her study, but the police think Raven might have known about it. She'd probably been there to sign contracts for her events – that kind of thing. It would have been easy enough to pinch it around the time of Lovelace Sunday. All the toing and froing would have allowed her to slip in and hunt for the key. She might have lifted the gun as an insurance policy, in case of emergencies if any of her plans went wrong.'

'Wouldn't Diana have noticed it was gone?'

'I guess it depends how often she unlocked the drawer.'

Eve sighed. 'So the thinking is that Raven arranged to meet Diana with the intention of killing her?'

'That's right. There's evidence that she made the appointment by phone, so the precise time of their meetup's unknown. Sebastian and Sapphire were out, so they didn't see her go, but the police have one extra clue.' He put down his fork and took a notepad from his jeans pocket. 'Apparently Josh Standish went to see Diana at the manor at around four thirty yesterday afternoon.'

'That's right. He was leaving when I turned up.'

Robin nodded. 'He mentioned seeing you to Greg. He said Diana was really down. Not surprising after everything that had happened. She was despairing about the manor. Josh thinks she felt trapped: that it would be wrong to sell the place from under Sebastian's feet, but that carrying on seemed exhausting. He was worried about her, and at six thirty, he went to call on Irene Marston. The pair of them sat down in her cottage to thrash out ideas that might help Lovelace's finances. He wasn't sure any of them would work, but he wanted Diana to know she wasn't alone with the problem.'

Eve could imagine that having a boosting effect. Diana had seemed very isolated; Sebastian was no help.

'At seven thirty, Josh took the notes they'd made and went up to the manor to show them to Diana. There was no reply when he knocked, but he let himself in and left the ideas on her desk with an explanatory note. He's got keys because he oversees security.'

He was yet another person who could have accessed the gun then, but realistically, pretty much anyone might have got their hands on it. People had been in and out the whole time in the run-up to Lovelace Sunday, and again on the day.

'Anyway,' Robin took a slug of his wine, 'the police found notes Diana had written in response to their list of ideas, and her prints were on the paper Josh left, so it's clear she returned to the house after he left at seven thirty-five. Her death must have occurred after that. The pathologist's estimate is between six and nine last night.'

'And what about alibis for the other key players? I guess the police checked, even if Raven's suspect number one?' Palmer was lazy, but the rest of the team weren't.

'That's right. Josh went to the White Lion for a drink straight after leaving the manor and stayed until closing time. That's borne out by the landlord and other punters.

'As for Sebastian, he was with Sapphire. They'd gone for a walk – taken a picnic and a bottle of fizz with them, so they say.'

'What about Ralph Roscoe?'

Robin gave her a meaningful glance. 'At his rented cottage with his wife, Erica.'

Eve swallowed the mouthful of pasta she'd just taken. 'His *wife?*'

He nodded. 'It brought me up short too. Didn't Raven say she'd seen Cammie and Roscoe kissing?'

'Yes.' What a toad. She wondered if Cammie had known. And if this Erica knew her other half had been disloyal – unfaithful probably – it might mean she was another suspect for Cammie's murder if she'd been present on Lovelace Sunday.

'I can imagine what you're thinking,' Robin said, 'but Roscoe's wife was down in London from Thursday to Wednesday. The police have checked. They're not best pleased that Roscoe didn't mention her existence previously. So where does this leave us?'

Eve frowned. 'The case against Raven looks persuasive, but I need to dig deeper. There are too many unanswered questions. I don't even know what Sebastian's secret is yet, but that's a priority. I'm clear he might have killed Cammie to protect it. And then there's finding out who's been nipping in and out of Lavender Cottage and why. And what Cammie had found that might raise Lovelace's profile. It could be unrelated, but it's a loose end.

'If Raven's innocent, then Sebastian had the strongest motive. Cammie was a threat and Diana's death is in his interests too. There was always a danger she'd change her mind about selling the manor. Now he gets the place straight away.' Eve thought it through. 'Diana could have told Sebastian about meeting Raven, enabling him to watch them secretly and take Diana by surprise the moment Raven left.'

Robin nodded. 'His alibi's weak.'

Eve agreed. He could have convinced Sapphire to lie to save him time and trouble. If Raven's guilt seemed certain it might have felt unimportant – a harmless fib.

'But if Sebastian's guilty, why would Raven run?' Robin's blue eyes met hers.

'Because someone from Great Foley told her I'd been asking questions? She might have figured her past was catching up with her and decided to move on.'

Robin sighed. 'It's possible, I suppose.'

'Enough to consider other suspects,' Eve said. 'There's Ralph Roscoe too. I don't have a definite motive for him, but he was certainly interested in Cammie's research.' Once again, she wondered if it might be relevant. What was it that would have raised Lovelace's profile? Either way, she couldn't imagine why it would affect Ralph. 'He had a secret chat with Diana, the day before Lovelace Sunday. Plus he seems to be avoiding me.' He must have got her letter via the letting agency by now. 'I need to make sure I talk to him.

'As for Josh, he seems to be out of it, but Raven said she'd seen him have some kind of illicit discussion with Diana too.

She sneaked into his cottage; the chat wasn't just private, but secret.' That definitely needed explaining. 'I guess he might have been nervous Diana would sell the manor after all, just like Sebastian. And I can't think what that would do to Irene. If it weren't for her bad ankle, and Josh's alibi, I'd still be wondering about both of them.' She sighed and drained her wine. 'Josh Standish agreed to an interview tomorrow morning. And I'm speaking to Cammie's mother in London in the evening.' That would be hard. The woman hadn't been able to bring herself to come to Suffolk yet, according to Simon. Eve wondered if he'd told her about the burglary. It would have been horrible, breaking that news on top of everything else. 'In between times I need to work out how to find out more about Sebastian's murky past. I might try to find the Turnham brothers again too. See if they know about the forced window at Lavender Cottage.' She'd need to speak to Simon about that. What were the chances of persuading him to offer a reward in return for information? He wasn't their number one fan. 'And if I haven't heard back from Ralph Roscoe by tomorrow I'm going to doorstep him. I can't leave it any longer.'

Robin reached across and stroked her cheek gently. 'Let me know when you're going to do that,' he said. 'I'll come and hang around outside.'

A thought crossed Eve's mind. 'Robin, do you know if Raven took the comb with her, the one I found?'

He opened up an email on his phone. 'No,' he said, after a moment. 'Greg says that and the wellington boots were left behind.'

Eve felt a little shiver. Raven had hated her parents by all accounts – cut them off ruthlessly and completely. Yet she'd kept those two items from her former life. They must have been special to her.

Eve could see Raven leaving the boots, albeit regretfully. They were cumbersome and it would certainly attract attention if she ran off wearing them on a warm May day. But the comb was eminently portable and useful day-to-day, yet she'd left it behind.

She frowned. It could have been an oversight, but what if Raven hadn't run at all? And if she hadn't, where the heck was she?

28

Eve was wakeful for a lot of Friday night, her mind tussling with Diana's murder and Raven's supposed flight. None of her suspects had a clear opportunity for the latest killing. Whatever the truth, she'd just have to carry on – research the obituary and try to answer the mini mysteries she'd identified. If she worked away at those, maybe the mist would clear.

The following morning at ten, she was standing outside Josh Standish's tiny cottage, ready to get on with the job. His dwelling was on the manor estate, facing the lane through the hamlet, side-on to the big house, on an offshoot from the main driveway.

Josh had an alibi for Diana, but it was a complicated one, built on notes left on desks and fingerprints. Either way, Eve had questions. She wanted to know why he'd followed Cammie so closely before her murder, what sort of relationship he'd had with Diana, and if Raven still had an emotional hold on him. Anything he told her might be relevant.

As she knocked, Eve peered through a frosted glass panel in his front door. A moment later, she saw an inner door open off the hallway and the general shape of Josh walk through.

Though the details were obscured she noticed him close the door he'd just come through before continuing. Wasn't that a bit odd? It made her wonder what lay beyond. But maybe he was just untidy, his kitchen full of dirty crockery.

His expression was grim as he greeted her. He didn't feel the need to put on a show, she guessed.

'Thank you for allowing our meeting to go ahead when things are so awful.' Eve shook his hand. 'I was very sorry to hear about Diana.'

He nodded. 'She's been part of my life since I was a baby.'

The cottage was so close to the manor, there must have been precious little separation between his father's work and home life. And now Josh would be in the same boat. Eve wouldn't fancy that; he must always be at the beck and call of his employer.

'Hearing the speculation about Raven is such a shock too.' It was going back five years, but the storyteller was his ex-girl-friend. Her disappearance and the accusations against her must be having an effect.

The gardener's hands rose to cover his face. 'I was worried about her when Cammie first turned up. But I never really imagined...' He let the sentence trail off.

She found it impossible to tell if he was acting. He sounded natural, but his hands hid his expression.

Josh led Eve to a front room. There were photos of a couple with an intense-eyed dark-haired boy on the mantelpiece. 'You and your parents?'

Josh nodded.

There was another one too of just him and his dad, working in the grounds of the manor. Mr Standish senior was in the foreground, Josh further back, weeding a flower bed. Behind them was a marquee – they must have been preparing for a big event.

'That was taken the day Dad died,' Josh said. 'Diana's

engagement party.' He took a deep breath. 'I saw him drop to the ground.'

'I'm so sorry.' Josh looked young in the photograph, not much more than twelve. 'It must have been awful.'

He shook his head. 'Long time ago now. There's never been any money here, but Diana's done everything she can to help me.'

That was all very well, but his dad had died preparing for her engagement party. If Josh blamed her, his resentment had had plenty of time to mature.

'My mum worked the gardens too,' Josh went on. 'I helped after school and at weekends and took over when she died.'

He must never have had any free time.

As though he'd read her mind, he said: 'It's my life.'

Just like Irene. Lovelace seemed to swallow everyone in its orbit. 'It's a beautiful place. And I already had the impression you and Diana were close. Raven told me she visited you recently.' Eve didn't want to quote the storyteller in full: that it appeared they'd met in secret.

He frowned. 'Diana often popped in if there was something to discuss. What was Raven driving at?'

'She seemed to think it was significant.'

A huge sigh escaped him. 'She must have seen Diana come to talk to me about selling the manor.' He shook his head. 'That was Raven all over. Seeing conspiracy where there was none. If people left her out of a conversation she felt like she was being ignored. But it was nothing to do with her. Diana wanted to tell me she was making my continued employment a condition if she sold up. And that she'd insist the grounds remain as they are, with Lovelace Sunday still celebrated. She came to reassure me before she went public – and then of course she changed her mind. But it's like I said, after my father died, she always fought my corner.'

If that was true it meant his future had been certain, whatever Diana did. But of course, Lovelace might be more to him than just a job. It had been part of his and his family's life for so long. If he hadn't killed Diana to avenge his father's death, might he have killed to ensure she didn't sell? But he had an alibi, and no motive for Cammie that she could fathom.

'Diana sounds like a special person.' But deep down, Eve wondered about Josh's upbringing and all those hours spent working with no time to play. Yes, Diana had lacked money to bring in enough support, but that was no excuse for what was effectively child exploitation. 'Could I ask you about Cammie now? What were your impressions of her?'

'She was easy to talk to – both this time and when she stayed five years ago. She treated me as an equal.'

'Other people don't?'

'Diana was always looking after me, but as an employer. Peter was the same.'

'Did you and Cammie see a lot of each other, the first time she stayed here?' If Cammie had confided in Josh, the information might be useful.

He frowned. 'She'd occasionally come and help in the garden, very early in the day, before she started her own work.'

Eve didn't imagine Raven had liked that. Quiet time for them, alone together.

'I had the impression she wanted some peace – to be separate from the rest of her world. Her dad had just died.'

'And you seemed close more recently? As friends, I mean. I noticed you talked a lot.'

'We had a lot to say – or at least, I did to her. I didn't really want her swimming in the moat. It's a headache, being in charge of security and health and safety. And with all the kids looking on... I was worried they'd try it next.'

That might explain the way he'd dogged her steps. He'd certainly looked anxious.

'But yes, we talked. Of course, I wanted to know what she'd

dug up during her research. I live on Lovelace land. I'm interested in its history.'

'I get the impression you're not the only one who was curious.'

He raised an eyebrow.

'I've heard someone let themselves into the cottage Cammie was renting the night she died.' His look was inscrutable. 'And that someone's been in since too.'

'Really?' His brow furrowed now. 'I'd heard rumours about the first intruder. I didn't know about the second.'

'My colleague's brother owns the place. He's devastated that stuff's been stolen before Cammie's mum's picked up her belongings.'

'That's bad.'

Eve was pretty certain the recent break-in had come as a shock. As for the first, he might be telling the truth – he could have heard on the grapevine. Or maybe he was the Turnham brothers' ghost. He might have wanted to access anything that could help save the manor.

Eve got him talking about Cammie in informal mode, down at the pub, mucking in with preparations for Lovelace Sunday and so on. It would work well for the obituary, but something told her he was holding back. It was hard to get him to elaborate and there was a wariness about him.

At last, he stood up. 'I'm sorry, but I've got work to do. I might have to call it a day there.'

'Of course.' She rose too. What was he covering up?

29

After leaving Josh Standish's house, Eve walked straight up towards the manor. She'd parked her car up there with the thought of calling on Sebastian before she left. It would be wrong not to express her condolences, and she wanted to see his face. Cammie had been some kind of threat to him and now she was dead. And Diana could have halved his inheritance by selling up, and she was gone too. Sapphire was his alibi, but she seemed taken in by his charm. Cammie had clearly thought he was evil. Eve could imagine him committing murder to achieve his ends.

She crossed the bridge over the moat and knocked at the door of the manor.

It was Sapphire who answered. She was holding a small bit of card that seemed to be stuck to her finger.

She followed Eve's eyes. 'It's one of the display labels. We're altering the way the artefacts are laid out to make them more appealing.' She sighed. 'It's just so weird. I've been full of ideas about what Diana and Sebastian might do to improve things for ages, but I didn't think I'd be putting it into practice to take my mind off what's happened. And of course it's not working. What would, after something like this?'

Eve explained that she'd just interviewed Josh, and wanted to drop by to express her sympathy.

'That's kind.' Sapphire squeezed her eyes tight shut for a moment. 'We're just coming to terms with it all.'

Eve needed to make this brief exchange count. Something was still nagging her about Raven's supposed flight. If there was any chance she was innocent, now was the time to push to find the killer. No one would be on their guard, with the police presenting her as guilty. If Sapphire had provided Sebastian with a false alibi, now might be the time to get it out of her.

'Were you here at home when it happened?' Eve watched her eyes closely as she waited for her response.

The young woman shook her head. 'No. The awful thing was, we were off having a picnic, lazing in the sunshine in a secluded spot on the beach just down the coast. We were having the most perfect time. In fact,' she leaned forward and whispered, 'it's official now.' She held out her left hand and Eve saw the sparkling diamond engagement ring.

'Oh goodness, that's beautiful. Congratulations!' In the back of her mind, Eve wondered if she should say anything about Sebastian's flirting, but Cammie had already done that. It hadn't had any effect.

Sapphire's eyes glistened. 'It doesn't seem right to celebrate openly at a time like this. We cracked open a bottle of Champagne on the beach – though I was the main drinker. Seb was driving. I was in seventh heaven while Raven was killing Diana.' Her eyes were huge and not on Eve's now. 'We lay there until the stars came out, like a couple of teenagers.'

Eve imagined the scene. Sapphire, happy, getting tipsy on champagne. Did she remember every moment of the evening? Sebastian could easily have slipped her something.

'That sounds so romantic,' she said aloud. 'I remember

falling asleep in a field once with a boyfriend and waking up to see the moon had come out.'

Sapphire sighed, but before she could comment, Sebastian appeared out of the shadows.

'Eve came to give her condolences,' Sapphire said.

'Thank you.' His voice was low. 'I can't believe Diana's gone. We had our differences, but she was everything to me.'

The words sounded so rehearsed it was embarrassing. Surely Sapphire must notice? But she looked round at him and stroked his arm before he pulled her into a hug. Eve wondered how she felt. She wouldn't have that same feeling of connection with Diana of course, but she'd looked emotional. All the same, deep down she might be excited to get to work on Lovelace, especially now she and Sebastian were engaged. It was her future.

'Sebastian's been telling me about Raven,' Sapphire said. 'We never talked properly. She sounds rather frightening.'

And of course, she was. For the umpteenth time, Eve thought of her depositing the defenceless spider into the hands of that small girl.

Eve nodded. 'It's nice to get your good news at least.' She turned to Sebastian, her eyes on his. 'Congratulations on your engagement. The picnic sounded so romantic.'

His eyes were sharp. 'Thank you.'

He looked uncomfortable, but it was hard to know the cause. It might be because Eve had seen him flirting, or because she'd overheard his row with Cammie. But it might also be because his alibi was false and he'd killed, three times over.

As Eve walked back to her car, she looked up and saw a woman approaching Josh Standish's cottage. Tall and model-like, with long, dark hair. A second later he was outside greeting her. It was interesting to watch – he had an entirely different aura as he welcomed her, one hand on her arm, a smile transforming his face. A moment later they disappeared inside his cottage.

Perhaps that was why he'd been so twitchy towards the end of their interview: he'd been expecting company. And Sebastian wasn't the only two-timer, by the look of it. Josh's visitor wasn't the same woman he'd been entertaining in the White Lion earlier in the week.

Back in the car, Eve called Robin to say she was planning to doorstep Ralph Roscoe next. He was free and arranged to join her, though he'd stay out of sight. After a couple of minutes, she rang off and fished her keys from her bag, ready to drive to Wessingham. But as she put them in the ignition, she saw the model-like brunette emerge from Josh's house again. She'd barely been there five minutes. Had they argued? But Josh was with her, patting her arm – smiling. And what was she carrying?

The woman drove off and a second later, Josh headed across the grounds in the direction of a large shed.

Eve drove down the driveway, wondering what the gardener and his visitor had been up to. She was just level with his cottage when she noticed some small dark patches on the gravel outside. She was fairly sure they hadn't been there when she'd visited him a short while earlier.

Looking over her shoulder, she saw Josh enter the distant shed he'd been making for. Taking a deep breath, Eve turned off her engine and nipped across to investigate the dark patches.

They were little deposits of earth – like tiny molehills, where no molehills should be.

The puzzle was high in Eve's mind as she drove to the house Ralph Roscoe had rented, but she forced herself to switch focus. If she managed to speak to him, she needed to get a lot out of the interview. She was still processing the fact that he had a wife, though of course, Cammie had had an affair with a married man before. It altered the dynamic, even if the police were sure Erica Roscoe had been in London when Cammie was killed. Cammie had been a potential threat to Ralph's marriage. At the very least, they'd been seen kissing. If she'd decided she wanted more out of the relationship she could have threatened to tell Erica.

Eve knocked on the door of the fairy-tale thatched cottage, surrounded by trees and birdsong, secluded in its tucked-away back lane in Wessingham. There was a car parked outside – a gleaming red Mercedes. Perhaps she'd be in luck.

30

Eve waited a full five minutes outside the Roscoes' rented cottage, and knocked again twice, but no one came to the door. She gave a quick sigh. This was getting irritating.

She hoped Robin wouldn't have a wasted journey, though it was just as well she'd called him. He'd hate her going into such an isolated house without backup.

She was prepared to wait for Ralph or Erica to come back. The lane curved round as it reached the cottage and she crossed over and found a place to lurk, tucked behind a thick sprawling tangle of honeysuckle, which had wrapped itself around a tree.

All was quiet, except for the birdsong. Eve was conscious of the sweet smells of the countryside and the warmth of the sun. Within a minute she got a text from Robin.

In position! Hidden by trees, right by cottage. Assume you're still outside? Yell if there's any problem. xx

Eve's heart sank. They could be there for hours. She'd been encouraged by the presence of the car outside, thinking the couple must be within walking distance, but maybe they had two vehicles. They could have gone out for the day.

Hope this isn't a colossal waste of your time... xx

But in fact, it was only twenty minutes before she saw movement. Ralph Roscoe was strolling down the lane towards the house. The way he walked said nonchalant, but the quick glances to left and right said otherwise. Eve ducked her head back behind the climber. His behaviour made her wonder. Was he this wary every time he came home? It made him look suspicious.

Eve felt her heart rate increase, but Robin was just outside the house; he'd break in if need be. He'd certainly hear her if she yelled; the place was so small. She took a deep breath and stepped into the lane.

'Mr Roscoe!'

He jumped and turned, his face falling.

'I'm so sorry to spring out at you. I knocked just a short while ago and the day was so lovely, I thought I'd hang around for a bit in case you came back. My name's Eve Mallow. You might recognise me. I was one of the Lovelace Sunday volunteers.' She held out a hand. 'I'm so sorry for your loss. I can't think what you must have gone through.'

She could see a yellowing bruise on his handsome face, and scabbed-over scratches on his hands. The landing must have been painful. The gorse was prickly, but its cushioning would have saved him from worse damage.

He raised an eyebrow. 'I got your letter, and now, here you are.' His tone was weary and mildly accusatory. 'I haven't felt much like talking. I've had it up to here with journalists. I could hardly move for them in the immediate aftermath.'

That was understandable, but Eve had explained what she was after in her letter. How she was only interested in what

Cammie had been like as a person. How she'd love to hear about her skydiving, back when she was at university. Eve suspected he didn't want to talk about their relationship. Because he'd let her down years ago, maybe, and because he'd been seeing her on the sly more recently. And maybe because he'd killed her.

She swallowed and came out with her usual patter. 'I don't blame you at all. It's just that I heard you used to attend some of the same clubs back in Cambridge and it's invaluable to have someone who shared in her adventures and saw what she was like in that environment. I spoke with Phoebe Richmond, but she didn't have the sort of insights I'm after.'

'Phoebe... wow.' His eyes were far away for a moment. 'I haven't thought of her in a while.'

'If you could just spare me five minutes? I'd be so grateful. I'm about to start writing up my article and it would fill some gaps.' She'd never normally be so pushy. It was against her principles, but the man might be a murderer, in a case where Palmer was focused on only one suspect. She had to get on with it.

Roscoe sighed. 'All right then. Come in.'

Eve thought of the hiding place Robin had found, just round the side of the house. She'd got backup. It would be okay.

Inside, they sat in a sun-filled sitting room with a dusty pink and willow-green colour scheme. It was very pretty. Eve wondered what Ralph Roscoe was doing here. As a business angel she appreciated he could probably work from anywhere, but why spend money on a temporary home in the depths of Suffolk? Roscoe was smartly dressed, and his car was the sort you saw advertised in the glossiest magazines, but surely businesspeople were mindful of how they spent their income?

'It's a beautiful cottage,' she said aloud. 'Are you here for long?'

'Long enough to get a proper break. I'm still working of course, but being in the countryside is a tonic. London can be wearing – endless nights out, crowds and noise.'

Eve loved crowds but even she had enjoyed moving to a Suffolk village, and getting to know a smaller group of people up close.

He motioned her to a seat on the chesterfield sofa but didn't offer her a drink, which was hardly surprising. She took out a notebook to show she meant business.

'So, perhaps you could tell me about those skydiving sessions?'

He frowned. 'You'd think leaping out of a plane would be the perfect activity for her, wouldn't you? But it was almost too tame – with an instructor looking on and all the safety checks. The carefully chosen landing points.' Roscoe's eyes met hers. 'She preferred the secret night-climbing she did – scaling buildings, breaking the rules. The bigger the risk, the more of a kick she got out of it. I wondered if it was hereditary. You know her father was a racing driver?'

Eve nodded. 'Were you with her for the night climbs?'

He grinned at last, seemingly caught up in the memory. 'I was. It was hard to get in –

there was so much secrecy – but it was worth it. That shared adrenaline. What a buzz!'

'Phoebe said you and Cammie broke up when you graduated.'

The fond look in his eye was gone, replaced by a cold stare, directed at Eve. 'But that doesn't relate to Cammie's character, so you won't want to ask me about it.'

Neat. But Eve wasn't beaten yet. 'I'm sorry, I didn't mean to bring up a painful topic. I know how it hurts, being dumped. My husband walked out on me a few years back.' Eve was actually delighted about it, now she'd seen sense, but it was a useful fact to slip in.

Roscoe sat up straighter. 'Is that what Phoebe told you? That Cammie dumped me?'

'Oh, sorry. Something made me think... but it sounds like I

misunderstood.' It was enough to confirm her previous hunch. Ralph had finished with Cammie, and she'd gone off caving – burying her feelings with some consuming adventure. The thought that Ralph might have borne a grudge all these years, and killed Cammie because of it, seemed dead in the water.

'I got involved in a start-up in the States,' he said. 'A long-distance relationship was never going to work at that stage.'

Certainly not, if you started off by dumping your partner. Though to be fair, they'd been young. It sounded like bad timing. 'How did you find her more recently? Was it coincidence that you met up again at Lovelace?'

He hesitated. 'Yes, yes it was. The slower pace of life here gave me time to get interested in local history. My work's very desk-bound. I'm always on the phone, helping the companies I invest in with advice. Either that or I'm on my laptop, going over figures and business plans. Volunteering in the run-up to Lovelace Sunday was the perfect antidote.'

'You must have got to know Diana quite well.' Eve was wondering about the secret talk she'd seen them have.

His eyes narrowed and he folded his arms. 'We chatted, naturally. She confided in me about some of the headaches Lovelace caused her. But you're here to talk about Cammie. Let's get back to it.'

He was cagey. 'Yes, of course. Did you notice much change in her, since university days?'

'She was just as competitive and adventurous, but more mature, and underneath it all, sadder, I think. Though she buttoned that feeling up tight.'

'Sadder?'

'She had a difficult relationship with her dad. She loved him to bits – far more than her mum – but he was seldom around and then he was killed in an accident on the track. I had the impression Lovelace had been like a second home to her, but that things had changed there, with the old man's death, and the strained relationship between Diana and Sebastian.'

Eve nodded. Cammie had certainly suffered a lot of loss. She shook her head. 'Poor woman. And then to die so horribly. How was she on the day of the balloon flight?'

'On a high. And that was just like old times. She didn't want anyone fussing over the arrangements, she just wanted to be up there in the wide blue yonder.' He bit his lip. 'Those streamers saved my life. Some of them fell inside the balloon and made me look down, so I saw the fire when it was still small.' He put a hand up to his forehead. 'I should have looked for the fire extinguisher. Shouted to warn Cammie. Kept my head. But jumping was instinctive.'

He looked genuinely shocked – his face white. If he was lying, he'd have had a lot of practice by now, but surely no one could fake that pallor.

It was time to start delving into areas important to the case.

'I gather you and Cammie got quite close again.' Her eyes met his. 'I won't put that in the obituary, I'm not muckraking, I just want to know the kind of appeal she had and the sort of relationships she formed.'

His steady, unfriendly gaze was on hers. He didn't say anything.

'Someone said they saw you kissing,' Eve persisted.

For a moment, Eve sensed Roscoe was undecided about his response. When it came, it felt like acting.

He laughed. 'I'd forgotten what life in a small village is like! But that was just a bit of flirting. We were old friends, don't forget.'

But Ralph was married. Eve wouldn't fancy the idea of Robin kissing an 'old friend', and they were only dating.

'Do you think there was anything going on between Cammie and Josh Standish?' If Eve detected jealousy, it would prove Roscoe's clinches with Cammie had meant something.

But Roscoe looked both casual and nonplussed. 'The gardener? No, I don't think so. He's already got a posse of women who follow him around from what I've seen. Didn't you notice them at Lovelace Sunday? They love that he's Seth Pickford's modern-day equivalent. He's part of the manor myth. He and Sebastian have leaped on the same bandwagon.'

The manor's legend certainly seemed all-powerful.

At that moment, a phone rang from somewhere outside the room they occupied. The suddenness made her jump, but not as much as hearing someone pick up.

She and Roscoe weren't alone after all.

The voice was a woman's – muffled. 'Oh no, again?' She sounded exasperated, but reined it in quickly. 'No, no, I'm so sorry. It shouldn't have happened. No, please let me call the electrician we normally use.' Then she said something about settling up 'our end'. After she'd rung off, she muttered something loud and irritable about mothers, but Eve was distracted.

The woman who'd answered had to be Ralph Roscoe's wife, Erica. *Heck.* She'd probably heard Eve say Cammie and Ralph had been caught kissing. No wonder Ralph had looked so awkward. Eve was surprised he'd gone for laughing it off, rather than flat-out denial.

And what if Ralph was guilty? Having two people to contend with rather than one sent her heart rate ramping up. She was ready to yell her head off if things got out of hand.

A second later a woman appeared, petite and shapely, her long honey-coloured hair piled up on her head.

'My wife, Erica,' Roscoe said.

Eve's adrenaline was still going after being wrong-footed. Erica had been very quiet. She must have been listening in deliberately. The cottage was so tiny she'd almost certainly heard every word. And she clearly wasn't bothered that Eve knew that. She could have left the phone to ring – let Ralph get it.

Eve stood up, held out a hand and assessed the woman in front of her. She looked expensive, with her perfect-yet-subtle make-up and expertly styled hair. Erica gave her a bright smile and shook hands, though her large eyes had a glint to them. The whole thing was bizarre.

'I'm so sorry.' Eve decided it was best to be upfront. 'I wouldn't have touched on such personal topics if I'd known you were there.' In fact, she felt irritated rather than sorry. She couldn't claim the moral high ground – after all, she'd pushed her way in – but she *had* been deceived. Why hadn't Erica Roscoe answered the door when Eve first knocked? And then hidden away like that instead of announcing herself? And if she was going to take that approach, why appear now?

Erica's eyebrow rose, her mouth quirking into an ironic smile. 'I knew Ralph took Cammie out for the odd evening. I didn't expect them to be chaste. It wouldn't be natural, after their past relationship. There's a lot to be said for don't ask, don't tell.'

But Eve didn't believe anyone could be that nonchalant. She'd make a fine suspect for Cammie's murder if the police hadn't confirmed she'd been in London on the day of the balloon launch.

As Eve walked towards the door, her head was still spinning with thoughts and questions, but not so much that she didn't spot some post on a side table. There was a type-written letter half hidden under an envelope.

My dear Erica,

Based on past experience, Hector and I would love to come on board.

She couldn't read the rest but she noticed Erica's name and

address, typed just above the salutation. She was Erica Bond there. She must have kept her maiden name.

It made Eve wonder again if Cammie had known Ralph was married. It all depended on what social media he had and if he and Cammie were connected. Erica having a different surname could certainly have muddied the waters.

If Cammie hadn't known Ralph was attached when he started flirting, finding out suddenly would have hurt. Threatening to tell Erica would be a way of hitting back. Perhaps it had cost her her life.

31

Shortly after an early lunch, Eve was heading back towards Lovelace-by-Sax, this time with two overexcited passengers, Viv and Gus. Viv's effervescence had clearly rubbed off on the dachshund, who was looking this way and that from his harness in the back of the car, tongue lolling.

Viv clutched five ten-pound notes. She was grinning. 'I *knew* we could get Simon to see sense. And you mustn't worry. If it's an official reward for information, it doesn't count as bribery. Besides, it was your idea; it's no use going back on it now.'

Eve wasn't planning to, despite her misgivings. Fifty pounds meant there was an excellent chance the Turnham brothers' crew would talk to them without having to rope Lars in again. But what would they do with the money? That was what worried her. Still, it was all in a good cause. If the latest Lavender Cottage break-in had happened the night Lars spoke with them, they might know something.

Viv was chewing her lip now, as though she was finally thinking through the ramifications. 'Do you think they might have pinched the stuff themselves?'

'My gut instinct is no. Thieving's a far cry from breaking in for a bet, like they intended the night Cammie died. It seems too planned for them. They're bored youths rather than hardened criminals.'

'I hope they tell us the truth.'

'Me too.'

Tammy said the gang were regularly at the playing field at this hour, out along a lane leading right off the main route through Lovelace-by-Sax. Eve made the turn. Ahead of her she could see a meagre collection of swings, two for toddlers and two for more grown-up children. Two lads occupied those, lounging heavily. Others were leaning against the swings' frames, smoking. There were no younger children to be seen, which was hardly surprising. The lads were an intimidating sight.

Eve parked and got Gus out of his harness. Viv leaped out of the car.

'Let's show them the colour of our money!' she said.

As they approached though, the youths seemed more interested in the colour of Viv's hair. 'Would you look at that!' one of them said, pointing.

Viv beamed. 'It looks so much better when the sun's out.'

The lad burst out laughing.

Eve butted in. 'Are you Joey Turnham?'

He shot a quick glance at another boy, which told Eve all she needed to know. She turned to him.

'So you're Joey.' Now she looked, she could see which his brother was too. They were alike: broad with wide, heavy-set faces. 'And you're Luke.'

Lots of shrugs. 'Who wants to know?'

Viv rolled her eyes. 'We do, obviously!'

One of the lads was stroking Gus. That was a step in the right direction. She must make a fuss of him later. She hoped he didn't feel used.

'We asked around to find out who knows most about what goes on in Lovelace-by-Sax,' Eve said. 'And your names came up. People say you've got your ears to the ground and we need your help. Viv's brother' – she nodded at her friend – 'has offered a reward for information.'

Viv still clutched the cash and Eve saw the boys glance at it.

'What kind of information?' Luke said.

Eve knew she had to tread carefully. The money was definitely a lure, especially as Simon had been so generous, but if they thought they were in serious trouble they'd probably run for it. 'About Lavender Cottage.' She held up a hand. 'He's not interested in anyone who's been hanging around in the garden or anything like that. He knows someone's been there. He saw the cigarette butts. But he was young once.'

'A *very* long time ago,' Viv put in.

'He said he used to muck around when he was a kid too.'

'He was a terror.'

They were sharing their audience with Gus now. Four of the lads were crouched down fussing him, though their eyes were on Eve and Viv.

'What he really wants to know is, did any of you see anything at the house on Wednesday night? There was a break-in and several valuables were stolen.'

'We never did it,' Joey said urgently. 'Is this some kind of trap? All the sweet talk and the money.'

He stood up, his eyes fiery. Eve hoped he was telling the truth. 'Not at all. If he thought you'd done it he'd have called the police, not asked for your help. But he did hope you might have seen something. He wants to know who was responsible.' Eve kept her eyes on them. 'And how they got in.'

There was an exchange of glances as she uttered her last sentence.

'You've got an idea about how they got inside?'

More sidelong looks from one brother to another.

'We did go round the back Wednesday night,' Joey said. He looked at the ground. 'Someone had forced a window – I spotted it. Maybe they wanted to get in for a laugh, but I reckon they left it.'

Eve was pretty certain one of *them* had done the forcing, shortly before their mobile rang and they dashed off in search of other entertainment. It would fit with what she'd heard from her position in the neighbouring field, but she wasn't going to push it.

She nodded. 'If so, maybe the thief was able to get in quite easily, without any further work.'

'Could be.' He still didn't meet her eyes.

'Did you go back there later at all? If you saw anything, it could be helpful.' There was a danger they'd make something up just to get the money, but Eve couldn't do much about that.

Interestingly, the lads looked just as shifty as before.

'Why would we go back?' Luke said.

Perhaps to pick up where they'd left off, thought Eve. They'd been planning to break in on Sunday night as a dare, but the intruder then had frightened them away. She could imagine them wanting another go. And not wanting to admit it.

'To fetch something you'd dropped maybe? Or just for somewhere to hang out?'

Luke's shoulders went down. 'Yeah, of course. Thinking about it, we did go back.' He shook his head. 'It was weird, because we saw someone in there on Sunday night too. And then on Wednesday there was someone there again. It was like a flipping station – people coming and going.'

'That's interesting. Do you think it was the same person?'

Joey shook his head. 'Nah. I didn't see the person on Sunday but I caught their shadow. They were tall. Bulky. But on Wednesday it was a woman.'

Eve caught her breath. Who the heck could that have been?

'It was bright – full moon,' Joey went on. One of the other

lads butted in with a wolf howl, which excited Gus into a bark, much to the group's amusement. 'Anyway, I only caught sight of her from behind,' Joey resumed, 'but she was thin, with long hair. Couldn't really tell the colour.'

'You can't guess who she was?'

He shook his head. 'Mentioned her to a few mates, down the White Lion.' He talked as though he was at least forty. 'But none of them could think who she'd be.'

As they drove back to Saxford, Viv called Simon. 'We spent your fifty pounds!'

32

Eve made a great fuss of Gus when they got home.

'You were brilliant.' She gave him a cuddle, then he skipped about looking confused but happy. 'They were definitely more relaxed with you there.' Though the money had helped, obviously.

She sensed Viv had enjoyed the feeling of power that came with bribery. *Worrying*. On the upside, they'd told the lads that Simon would be installing security cameras now, so they'd best not hang out at Lavender Cottage any more. Eve had made a big thing of how helpful they'd been, and said she'd put the word out. Just for a second she'd seen a flicker of pride in one of the boy's eyes. It had to be said, Joey Turnham had looked horrified, but you had to start somewhere. If a few of their neighbours thanked them in the street, they might get to like it.

'I wish I could take you with me this afternoon,' Eve said to Gus. 'But I'm going by train, and I'll be interviewing Hazel Carrington as well as seeing the twins.' She'd contacted her children as she usually did when she was headed for the city. She grabbed any chance to see them. Today, her stomach fluttered at the thought. It was part excitement, part nerves. Her son, Nick, was bringing his new girlfriend, Fiona Prentice. It would be the first time she'd met her, although she'd helped Eve research something a few months earlier – she was an academic at the British Museum. 'Tammy's going to come and give you some supper as soon as she's finished at Monty's.'

Tammy and Lars had held the fort at the teashop that afternoon, during her and Viv's escapade. Viv was going to give them a bonus.

Gus did an ecstatic dance at the mention of Tammy's name. Eve sighed. She was used to being the less exciting dog servant.

On the London train, Eve took out her notebook, ready to make a timetable. She needed to get the comings and goings at Lavender Cottage straight in her head.

Lavender Cottage

Sunday 15 May: Cammie Harrington killed. Male intruder (? tall and bulky), seen inside by the Turnham brothers' gang. Nothing taken as far as anyone knows. Poisoned smoothie not removed.

Monday 16 May: Stella Hilling arrives early to clean, drinks the smoothie. Discovered by me and Simon at lunchtime, dead. Police arrive and maintain a presence all day. Spare key removed. House sealed off.

Tuesday 17 May: police still busy at Lavender Cottage.

Wednesday 18 May: police tape and barriers removed from Lavender Cottage. Turnham brothers discuss the previous intruder with Lars in the evening. Viv and I watch from the cottage and later from the field. Turnham brothers leave garden, probably having loosened a window. They return later to find someone has made use of their handiwork. Intruder this time appears to be female, thin, with long hair. Several items stolen.

Thursday 19 May (evening): Diana Pickford-Jones shot dead. Raven Allerton disappears.

Eve sat staring at her notes. Could Diana have stolen some-thing from Lavender Cottage that made her a danger to the killer? Her hair was shoulder length but in the half-light it might have appeared longer. Or was the female the Turnham gang spotted the murderer, removing something that might incriminate them? Of the suspects present on Lovelace Sunday, the long hair was a match for Raven, and possibly for Diana. Unless it was a man, wearing a wig... Sebastian was slender.

But if it was the killer, why hadn't they removed whatever it was when they planted the poisoned drink? Theories started to gather, but Eve was interrupted by her mobile ringing.

Hazel Harrington. She felt a twist of concern. Why was she ringing now?

'Eve, I'm afraid I can't meet you this evening after all.'

She didn't sound upset, or apologetic. Just matter-of-fact – and in a hurry.

'That's a shame, only I'm on the train now.'

'What a nuisance, but there it is. An important work contact's just called. They're only in the UK until tomorrow morning; if I want to see them it has to be tonight. Perhaps you could email me your questions.'

Eve felt her teeth clench automatically. She got that she was well down the pecking order, but this was just plain rude. And didn't Hazel want to pay tribute to her daughter? 'Perhaps you could give me five minutes now. A conversation always works better and it will give me something to do on my journey.' She'd been tempted to say 'unnecessary' journey, but she'd be glad to see the twins.

There was a heavy sigh from down the line and a tut from the gentleman opposite, who rustled his newspaper for emphasis.

'*I can't give you long.*'

'I wouldn't expect it.' *Not based on current behaviour, anyway.* Eve picked up her notebook and bag and walked into the vestibule by the loos. 'I'd love to hear about your relationship with Cammie. What she was like growing up.' Eve pulled up short. This must still be painful territory, however distracted Hazel was by her business dealings. 'I'm sorry. I realise the questions are hard at a time like this, but your knowledge is unique. If you have a story from Cammie's childhood that sums her up for you, or any special memories, that would be hugely helpful.'

'*Right, right.*' Hazel still sounded rushed, as though she was dragging her mind to the matter in hand.

Eve scribbled notes as Hazel relayed details of the schools Cammie had attended, her academic achievements and her move into television work. Eve could have got it all from Wikipedia. In fact, she already had, in the main. There was nothing that told a story, and certainly not of a mother–daughter relationship.

'What about family holidays? Could you tell me about those?'

Hazel mentioned skiing trips to Chamonix, and getaways to Bora Bora.

'And what type of activities did you usually do together?'

'*Well, we didn't normally do the same things of course.*' Hazel sounded mystified. '*Cammie needed beginners' tuition for the skiing, for instance. She didn't reach my standard until she got too old for family trips. And naturally the young ones want to do different things in the evenings. The resorts have excellent facilities.'*

When Eve asked if it had been emotional, dropping Cammie off at boarding school at the beginning of term, Hazel said she'd never done the school run herself. Once again, she sounded perplexed.

When Eve rang off, she stood there by the loo door, which rattled as the train whizzed towards London, feeling a mixture of shock and outrage. Raven had been right: she and Cammie *had* had a lot in common. It left her with an almost desperate desire to see the twins and hug them. She must remember not to look too weird and over-emotional in front of Nick's girlfriend.

Eve went back to her seat and wrote up rude notes about Hazel Harrington. She'd modify them into something more measured for the obituary. Probably.

In London, she got the tube from Liverpool Street to the restaurant where she'd planned to entertain Cammie's mum and browsed her phone as she ate.

Simon had emailed with an update. He'd been through Polly's inventory for Lavender Cottage and worked out which items were missing. The answer was a small mantel clock with a wooden frame and decorative scrollwork, a pewter vase, a pair of brass candlesticks and a tiny picture of an owl. Simon said he'd phoned Polly to warn her but although she was cross, she said they weren't valuable. She'd picked them up at junk shops. The police had used photographs they'd taken of the cottage's interior to work out if any of Cammie's belongings had also been taken. They'd found three things missing: a silver letter opener with her initial engraved on it, a pen (also silver and personalised), and a silver and jade necklace. Eve wondered if the letter opener and pen were part of a set. They had to be presents. No one bought themselves that kind of thing. Taking the list as a whole, it was a weird collection to pinch, but she supposed any of the items might have looked valuable.

But the Turnham brothers' description of the thief made her wonder. Statistically, the number of women arrested was way lower than the number of men. It didn't mean there were no female burglars, but they were fairly unusual. And if Eve had long hair, and was going out for a spot of housebreaking, she'd stuff it under a dark hat to disguise herself. She guessed either the intruder was new to the job, or the long hair was part of a disguise itself. Either way, it didn't point to your average burglar. She guessed the break-in must relate to Cammie's murder. What significance might the desk accessories have? Or had they been taken as a blind and it was the necklace that mattered? Or might the whole burglary have been staged? Maybe they'd been after something quite different. A note tucked into a book, say, that the police hadn't found. Polly had 'accessorised' the cottage with a lot of novels. Simon said they weren't individually itemised on the inventory.

In his email, Simon had fretted again over Cammie's mum's possible upset at the theft. Eve replied to reassure him on that score. She felt a bit low, but just as she'd paid the bill Robin texted to invite her to an early lunch and updates the following day. And within half an hour she was at the Blue Boar pub, peering through the crowds, and rushing over to hug Nick and Ellen, her stomach a bundle of nerves at seeing Nick's Dr Prentice for the first time.

On the train home, she felt a lot happier. She hugged thoughts of the evening to her. Of Fiona Prentice's friendly sparkling eyes and her fondness as she'd looked at Nick. Of how well Ellen and Fiona seemed to get on, laughing over the latest crazy inventions Ellen's patent law firm was dealing with. Of the sight of both her children looking so well and happy. They'd asked after Robin, with a twinkle in their eyes. It was largely down to their intervention that she and Robin had got together.

As she'd left, Ellen had taken her to one side, hooked an arm through hers and said how pleased she was about Fiona. Just for a second, Eve had felt wistful about her and Robin. There was a lot to be said for a normal relationship.

Still, they managed. And she'd got Gus. She took a taxi home, knowing what a warm welcome she'd get, and how pleased she'd be to see him.

33

The following morning, Eve went to the village store to pick up some breakfast things. She felt a little bleary from her late night and pottered around slowly. The store was empty, and Moira regaled her with gossip as she filled her basket.

'Well, of course, in my position, I do get to hear things. I know it's not really relevant to the case any more, after that dreadful Raven did what she did.'

For a second, Eve thought of the comb, abandoned in the bathroom at the shepherd's hut. Was the storyteller really starting a new life somewhere after killing Diana?

'All the same,' Moira went on, 'I thought you might be interested to hear the latest.'

Eve put a loaf of crusty white bread into her basket. They baked it over at the pub and it was still warm. 'It's always useful to hear background information.' She knew Moira would tell her, whatever she said.

The storekeeper beamed, but then her brow furrowed. 'Well, it's distressing news really.'

The frown had to be for show. No news was distressing to Moira.

'A friend of mine who works in Blenkinsop's in Blyworth tells me Sebastian Pickford's been fighting a drink problem. I gather it was completely out of hand for a year or so. He was getting through bottle after bottle of whisky, though in recent weeks he seems to have managed to pull back from the brink.' She shook her head. 'He's a very charming young man, of course, and he's had a lot to cope with, what with his mother dying young and then losing Peter. I'm sure we should all make allowances.'

But that was much less satisfying, obviously. Eve wondered if the rumours were exaggerated anyway. However much Sebastian had drunk, he'd managed to keep his modelling career on track.

'The thing I can't understand,' Moira continued, her frown deepening, 'is why he went to Blenkinsop's to buy his spirits. I mean, I appreciate there's no convenience store in Lovelace-by-Sax, but we're actually a lot closer to the manor than Blenkinsop's is.'

'That really is very odd.' Eve put her basket on the counter.

In fact, she found it entirely explicable. News of Sebastian's private business would have spread a lot faster if he'd done his shopping in Saxford. It was unlucky for him that one of the assistants at Blenkinsop's happened to know Moira. Everyone would be aware of his problem by the end of the morning.

She let the information play in her mind. For a second, she thought of the secret Cammie said Sebastian had been keeping, but drinking didn't fit with her words. It bugged her that she was still no further with solving that mystery. An answer might make things a lot clearer. As she unlooped Gus's leash from the hooks outside the store, she let her mind freewheel. How could she get more information? As she walked towards Blind Eye Wood, an idea came to her. *Heaven Jones.* She couldn't imagine why it hadn't occurred to her before. Eve had met the improbably named model while researching the obituary of another murder victim. She might not know Sebastian, but they probably moved in the same circles – it had to be worth a shot.

Eve considered her approach carefully as she walked. She and Heaven had got on well, but that didn't mean the woman would be happy to dish the dirt on a mutual acquaintance. In the end, she paused in the woods, letting Gus off his leash for a run about, and sent off an email, explaining the job she had in hand, and how she wasn't quite sure what to make of Sebastian. It was best to open communications with a general query. If Heaven knew him, and felt able to talk, Eve would steer the conversation onto any dark secrets being gossiped about in the modelling world.

After Gus had indulged in some invigorating scampering, they made their way to St Peter's and caught the morning service. Eve felt for Jim Thackeray, having to carry on and provide comfort to the villagers in his address, when the horrific events at the manor affected him so closely. As the congregation milled out, she overheard Moira passing on the news about Sebastian's supposed drink problem.

Within an hour, Eve and Gus arrived at the Swan in Wessingham, where she'd arranged to meet Robin. It tended to be a safe, private venue, thanks to the loyalty the Cross Keys commanded in Saxford.

They were sitting in a quiet corner of the pub's garden, in the shade of a lime tree. Gus had gone for a drink of water outside the back door but now he pottered over to them and settled down for a rest.

Robin and Eve each had low-alcohol beer. A clear head was essential.

'Your hunch about Peter Pickford-Jones's gifts to Raven was spot on,' Robin said. 'He did give her money. A lot of it. The police got clearance to approach her bank. Turns out she came in for fifteen thousand pounds, all told.'

'Heck.' Gus raised his head at the tone of her voice and she ruffled his fur. 'Hiding her wealthy background would have felt like much more of a betrayal under those circumstances.'

'I'd say so. And the police are now sure that Cammie told Peter,' Robin went on, 'and that Peter banished Raven from Lovelace. It's all in Raven's diaries.' He cocked his head. 'Greg read me a few extracts. They're full of hate. Palmer's all the more convinced she's responsible for both killings, and that Diana must have been onto her.'

Eve shook her head. She still had doubts about the woman's guilt. Suddenly, she knew what had been niggling at her. 'Would she really leave her diary behind like that?'

'Maybe she knew she'd look guilty anyway, so there was no point being encumbered with it.' His eyes met hers. 'But I've got my doubts about Raven too. She hasn't touched her bank account since she left, which might be expected, but she didn't withdraw money to tide her over beforehand either.'

That was odd. The chill Eve had felt swept over her again. Whatever the truth, the papers had bought Raven's guilt. They'd been full of photographs of Great Foley and her parents' palatial house that morning. It was shown next to shots of the shepherd's hut under a headline 'RICHES TO RAGS'.

'Whatever she did, she had a lousy childhood. I can see why she reinvented herself. Maybe the lack of care as a child meant she couldn't empathise properly with people as an adult. To be honest, I don't find the idea of her killing Diana hard to swallow. It's the small details that don't add up.' She frowned, thinking it through. 'She put on a front, Robin. She'd have hated people reading her diary – poring over her dishonesty, and the way Peter banned her from Lovelace. She'd have found it humiliating. She could have hidden it or thrown it away, but it's still there. It doesn't fit.'

He nodded as a waitress turned up with a mozzarella, tomato and basil panini for Eve and a ploughman's lunch for him.

The waitress retreated, pausing on her way to exchange a word with a waiter carrying a jug of Pimm's and lemonade.

Eve heard the words 'body' and 'Faverly Pits' and a gasp from the waiter. Suddenly she was on high alert again, hairs rising on her scalp.

And at that moment, Robin's mobile rang.

34

Eve watched Robin's eyes as he listened to the caller. 'Faverly Pits nature reserve? I know it.' He listened for a minute or so. 'Okay, Greg. Thanks.' He hung up and turned to Eve. 'I'm afraid Raven's body's been found.'

Eve put down her panini, her insides turning cold. She knew Faverly Pits was an old quarry with some perilous drops. 'What happened?'

'She was dumped there. Her body was covered with vegetation – deliberately hidden. But if she'd been found after months or even years, we might all have assumed she jumped, then crawled a short way before dying from her fall. The killer made an effort to make her injuries look consistent with that. The pathologist thinks they were made after her death, though that's small comfort. It was a blow to the head which killed her.'

Icy prickles spread up Eve's arms, like cold sea rushing over warm sand.

'When do they think she died?'

'It's hard to be precise, but probably around the same time as Diana. It's looking like the killer attacked them both in the woods at Lovelace. The CSIs have found traces of vegetation in

Raven's hair consistent with her being knocked to the ground there.'

'So it looks like the killer was using Raven as a scapegoat.'

Robin nodded.

Eve put her head in her hands. It was unbelievably ruthless. She'd believed Raven capable of murder but that felt like a betrayal now. She'd had a rotten upbringing, and someone had spotted her vulnerability and used it to try to cover their tracks. They would have let her friends and family believe she was a killer, and denied them closure by hiding her body. Such cruelty.

She forced herself to focus on the facts again.

'I suppose Raven could have stolen from Lavender Cottage. Something she discovered might have driven the killer to action.'

'Let's go back to the facts we have and take it from the top,' Robin said. 'We know the obvious things that were stolen. We can't hope to guess if the thief took anything extra – like a photograph or a scrap of paper.'

It was a depressing thought.

'If Raven was the thief, and she was killed for what she stole, then her murderer might have taken the evidence. We know they went to the shepherd's hut to pack a bag. But I don't think that fits.'

Eve followed it through. 'No, I agree. Unless the killer knew every item she'd taken from Lavender Cottage – which seems unlikely – they'd have left the irrelevant ones behind. The CSIs would have found them.'

Robin nodded. 'Exactly. So unless Raven stole the items and hid them somewhere outside the shepherd's hut, then I'd say we're looking for a different thief.'

'Agreed. And I can't believe the burglary was random. I think the intruder was waiting until the house was empty to get what they wanted. If it wasn't Raven, maybe it was the killer.'

'But if so, why not take what they were after when they planted the poisoned smoothie?'

Eve had been considering that problem. 'I can think of a number of reasons. They might not have known Cammie had the item at the time. News of the loving cup she'd taken could have alerted them to other things she might have.'

Robin nodded. 'True.'

'Or maybe it was something they needed to search for, and they ran out of time. Cammie could have come home at any moment. It was a short trip back to Lavender Cottage from the manor.

'And lastly, maybe they decided not to risk taking it then, in case the balloon crash failed, and Cammie returned home that night. She might have noticed something was missing and been put on her guard. Especially if she'd just had a near miss.'

Robin gave her a half-smile. 'All right, you've convinced me. Let's carry on with our chain of thought then. Worst-case scenario first. If the objects were a blind and the thief stole something previously unidentified then we're sunk.'

He prepared a mouthful of cheddar and pickled onion. 'We just have to hope it's one of the items we know about that's important. Let's focus on the things that belonged to Cammie.'

Eve nodded. 'They were a silver monogrammed pen and letter opener, and a jade necklace.' She pulled her phone from her bag. 'The photos Greg sent of Lavender Cottage ought to show them.' Her own hadn't featured either the letter opener or the necklace. The opener had been in a drawer, and she hadn't dared hunt around when the place was a crime scene. The necklace had probably been upstairs in the bedroom Cammie had used.

She swiped through the police photos, finding the pen and the letter opener first. 'Oh, that's interesting.' She handed the phone to Robin so he could zoom in on them in turn. 'I thought they might be part of a set, given they're both silver and engraved with a C, but they're quite different designs.' She sipped her beer. Now she thought about it, who brought a letter opener with them when they travelled? It was hardly an essential. 'The letter opener looks old, don't you think?' Her mind was suddenly on the loving cup again. Another engraved silver object. But the initial on the letter opener wasn't right for Louisa or her husband, Seth. 'When Simon emailed me his list, I assumed the C on the letter opener was for Cammie, but I'd say it's a good bit older than she was.'

She took her phone from Robin and scrolled to the photographs the police had recovered from Cammie's laptop – the ones of Lovelace Manor. Eve was pretty sure she remembered seeing a shot of the plaque that was mounted in one of the rooms there. She knew it told Louisa and Seth's story. Was there a C associated with the Lovelace legend?

But before she found the plaque, she discovered a photograph of one of the display cases, which housed a locket with a C on it, in exactly the same ornate design as the C on the letter opener. Eve shivered as she enlarged the image and read the label that went alongside the artefact: 'A locket belonging to Cecily Lovelace, Louisa's mother, who died when Louisa was an infant.' Eve kicked herself. She'd forgotten that was her name, though she was pretty sure Diana had mentioned it when she'd recounted the Lovelace legend.

She showed Robin the photograph. 'I think the letter opener's another manor heirloom.' She frowned. 'We know the loving cup came from the moat. I wonder if this did too. But I'm confused, Robin. Why the heck would anyone kill over an old silver trinket? I can't imagine it's all that valuable, and unlike the loving cup, it's not even associated with the love story.' She closed her eyes a moment. 'I'm wondering if your worst-case scenario is true. I imagine the letter opener's important – they won't have taken it by chance. But perhaps there was an extra unidentified item too, like you said – and that's what's really crucial.'

Robin swallowed a hunk of bread. 'Quite possibly. It might be the key to whole thing, but we have no way of knowing what it was.'

Eve nodded. 'I suppose we need to keep focusing on the who, until we can guess the what. Sebastian's slender. If he'd worn a wig, he could have been the second intruder at Lavender Cottage. He's sitting pretty now, with his new fiancée and his inheritance.'

Back at Elizabeth's Cottage, Eve spent the next few hours going through what she knew, writing up her notes and looking for patterns. Late in the day, she received two phone calls.

The first was from Viv. Eve filled her in on the discovery of Raven's body, confirming rumours already circulating in the village. They spent some time sharing their shock and running over the implications.

After that, in the heat of the moment, Eve made the mistake of revealing her plans for the following day. She wanted a closer look at Josh Standish's set-up. Why had the woman she'd seen left his house so quickly, perhaps trailing the mud Eve had spotted on the driveway? She had a hunch about it, but she needed proof.

'*Can I come?*' Viv's voice was pleading. '*It would be safer that way. And if you're going early I can fit it in before Monty's opens. Please.*'

'Oh, all right then. But we'll have to be really quiet. No stage whispers and no giggling.'

'*As if I would.*'

Hmm. It wasn't what Eve had had in mind, but she'd never hear the last of it if she said no.

It was after supper when she received the second call. She glanced at her mobile.

Heaven Jones. She must be ringing about Sebastian. Eve snatched up her notebook as she answered.

'Heaven! Thanks so much for getting back to me. How are you?'

'*I'm well thanks.*' Her deep melodic voice conjured up an image of her as she was when they'd last met. She'd been wearing what appeared to be a very large pillowcase with arm and leg holes, teamed with silver sandals, yet still looked the epitome of elegance. '*I was intrigued to get your email. I've met Sebastian Pickford several times.*'

The way she paused told Eve she'd get something interesting, even if it didn't unlock the case. 'If you have any insights you're prepared to share, that would be amazing. It's not him I'm writing about of course—'

'*Don't worry.*' Heaven's tone was serious. '*As soon as I saw there'd been killings at Sebastian's family home I wondered about him. He's used to everything falling into his lap and I've seen him when things aren't going his way. He gets a lot of work, but if he's turned down, things get ugly. Nothing overt – he tends to drip poison about people who've crossed him into the ears of anyone who will listen. And he has clout. Some of the glossies reckon women buy them just for the adverts he's in. Can you imagine? He must be making a small fortune, but he doesn't like to work too hard and mostly he's allowed to call the shots.*'

It sounded deeply irritating. Eve knew how dedicated Heaven was – the long, gruelling schedule she worked to. 'I'm surprised he gets away with it.'

'*I believe it's boiled-frog syndrome. He made himself charming at the outset, and now he knows he's too valuable to lose.*'

None of it came as a surprise. It fitted with the impression

Eve had of him. Her mind flitted to Sapphire. Was she really going to marry this man?

'*He's got the perfect bone structure for modelling of course,*' Heaven went on, '*but he's actually a little outside the standard dimensions. He got picked up by luck. He was spotted at a party – a bigwig at the agency which took him on overheard him telling the story of his great-grandparents – the pair who eloped. The word is, it captured their imagination. Apparently they could see him as a Hollywood-style romantic hero. They were convinced his high cheekbones, cleft chin and backstory would be a perfect package for the top brands. Turns out they were right.*'

Sickening. 'Heaven, I've heard Sebastian might have been keeping a secret. Something really damaging – evil almost. The most I've been able to uncover is that he might have a drink problem and I guess it's not that. Do you have any inkling of what it might be?'

There was a pause. '*Honestly, no. I can imagine it being true, but the rumours haven't reached me. I've never seen him out-of-control drunk either, but of course, people can put away a lot if their tolerance is high.*'

'And sorry to be so direct, but could you see him committing murder?'

She heard Heaven take a long breath. '*Like I said, he came to mind when I heard about the deaths, but now you ask me point-blank, I'm not sure. I'd have said he tends to work in more insidious ways. He wouldn't find it morally repugnant, but he'd prefer not to get his hands dirty.*'

After she and Heaven had chatted more generally, Eve hung up. She thought through the murders. Rigging the balloon crash and planting the poison were both hands-off methods of killing, but shooting his half-sister and coshing Raven would be a whole different ball game. To say nothing of faking additional injuries, which was horrific. But what if Sebastian had got desperate – pushed into a corner because Diana had discovered his guilt, perhaps? Then the man Heaven thought she knew might ratchet up a gear.

What she'd said about his insidious behaviour was interesting. Causing damage subtly, under the radar – she could imagine Cammie referring to that as requiring the worst sort of guile. But she still had no idea of the specifics.

She sighed. 'I don't seem to be making any progress, Gus.' She bent to pat him. 'I need some concrete facts.'

She was lounging on one of the couches in her living room, Gus by her side, when she found one – though it was nothing to do with Sebastian. She'd finally got as far as looking at the Sunday papers and was leafing through the property section, marvelling at how much you could pay for a flat in London, when she saw a name she recognised. Apartments for sale as part of an exclusive development by Erica Bond Associates. Last few remaining.

Eye-wateringly expensive.

Erica Bond? That was a coincidence. It was Ralph Roscoe's wife's name, of course. Idly, Eve keyed Erica Bond Associates into Google and the familiar face of the woman she'd met appeared in front of her.

35

At a quarter past five the following morning, shortly after sunrise, Eve and Viv reached the space behind Josh Standish's cottage. Although it was part of the Lovelace estate, it was outside the gated land reserved for paying visitors. There was a right of way through the woods and they'd taken it, stepping quietly through the dew-soaked undergrowth. They'd come dressed for the occasion in old jeans and fleeces. It was sufficiently early to need them against the cold, but they protected their arms and legs too. The bark of the oak tree they chose to climb was rough.

Eve was glad the branches started so low down; she wasn't sure she'd have managed it otherwise. As it was, the climb was easy on a practical level, though she wasn't crazy about heights. As soon as they reached a point where they were well hidden, with a view over Josh Standish's garden wall, she signalled to Viv that she was going to stop. Viv followed suit. She was ignoring Eve's strictures about keeping three points of contact with the tree. For a second Eve imagined her falling and them having to call an ambulance, rousing Josh from his sleep, with some very awkward explaining to do. She mimed to Viv to hold on tighter and her friend rolled her eyes.

At last, Eve felt slightly more relaxed. She became conscious of the dawn chorus and the pink light through the trees as she pulled the pair of mini binoculars from a zipped pocket in her fleece.

A moment later she was breaking her own rules to adjust the focus. She wanted to know what was behind the door Josh had shut so firmly when she'd visited, and if it had anything to do with his female visitor.

It was as she'd thought. Plant pots, sitting in his conservatory at the back, and outside in his garden too. A lot of them. Some seedlings, some more advanced. Lavender, salvia, rosemary, hardy geraniums. Nothing dodgy, so why be cagey about it? But it looked like he was growing them on an industrial scale and Eve couldn't see the plants they'd been cut from in his small paved garden. Was he secretly profiting from the flowers and shrubs he tended at the manor? Taking cuttings and selling them under the radar, cash in hand?

Viv nudged her and she handed over the binoculars.

If she was right, it was hardly the crime of the century. It might make life a little bit more comfortable, but she supposed it could have got Josh the sack. He'd said Diana had fallen over herself to help him, but she'd only got his word for that. All the same, the idea of him killing Raven and Diana over it seemed ridiculous. And why would he have murdered Cammie?

Viv widened her eyes to show she'd noted the plants. Eve had just indicated that they could climb down again, when they heard voices. She froze and put her finger to her lips but her sudden halt had surprised Viv. She grabbed the branch she'd just let go of and for one awful moment her foot slipped. Eve could hardly breathe, but at last Viv managed to get her toe into a crack in the bark and regain her perch. Down below the voices continued without any pause.

Whoever it was was over the wall, in Lovelace's gated grounds. Eve breathed a sigh of relief; they were unlikely to be seen.

She held her hand out for the binoculars to an irritated look from Viv. With their aid, Eve could just see the two figures, though they weren't close enough for her to hear their words. One was Josh Standish. The other was a woman Eve hadn't seen before, with long, glossy hair, a well-cut fitted dress, and some funky-looking sandals: black platform heels and lots of straps. Designer rather than hippy.

Josh had his arm around the woman's shoulders and she was gazing into his eyes. It brought back Ralph Roscoe's words about Josh's admirers. Maybe he took lovers for a night under the stars, using Lovelace's charm as part of his seduction technique. Eve remembered Cammie mentioning Sebastian doing the same thing. There was a lot of overlap between them. As for Josh, using the garden wouldn't have gone down well with Diana but again, one murder would be extreme in the face of the sack, let alone three deliberate killings and a fourth by accident... And she certainly didn't see how it could relate to a stolen letter opener.

Josh and his companion passed out of sight.

'How long do you think we'll have to wait here?' Viv said. 'I could do with the loo.'

Eve had images of a hot drink floating through her head. 'I don't think we can risk it yet.' She'd been banking on leaving before Josh woke up. Now, he might appear at the back of his house any moment and see them descend.

Eve turned the binoculars back on his cottage and five minutes later, he did appear. He picked up a lavender plant and disappeared with it – back to the front of the house.

'A plant for his lady friend?' Viv whispered loudly.

'I wondered if he'd been selling them, but perhaps it's a free gift. Then again, he's got several women on the go, from what

I've seen. If he's not faithful, he might be taking each of them for all they've got.'

'A cad and a bounder?'

'It's possible.'

They waited for ten more minutes. Eve was just about to give in, and trust to luck, when they saw Josh recross the lawn inside the main grounds. Back in the direction he and the woman had come from.

'Thank goodness,' Viv said, following Eve down as soon as he was out of sight. 'Perhaps he's going to clear up after his antics last night, so he doesn't get found out.'

'Sounds about right.'

'I'm not sure I can make it back to Saxford.'

'Don't worry, I've still got Simon's spare key for Lavender Cottage. You can go to the bathroom there.'

Once Viv had done the necessary, Eve locked up Lavender Cottage again and they walked towards the back lane that led to the small playground they'd visited on Saturday when they'd talked to the Turnham brothers. It had seemed like the least conspicuous place to park when they'd arrived that morning and was close to the right of way they'd used to access their vantage point. It was just after seven now, and people were starting to open their curtains, but the hamlet was still quiet.

'So, tell me the latest then,' Viv said.

Eve passed on her discovery relating to Erica Roscoe, otherwise known as Erica Bond.

'It turns out she's a property developer,' Eve said. 'She takes beautiful old buildings and turns them into luxury flats, keeping as many of the original features as she can. She goes for character properties and gets high prices because of it.'

Eve had had a lovely time, satisfying her curiosity. She'd found several of Erica's classy developments and even got as far as a feature article which showed her and Ralph's swanky pad in London and Erica's family home in Hampshire. Her parents still lived there apparently. They must rattle around – it was almost as big as Lovelace and a lot smarter. But it turned out Erica's mother was the chief executive of an investment bank and involved in a number of charities; perhaps she had to do a lot of entertaining. The article included an interview with her cook and housekeeper – it sounded like quite an operation.

Ralph's photo didn't appear in the article and neither of them seemed to have Facebook. Eve still thought it was possible Cammie was unaware of their marriage. But it was Erica's career that sent her heart racing.

Viv looked at Eve. 'You think she was after Lovelace?'

'Well, we know Diana was thinking of selling just after her husband died, only she pulled back after a week and decided not to. Maybe Erica and Ralph got wind of that and thought they might persuade her to change her mind again. Either way, I intend to find out. The future of the manor means a lot to Sebastian. I gather he's always referred to it as his birthright and if it was sold, it would have halved his inheritance too. If Erica Bond made Diana a good offer he might have worried she'd crack. And maybe Cammie's research ties in as well, though I can't think how. I'm going to go back and hammer on their door as soon as I'm able.'

36

Later that morning, Eve was back inside Ralph Roscoe and Erica Bond's cottage. Her insides squirmed as she thought of Robin, hanging around outside again. He was between his Monday jobs. He'd said he was glad she'd asked, but she guessed it was hardly convenient.

She'd kept knocking until Ralph opened up. He'd threatened to call the police if she didn't stop bothering them, but she'd suggested they hear her out first.

Now, the couple were looking at her as though she was something unpleasant Ralph had found on the sole of his shoe.

'You wanted to buy the manor.' Eve said it without preamble, then focused on Ralph. 'You were helping Erica by talking to Diana about it. It was more discreet that way, I suppose. I saw you having a secret conversation the day before Lovelace Sunday. That's why you were volunteering: to schmooze her.' She turned to Erica now. 'I guess you kept a low profile because Sebastian and the villagers are dead against the manor changing hands.' Eve felt bolder than she had on her last visit. If Diana had been weakening, there was no way they'd have wanted to kill her. And even if she'd turned them down, taking her out of the equation didn't fit. The chances of changing Sebastian's mind on selling seemed thin. Certainly too thin to kill Raven and Diana on the off chance. Unless Ralph's hand had been forced, of course. If Diana had worked out he'd killed Cammie it would be a different matter.

'There was no "schmoozing" required.' Ralph put the word in inverted commas, his lips pursed in a look of distaste. 'Diana had agreed to sell, soon after her husband died. The paperwork was signed weeks ago. The meetup you saw in the woods was just to check in. She was keen to know how everything was progressing.' He shook his head. 'I visited her the day she died with the latest updates. Everything was on track. I know she said publicly that she'd changed her mind, but that was just for show. To get everyone off her back.'

'Yet she went to the lengths of inviting Cammie here, supposedly to turn Lovelace's fortunes around.' But of course, Eve knew why Diana had really invited Cammie. She'd seen an opportunity to look the woman in the eye – to try to understand how she could hurt her so badly.

'All part of the show, I assume,' Ralph said. 'I was surprised by that too, but when I talked with her, she was determined to press on.'

'Have you told the police the full story? Someone could have killed her to stop the sale.'

'I had the same thought, but only for a moment. It wouldn't explain Cammie's death. If anything, she'd have made it more likely Diana would have held on to the place, if she'd managed to make it more profitable. It was in Sebastian's interests to keep her alive, though he had a motive for Diana, to get his hands on Lovelace.'

'Diana told me she'd come to her senses over the sale – that she had a renewed commitment to keeping the manor in the family. I understand she thought it would be unfair to pull the rug from under Sebastian's feet.'

Ralph laughed now, a hollow sound, which made Eve feel foolish for taking Diana at face value. 'I'm afraid she wasn't quite honest then. She hated Sebastian. It seemed to me that it was one of the reasons she wanted to sell: to punish him.'

'For what?'

He shrugged his large shoulders. 'How would I know? But that's the impression I got. I asked if he might contest the sale, but she said he hadn't got a leg to stand on. I think she meant more than just legally.'

The plan gave Sebastian a heck of a motive, if he'd found out Diana was double-crossing him. And Eve could see his motive for Cammie too, thanks to the conversation she'd overheard. Cammie had known his damaging secret, whatever it was. Then Raven would have been his scapegoat. But what about the burglary? The history of the manor had to be relevant.

'What would have happened to Josh Standish and the gardens if the sale had gone through?' She'd heard his story, but it needed verifying.

Ralph rubbed his chin. 'Diana was adamant about that. Josh was to stay, and the gardens were to be maintained in consultation with him. She even set a lower limit for his wages – talk about driving a hard bargain.'

'But it went with our plans.' Erica spoke for the first time. 'It would have been a selling point. The development would have been very select – people would expect high annual costs. We wouldn't want the manor or the grounds to lose their character and the new occupants would have been able to use the gardens for outdoor entertaining. Imagine a dinner party in the walled garden. The agreement to maintain the grounds helped Diana get listed building consent for a sympathetic conversion. The place is going to rack and ruin as it is. The planners saw sense.'

Ralph nodded. 'Lovelace Sunday would have continued too, with full public access to the gardens for the day.' His brow furrowed. 'As for the gardener guy, Diana must have been fond of him. Either that or in his debt. She went to a lot of effort.'

It showed Josh wouldn't suffer as a result of Diana's plans, anyway. In fact, it was possible he'd have got a pay rise. And he had his alibi for her and Raven. It was complex, but that didn't mean it had to be false.

A lot of her questions were answered, but she had a couple more. 'What made you join Cammie for the balloon ride?'

He shook his head. 'It was last minute and complete chance. She was teasing me about her research, and I was keen to know what she'd found out. It could have affected Erica's decision to buy: made the place an even better bet, or less good. She hinted she was about to spill the beans, so after a moment's thought I decided I'd dash after her and leap on board. Only of course she never got the chance to tell me.'

A sudden suspicion crossed Eve's mind. 'Wait a minute. You didn't have a go at getting the information another way, did you?'

Ralph glanced at Erica.

'Someone let themselves into Lavender Cottage, the night Cammie died,' Eve said.

'I draw the line at plundering a dead woman's belongings in search of secrets.'

But Cammie had hinted she'd found something important. Something that could really put Lovelace on the map. It could have affected Erica's profits by hundreds of thousands. Eve wasn't sure Ralph Roscoe was telling the truth. Of course, if he had been inside, it would show him up as supremely callous, thinking only of money when his ex-girlfriend had just died. But it would also mean he was innocent. The killer would have removed the poisoned smoothie.

'What made you stay on in Suffolk?'

'We've approached Sebastian,' Erica said.

'I spoke to him,' Ralph added. 'I thought his perspective

might change now he's taken over the reins. I don't honestly think he'll budge.' He sighed. 'If I could just make him see that owning a place like that's not a bed of roses. I'll have one more go at least.'

Erica stretched elegantly. 'And then I vote we cut our losses – take a proper holiday. It's time we had a break.'

It must be such a strain, all this wheeler-dealing...

Eve didn't like Roscoe, but she imagined he was right: the reality of owning Lovelace would be crushing. The manor would probably swallow Sebastian's handsome earnings, though Sapphire's expert help might make a difference. And if he was guilty, she'd lied for him too.

It was lucky for Sebastian that Josh had introduced them.

'Do you think Sebastian ever found out Diana was still planning to sell?'

Ralph shrugged. 'He certainly didn't admit to it, and I didn't give the game away. But he might be a good actor, and I'll bet he was on edge about it.'

Eve bet he was too.

37

Robin had a gardening appointment to get to.

'Would you mind dropping me off at Lovelace?' Eve gave him a sidelong glance. 'After this morning, my next job has to be talking to Josh about the mysterious plant collection he keeps in his conservatory.'

He had his hand on the ignition key, his eyes on hers.

Eve gave him a half-smile. 'Don't worry. I'm going to ask if I can buy him a drink at the White Lion. If he invites me into his house, I'll say I couldn't possibly impose.'

'And you'll get the bus back?'

She nodded, and at last he turned the key.

Ten minutes later, Eve was standing at Josh Standish's door, receiving no answer. She sighed. Forty-five minutes until the next bus was due and she might be leaving with nothing to show for her efforts.

She knocked again, looking up towards the manor to the right of Josh's cottage, then over her shoulder towards the main road that ran through the hamlet. There was no sign of him.

But as Eve knocked a third time, she heard crunching on the gravel behind her and turned to see Sapphire striding towards her, Sebastian just behind.

'I expect he's in the White Lion,' Sapphire said. 'We arranged to meet him there. I wanted to talk about the future.' She shook her head. 'I know it seems awful to focus on anything practical at a time like this, but Lovelace has been struggling for decades and we think it's best to press on. Keeping a grip on normality helps to push away the dark thoughts. It's all been so awful.'

'Of course.' She did look strained, her face pale, but there was an energy there, when she talked about the house – a tiny spark in her tired eyes.

'I've been making a timeline through the house,' Sapphire said quickly. 'I'm putting memorabilia from Louisa's childhood in what was her bedroom, then displaying other artefacts in chronological order in themed rooms, ending with items from her and Seth's married life in the drawing room.'

'That sounds good.' Eve was caught up in her breathless enthusiasm. It did sound more appealing than what Diana had had. The existing layouts had been traditional and rather dry.

Sapphire flushed and smiled. 'Visitors will see the sketches Louisa did of Seth when she was a teenager through a glass panel in one of the floorboards of her bedroom. That's where she hid them. And then the formal photograph of them that still remains will be on the mantelpiece in the drawing room, just where a married couple might place a framed photo. I want to give visitors snapshots in time.'

'I'd love to take a tour, once you've finished.'

'We should arrange that,' Sebastian said, stepping forward, his tone warm, expression seemingly genuine. But Eve knew he had two faces: the mask he showed to Sapphire and the real one underneath.

'Thanks.' But for now, she wanted to focus on Josh. 'I might come over to the White Lion myself,' she said, glancing at her watch. 'I'll end up missing lunch otherwise. I'll let you two get on with your discussions with Josh though. I can catch him once you've finished.'

'Oh, but you'd be welcome to join us,' Sapphire said. 'We saw the news this morning – that Raven Allerton's body's been discovered, and it looks as though she was killed too.' She blinked quickly. 'I can hardly bear it. Just when we thought – however terrible recent events have been – that they were at least over. After your past involvement in murder investigations, we'd be interested to hear if you've got any ideas. I'm sure Josh would be too.'

'Absolutely,' Sebastian said. 'Please, do join us.'

Eve's stomach knotted. If Sebastian was the killer, he had every reason to want to know her thoughts. She wouldn't unbutton in front of him, however warmly he encouraged her.

He went ahead, pushing the pub door open as Eve and Sapphire followed. Josh was sitting in a corner at a small round table.

'There's room enough for four,' Sapphire said. Sebastian passed her a chair. Josh Standish was unsmiling.

'I don't want to intrude.'

'You aren't in the least.' Sapphire turned to Josh. 'Eve was knocking at your door, so I brought her over.'

'What would everyone like to drink?' Sebastian stood, handsome in his designer suit, ready to spend some of his substantial earnings on a round. Eve got out her purse, but he waved aside her offer to contribute.

'A Coke, please.'

Josh asked for a half of Adnams and Sebastian strode towards the bar.

The gardener turned to Eve next. 'You wanted me?'

She hesitated, but Sapphire was getting up. 'Let me help you carry, Seb.'

This might be as good a chance as any. She took a deep breath and remembered her plan.

'Yes. When I was at Lovelace the other day, I happened to see a woman leaving your place with a pot plant. I guessed you must sell cuttings from the manor estate, and I wondered if I could buy one for my garden.' She held her breath. Would he buy her story?

'I'm afraid I don't sell plants. That was just a single cutting for a friend.' His tone was final.

Up at the bar, Sebastian was chatting to the landlord, turning on the charm, Sapphire on his arm. They seemed engrossed, but Eve didn't know how long she'd got.

'Actually, I saw two people buying plants from you. On separate occasions.' It had to be worth the bluff. If Eve was right, he wasn't just selling plants, he was selling a dream: acting like the modern-day equivalent of Seth Pickford, as Ralph Roscoe had said. Customers were charmed by him and went off with plants they probably thought of as lucky. Eve wondered how much he was selling them for.

'Ah.' Josh sighed. 'All right.' He glanced at the bar now too. Sebastian was paying for the drinks. 'Diana told me to feel free to sell them as a sideline, but it's unofficial. I don't want Sebastian to find out. Diana wasn't able to pay me as much as she'd like, so she was keen for me to find other ways of bringing in money from the estate. Sebastian would have insisted the profits went to help shore up the manor, so it was our secret.'

'I understand,' Eve said. Her gut instinct said he was telling the truth.

'I'm glad you still want a plant. I was worried people might not, after what's happened in the last week.'

'That's not to do with Lovelace though, is it?' She hoped her eyes wouldn't give her away. Of course it was to do with Lovelace. 'I mean, what with the drugs the police found at Cammie's rented cottage and Raven Allerton's secret history, it seems as though the drama revolves around incomers, though poor Diana got caught up in it.' The press's attention had continued to focus on Cammie's celebrity lifestyle and Raven's lies. The manor had fallen out of the news.

Josh nodded. 'I suppose. What plant would you like?'

'A lavender would be lovely.'

He nodded. 'Come by tomorrow at nine and I'll have one ready.'

'How much?'

He paused. 'I've got one in a two-litre pot you can have for a tenner.'

Eve had a feeling he'd geared the price to suit his audience. She imagined a hardened Lovelace enthusiast would pay way more. Ten times as much? It was entirely possible.

38

Eve spent that afternoon working a shift at Monty's. By the time the last customers trailed out she had a sinking feeling inside. Information on the murders had been whirling in her head for hours but there'd been no time to string her thoughts together or chat things over with Viv.

'What's that face for?' Viv said, as she started to clear away the leftover cakes from the display stand. 'You look like a camel with indigestion.'

'You do know how to make a person feel good.'

'I suppose it's the case that's bothering you.'

'Ideas have been creeping in all afternoon, but the shouts for more scones and fresh pots of tea have driven them out again. And that crying baby didn't help.'

'Why don't we pick up Gus and head to the Cross Keys when we've finished here? I'm ready to slip into Watson mode.'

Half an hour later, Eve and Viv were sitting at their usual table inside the pub as Gus and the pub schnauzer, Hetty, performed their ritual greeting. As ever, the sight made Eve smile. Opposites clearly attracted.

'Right, pour out your thoughts,' Viv said, taking a sip of her Sauvignon Blanc.

Eve tried to order everything in her head. 'Okay, it's horrific, but we now have four people dead. Cammie, then Stella Hilling who got caught in the crossfire, then Diana and now Raven. Though in reality the last two deaths probably occurred around the same time.'

Viv gave Eve a small sideways glance and took out a brand-new notepad from her bag. 'I thought I should get myself organised for our catch-ups. Take a leaf out of your book. I hope you're pleased.'

'Astounded. I mean, delighted.'

'Rude.' Viv got scribbling. 'Right. The four victims.'

'The recent discovery that one of the items stolen from Lavender Cottage was a letter opener, almost certainly owned by Louisa Lovelace's mother, seems like too much of a coincidence. I'm starting to wonder if the whole series of deaths relates to the manor and the research Cammie was doing. It seems all the more certain that the same person's responsible for every life that's been taken.'

Viv nodded and made a note. 'Sounds logical.'

'I still can't work out why the letter opener's significant. I think they probably stole something extra – some bit of the puzzle that's crucial. Something that the killer's aware of and we're not. That missing jigsaw piece will reveal why the letter opener's important – maybe the loving cup too – and if we manage to link those things, I assume the picture will become clear and the killer will be in real trouble. That must be why they risked breaking into Lavender Cottage. Either piecing together those clues will tell us their identity, or it'll bring about something else they desperately want to avoid.'

Viv sipped more wine. 'Right. So where are we with suspects?'

Eve rallied her thoughts. 'Ralph Roscoe seems unlikely now. Diana's death wrecked his and Erica's chances of buying the manor. Plus, the police's entire focus was on him for the balloon crash, and they found no proof. I wouldn't trust Palmer of course, but Greg Boles is another matter.'

'Okay.'

Eve suspected Viv was doodling now and tried to peer, but her friend sat up straighter so she couldn't, and started scribbling again.

'Josh the gardener's been earning money illicitly on the side, but he says it was with Diana's permission and I think I believe him. It fits with the way she treated him and he sounded honest. Plus, it would be quite something to kill four people to protect his secret. He's got more at stake than some – the sack would mean losing his home as well as his income, which would be devastating. But I'm not convinced Diana would have been that harsh, even if she hadn't given her approval as Josh claims. Beyond that, I don't get what relevance the Lovelace artefacts would have for him. Plus, he's got an alibi for Diana. If the police are right, she was still alive when he arrived to spend the evening at the White Lion on Thursday.' Eve remembered the details. Josh had left a list of ideas for Lovelace's future on Diana's desk. That list had had Diana's prints on it, proving she'd returned after Josh had called, before heading out to meet Raven that fateful evening. She'd even made her own notes in response to his suggestions.

Viv was writing something heavily in her notebook now. Eve saw her underline whatever it was.

She made an effort to focus. 'And so we come to Sebastian and Sapphire.'

Viv nodded. 'Sapphire was definitely at the stately home where she works on Lovelace Sunday?'

'That's right. No doubt about it. And officially she and Sebastian alibi each other for Diana's murder. That probably holds good for Raven too, depending on the precise time of her death. But Sebastian's well off for motives. We know Cammie knew something damaging about him, and if he found out Diana was secretly still intent on selling the manor, he had every reason to kill her. The significance of the artefacts Cammie found is still a mystery, but they're his family heirlooms.'

'And Sapphire would have had to lie for him?'

'Yes, but at the time, it seemed almost certain that Raven had killed Diana, so she could have done it to save him bother, feeling sure he was innocent. Beyond that, they were having a boozy picnic together. It's not impossible Sebastian slipped her something to make her sleep. She might not even know he left. He could have sneaked off to kill both women, then crept out during the night to move Raven's body to the old quarry.'

Viv shuddered. 'Do you think it's worth thinking back again, over the old connections from when Cammie stayed at the manor before?'

'Maybe.' Eve took her phone out and found the pictures Phoebe Richmond had sent through. 'These are the most unguarded records I've got from that time. The photos Cammie sent to an old friend, not the ones she put on Instagram.'

Eve wasn't sure how relevant they were now. She'd already worked out about Cammie's affair with Peter, and decided that Sebastian's boasts about his own fling with Cammie were lies. But she was stuck, and looking at the pictures might unlock something.

She was just showing Viv a photo of Diana's husband when Jo Falconer brought their meals. She set Eve's caramelised onion and goat's cheese tartlet down in front of her and did the same with Viv's pasta.

'I hope you're going to put your phones away and concentrate on my food now.'

'Naturally.' Viv grinned and put her notebook down as Eve withdrew her phone from under Viv's nose.

Before she'd had the chance to switch off the screen, Jo peered at Peter's picture.

'Who's that then?'

'Peter Pickford-Jones. Diana from the manor's late husband.' Eve went through her database for him mentally. Died two months ago, an invalid and a recluse for a year or two beforehand. Once the life and soul of the party according to the White Lion's landlord. He'd tried to persuade Diana to sell Lovelace, yet he and Sebastian had some kind of bond. Irene had heard him calling for Sebastian when he was very ill.

'Interesting.' Jo had her hand on one hip. Furrows creased her brow. 'Had him in here several times. I didn't know who he was. Sorry to hear he's dead, though I can't say I'm surprised. He looked ill. I was worried about him. Almost wondered if we shouldn't serve him, but he never seemed drunk or caused a row.'

'Why wouldn't you serve him?'

Jo's chest rose with a deep breath. She looked sad. Resigned. 'I could tell he was an alcoholic. You don't spend long in my profession without getting to know the signs.'

That was new. But it made sense, now Eve thought about it. Jim Thackeray said Diana had kept him at a distance for the last years of Peter's life. Maybe Peter was frequently the worse for drink and she didn't want Jim to know his trouble.

'When did he come in?'

'Last year, certainly. Maybe a bit the year before too. He always came with that brother of Diana's, only I didn't know who he was at the time. Saw him this year at Lovelace Sunday. The pair of them would settle in for the night. Diana's brother was irresponsible. It got my goat.'

As Jo pottered back to the kitchen, Eve put her head in her hands.

'What is it?' Viv said.

'It's things making sense. I knew Peter had stopped drinking in his local, the White Lion. If he was an alcoholic, Diana probably persuaded him not to go. She must have been so scared for him.' Eve was certain she'd carried on loving him throughout their long marriage. 'But Sebastian... Sebastian was enabling his drinking.' It was all clear now. 'He brought him here and plied him with booze. So much so that Jo was worried. And Sebastian went into a supermarket in Blyworth so he could buy Peter spirits somewhere nice and anonymous.' Only one of the store workers knew Moira and had gossiped, thinking it was Sebastian who had a drink problem. 'Irene heard Peter calling out for Sebastian, shortly before he died, saying that he understood what Peter needed.' A horrible creeping cold filtered through Eve, like icy water sopped up by a cloth. 'It was deliberate, I'm sure of it. He knew Peter wanted Diana to sell Lovelace. Helping him to drink himself to death neutralised a threat.'

It fitted with Sebastian's character, the way Heaven Jones had described it. Insidious. She put her wine down. Didn't feel like it any more. 'I think Cammie had guessed what he'd done. And she loved Peter too. It was way more than a fleeting affair. She was back at Lovelace visiting him just before he died. I think that was Sebastian's dark secret.'

Back at Elizabeth's Cottage, Eve made herself a hot chocolate and cuddled up with Gus in the living room.

'Cammie asked Sebastian if Diana and Sapphire knew what he'd done. I'm guessing Sapphire probably doesn't, but I'll bet Diana did.' It would explain why, after years of refusing to sell Lovelace, despite Peter's entreaties, she'd finally changed her mind. Why she was planning to ruthlessly pull the rug from under Sebastian's feet, secretly going ahead with the sale. She'd never have forgiven his actions and had come up with the ultimate punishment. Eve empathised. The mere thought of what Sebastian had done left her heart hammering from impotent rage. 'But even if Diana knew,' she went on, 'Sebastian might not have known that she did. He could still have killed Cammie to keep his secret. He probably guessed that if Diana found out she'd do everything she could to hurt him.'

Later in bed, the window open, the soft night air stirring her curtains, facts continued to drift in Eve's head.

What had she got? What about the artefacts? The loving cup – gifted to Louisa Lovelace and Seth Pickford – might be just as important as the letter opener, but immediately after Stella Hilling's death it was in police hands. The killer had missed their chance to steal it before it was discovered.

So what if the cup *was* just as important? What if it took that as well as the letter opener and the unknown missing jigsaw piece to complete the picture? The picture the killer was so desperate to hide...

Eve turned onto her side and reached for her phone, waking it up so she could look at photographs of the two artefacts again.

A battered loving cup. Something that should have been treasured and kept safe, but which the police had confirmed had spent time in the manor's moat. It seemed quite likely Cammie had found the letter opener in the water too. She'd been intent on exploring. Once she'd discovered one interesting artefact, Eve could imagine her excitement. She'd want to keep going.

So both items might have been in the moat. She looked at the photographs. A symbol of Louisa and Seth's love for each other, and a perfectly ordinary though decorative desk item, inherited from Louisa's mother.

But what linked them?

39

Eve got almost no sleep that night. In the morning, she went through her notes and all the evidence she had so far, from the map of the balloon crash debris and her memories of Lovelace Sunday, to the latest murder. She found herself replaying a haunting video of Cammie and Ralph, up in the balloon, Cammie tatting around inside the basket initially, making everything shipshape, then focusing on the crowd below. The streamers shooting into the air. Ralph glancing down and shrinking back as they fell into the basket.

Something about it gave her the faintest feeling that she'd been missing something. Somewhere, on the very edge of her consciousness, there was a stray thought to pick up on, but it was too wispy to grab hold of.

Gus had woken up and come to join her. She stroked his head. 'Let's get sorted, and after your walk, I might head off early to Lovelace Manor.' Being at the crash site in person might help.

She'd lost Gus at the word walk. He was already lolloping down the stairs.

. . .

Eve was due to pick up her lavender plant from Josh Standish at nine, but there was plenty of time to walk to the crash site first. Early would be best; she hoped not to be seen. She parked her car in the back lane then walked through the woods, just as she'd done when she'd gone to peer into Josh's cottage.

The public right of way took her through the trees on Lovelace land, adjacent to the gated manor grounds which were separated off by a high stone wall. Eve was just walking past a locked iron gate, giving her a view of the gardens beyond, when she heard soft voices. She quickened her pace to get past the opening and hide from whoever was on the other side. She glanced at her watch. Seven fifteen. Whoever it was, they were out early.

Standing to one side of the gate she glimpsed the people she'd heard: a trio, two men and a woman. Once they'd passed, their backs to her, she dared to take a better look.

Josh Standish and a pair Eve didn't recognise. A moment later, the unknown man and woman linked hands. Eve saw his expensive-looking watch glint in the morning light. After that, he pulled the woman closer and turned to smile at Josh. It was weird. It reminded Eve of a couple she'd once seen emerging from the vicarage after talking to Jim Thackeray about their forthcoming wedding. Eve was sure this pair was a couple too, but what were they doing here at this hour? And what was Josh doing, escorting them? Just before Eve turned away, she saw Josh hand something to the man. A flash of reflected sunlight bounced off the object, dazzling her, and for a second she closed her eyes.

Eve walked on, her mind full of what she'd just seen. The path through the woods took her round past the gated manor grounds to an archway which opened onto a clearing. Beyond that was a thicket which overlooked the crash site.

She glanced around, preparing to dash from the archway to the thicket. She had a perfect right to be where she was, but seeing Josh had made her nervous. There was more going on here than she understood. She didn't want to be noticed. There was just a stream separating the clearing from the gardens he tended. She'd be completely exposed until she reached the thicket. She held her breath, but apart from birdsong, all was quiet now Josh had left the area. An instant later, she ran for it.

A memory drifted into her mind: the discovery of a designer jacket in the manor's walled garden. Moira had been able to identify the owner thanks to a membership card for some exclusive club in the pocket, but it was Josh who'd leaped into action, offering to trace them, even though he must have been busy.

Now, Eve wondered if Josh had let the owner of the jacket in himself. It would explain why he'd wanted to take care of its return personally.

She glanced in the direction of the walled garden. Was that where he and the couple had been, minutes before she arrived? And was that where he'd emerged from, the morning she'd seen him with the young woman? It seemed likely. Her eyes rested on the middle distance. He'd walked back in the direction of the walled garden after the woman had left last time. Maybe he'd come back again this time, after saying goodbye to the couple.

Eve kept an eye out, but she wanted to focus on the field where the balloon had crashed: to take her mind back to that day. If she lingered too long, she might have Sebastian and Sapphire pottering around as well as Josh.

She looked out at the field, then to the scrubby land just over her shoulder. Then she closed her eyes and visualised the scene again: the balloon drifting low over the gorse, the streamers shooting into the air. She replayed the video on her phone and watched as Ralph Roscoe started at the sight of them, then looked down into the balloon's basket, where they landed. Cammie had started momentarily too, as the streamers shot up. A reflex reaction, but she overrode it. Continued to stare at the ground, all her focus there.

Why hadn't Cammie looked inside the basket like Ralph?

Movement caught Eve's eye. Josh Standish was coming back now. She shrank into the thicket, peering from behind a plum tree. As she watched, Josh entered the walled garden and emerged again a moment later, carrying an outsized canvas bag. Spilling from its inside, she could see a colourful blanket and the top of what looked like a rolled-up mat.

He glanced left and right as he emerged, then turned back towards his cottage.

It looked as though the couple had been camping out.

Half of Eve's mind was still on Cammie and Ralph Roscoe, up in the balloon. But Josh's activities were distracting. She already knew he was selling manor cuttings as a sideline to bring in extra money. And at a guess, he normally sold them for a lot more than the ten pounds he'd charged her. She wondered how much he might get for letting rich visitors into the walled garden on the sly. A lot, she imagined, from the right sort of person.

Lovelace's myths and legends would make an overnight stay an attractive proposition. People believed the place had magical qualities: it made you lucky in love, and was associated with fertility and passion. The coming of spring and summer. Eve could imagine any number of singles or couples paying a handsome amount to be smuggled in overnight, given comfortable bedding, sleeping out under the stars. All very exclusive and secret.

In this day and age, you'd expect it to get out, of course. Someone would post a photo to Facebook or Instagram. And now the glinting object Josh had handed the man made sense. A phone, it had to be. Maybe Josh had a rule: no modern technology. He probably told them to come and find him at the cottage if they needed anything. Eve could imagine the visitors complying; they might believe broadcasting their experience would destroy the magic.

How much might a rich enthusiast pay to stay in a garden with centuries of history, and a love story which had inspired plays and songs? Five hundred pounds? A thousand? Eve could imagine that and more, if they were seriously wealthy. All Josh needed was a fine night.

Heat rushed over her. His scheme would have been kaput if Diana had sold the manor. Ralph and Erica had bigged up the grounds as a selling point. Residents would have been able to hold parties in the walled garden. He'd no longer have had the run of the place – and he might be making a small fortune out of this particular venture. Officially, Josh was under the impression that Diana had decided against the sale, but he must have worried she might change her mind again. And maybe he *knew* that she had.

As soon as Josh was out of sight, Eve darted back from the thicket to the archway and on into the woods. Her palms felt sweaty and her mouth dry.

Cammie could have discovered his lucrative sideline, and Diana might not have sanctioned this one. It was a whole different ball game to the plant sales. What if Cammie had threatened to tell, thinking he was taking Diana for a ride? Eve was convinced she had still been fond of the woman, despite their complicated past. Would Josh have killed to keep her quiet?

As Eve slipped through the trees, back towards the exit that would lead to her car, her mind ran on. Would Josh really kill Diana? He was always talking about how kind she'd been, looking out for his interests, but his feelings towards her might be mixed. His father had collapsed and died in front of him on the day of her engagement party. Might he blame her for his death? It seemed possible. And guilt would explain the special attention she had always paid Josh – her insistence that he be well looked after.

Maybe he'd hated her, all these years since.

40

Eve felt a little shaky as she let herself into her car. She was due to go and knock on the gardener's door to collect her lavender in a short while. If he looked her in the eye, would he guess her suspicions? Work out that he'd been seen tidying up after some clients? Her mind ran over the break-in at Lavender Cottage. She still couldn't work out its relevance, and she doubted Josh was responsible. Anyone could wear a wig, but he wasn't slender like Sebastian. He didn't match the Turnham brothers' description, but the girlfriend she'd seen in the White Lion would...

Eve needed to calm down.

She called Robin to update him, then hung up, rang the police station and asked for Greg Boles. He wasn't in. She requested DC Olivia Dawkins next, another bright spark on the team, but she wasn't there either. In the end she left a message asking for one of them to call her back.

It was almost time to go and pick up the lavender. Eve took a deep breath and began her walk towards the lane, ready to turn left for the main driveway to the manor and Josh's cottage.

By the time she reached his door she'd got on top of her feelings, swallowing down the tightness in her throat.

'I've come for the lavender,' she said when he opened up, holding out her ten-pound note.

She'd thought she sounded normal, but he raised an eyebrow and looked at her oddly. 'Do you want to come in for a moment?'

'That's okay, thanks.' Even she could hear the tightness in her voice now.

He disappeared, then returned with the plant.

'Thank you.'

It was as he took her money, his dark eyes on hers, that she heard movement behind her. She glanced over her shoulder to see an elderly man moving slowly past the driveway. His presence made Eve bolder. Maybe she should challenge Josh after all. She had a witness.

'I saw you again this morning,' she said, trying to keep her voice strong and steady. 'It's not just plants you've been selling, is it? I imagine an overnight stay in the walled garden fetches a lot more than a pot of lavender.'

Josh's hand went up to cover his mouth, then dropped to his side. 'I don't like being spied on.'

'I was out walking early. I'm not sleeping so well these days.'

There was a moment's silence.

'My pay's a pittance,' Josh said at last.

'I get that, but your illicit sideline gives you a potential motive for Cammie and Diana's murders.' She watched him closely. Had Cammie found him out? And did he realise Diana had decided to sell Lovelace after all?

But his brow was furrowed, his jaw slack with shock. 'What do you mean?' He looked genuine.

'You spent a lot of time following Cammie around. If she kept tabs on you too, she might easily have discovered what you were up to. I think she'd have felt you were taking advantage – making so much money in secret.'

His eyes were wide, but Eve could see it wasn't fear. He looked horrified. 'I'm sure she never knew and if she had found out I'd never have killed her! I imagine she'd have told me to stop, and I would have.'

'Why did you follow her all the time?'

Eve couldn't believe it was purely concern over health and safety. He hadn't paid anyone else that much attention.

At last, he sighed. 'I wanted to know about her research, but in the end, I decided she was teasing everyone with her hints and secret smiles. She claimed she'd put Lovelace on the map, which would have been great from my point of view, but I never saw any sign of it being true. And the more secretive she was, the more people like Ralph Roscoe kept asking. I think she liked it.'

So Josh was another person who'd wanted to keep tabs on Cammie's progress. Eve remembered telling him about the intruder at Lavender Cottage the night she died. He said he'd already heard about it on the grapevine.

'Was it you prowling around at Cammie's place, the night of Lovelace Sunday?'

He looked down at the ground for a moment. The elderly man had passed the driveway now, but it was too late to change tack and she was getting somewhere. Her blood felt heated as she glimpsed the goal in sight.

'It was,' he said at last. 'I slipped in to see if I could find any notes on her work. If she had the key to bringing in more visitors, I wanted to know. The more buzz there was around the manor, the more likely Diana was to keep hold of the place. I'd cope fine if it was sold, but I love it here. It's been my life.'

'Did you find anything?'

Josh shook his head. 'It was as I'd thought. I was thorough – took hours over it – but there was nothing. I feel ashamed for trespassing now, but I thought her death was an accident and I didn't see how it could hurt. I never knew her well, so I suppose I was more detached than some people.'

It had been Josh all along then – if he was telling the truth. Ralph Roscoe had meant it when he said he would have drawn the line at sneaking into a dead woman's house. But so many people had wanted to know what Cammie had been up to.

Josh sighed again. 'It's crazy to imagine I'd kill to carry on letting out the walled garden. If Cammie or Diana had found me out, I'd have taken my savings and moved on. I've got a good nest egg now. And before you say it, yes, I realised Diana might sell at any time, but it wouldn't be the end of the world.'

He hadn't known the sale was back on then, unless he was a good actor.

'Diana was always good to me,' he went on. 'She felt so bad about my dad dying on her watch. She never had the money to pay me well, but I was always first on her mind. You could tell. She didn't know I was having people in overnight officially, but she made sure she and Sebastian steered clear of the gardens once evening fell. I think she suspected.'

Logic told Eve that could be true. After all, *she'd* seen the signs. It was hard to believe Diana wouldn't have done the same at some point.

Josh put a hand over his eyes. 'Poor Diana.'

There was a catch in his voice.

41

As Eve walked back to her car and put the lavender in the boot, she replayed the scene in her mind. Her instinct was to believe Josh. There'd been genuine feeling in his voice when he'd talked about Diana, and Cammie had told her friend Phoebe how motherly she could be. And if he was telling the truth about letting himself into Lavender Cottage then he had to be in the clear – he'd have removed the poisoned smoothie otherwise.

So he looked unlikely, as did the Roscoes, who were relying on Diana to sell them the manor. It brought her back to Sebastian.

Eve had just slammed the boot shut when she heard a noise behind her. Turning, she saw Moira. What on earth was she doing here?

'Morning, Eve! You're here bright and early.'

For a moment, Eve was stuck for what to say. If she mentioned Josh's plant sales, the news would be all over Lovelace-by-Sax by mid-morning. 'I came for a walk in the woods the other day.' She thought on her feet. 'Now I'm missing a scarf. I just popped back to see if I could find it.' She couldn't claim to be walking for leisure. Moira would want to know why she hadn't brought Gus.

'Any luck?' the storekeeper asked.

Eve shook her head. 'Afraid not.'

'That is a shame. And what news on the case?'

'Not much, I'm afraid.' Nothing she was prepared to share. 'What about you? What brings you here?'

'I was just having a quick cup of coffee with Irene. I was about to drive back to the store when I saw you down here. April's helping Paul until I get back. She's been such a wonderful support.'

Moira spoke as though she'd got the weight of the world on her shoulders. April was her sister. Her husband Paul sometimes minded the store too, but he wasn't great as a stand-in. He hated people.

'Have you seen the new display Sapphire's been working on, Eve? Irene's been telling me all about it. She's seen photos, but we can go one better. She made me a temporary key holder. She says I'd be welcome to nip in and look any time I like. I could show you round too.'

Eve was starting to see the little touches Diana had put in place to reward Irene for her hard work. No pay, but the grand title of chief volunteer and the right to enter the main house at will.

Now Moira had those rights. She could visit alone, but Eve had a feeling she wanted her as a decoy – an excuse to satisfy her own curiosity and beat Irene to a first-hand viewing. Eve was interested, of course, and the only way to find out the truth was to probe further. Sebastian was still her chief suspect, but it wasn't her habit to descend on people unannounced.

'I wouldn't want to disturb Sebastian and Sapphire. It's still early.'

Moira waved aside her worries. 'Oh, I'm sure they won't

mind. They know I've got a key and Irene says they're usually in their own quarters anyway.'

Irene says...

'And you really are owed, after all your hard work in the run-up to Lovelace Sunday.' Moira was clearly determined to see the latest developments. She probably hoped they'd bump into Sebastian and Sapphire too. The more she gleaned, the greater her pleasure later when she passed on the gossip.

'All right then.' Eve couldn't see Sebastian being a danger if she and Moira were together, and there were three cars on the drive in any case. It looked as though he and Sapphire had company.

Moira smiled, and trotted along with Eve at her side. Within minutes they were crossing the moat and Moira was using her keys to unlock the imposing oak door. She rang the bell as she went, but walked in with confidence. Eve could see how much she was enjoying her borrowed position. She tried to imagine what it would be like for Sapphire and Sebastian, with Moira – or more usually Irene – likely to materialise whenever they felt like it. Eve would hate it. She loved people, but having them on her turf without warning was a different matter.

Sapphire poked her head round from her and Sebastian's quarters while they were still in the entrance hall.

'Oh hello, Moira.' She sounded weary. 'And Eve, hello!' The smile in Eve's direction was a little warmer.

Moira explained their mission.

'Of course. Go ahead.' Though Eve thought her frown was a little anxious.

'Irene says we need to see Louisa's old bedroom first,' Moira said.

As they walked upstairs, Eve's mind was still on the case. Was she right to dismiss Josh on instinct? He could be lying about sneaking into Lavender Cottage the night Cammie died.

He'd know it would make him look innocent. Everyone had heard about the smoothie and had guessed the killer would have removed it if they'd had the chance. And Eve had fancied it was Ralph who'd been in there. He'd certainly looked tense when Eve asked.

As Eve and Moira walked along a corridor, Eve's thoughts turned back to the balloon crash. She mustn't lose sight of the question that had filled her head earlier. Why had Cammie's focus stayed on the ground as the streamers flew past her into the balloon?

As they walked along a second corridor, narrower than the first, Eve felt a tingle spread over her body. She slipped her phone from her pocket as Moira trotted ahead of her. In a second, she'd called up the map Robin had sent of the crash site. She checked where the half-burned battery had been found. It wasn't all that near the bits of basket that had come down, but then everything was far-flung, the area of debris wide.

As they reached the end of the corridor, Eve's mind ran on. The battery had been such a key discovery. The one thing that hinted someone on the ground could have been responsible for Cammie's death. But what if it had been planted…

'Here we are!' Moira opened the door to what had once been Louisa Lovelace's bedroom with a flourish.

But Eve hardly saw the room. Her mind was still on the battery, and a small, scorched patch of paving stone in the back garden of Lavender Cottage. Her skin prickled and she went cold all over. Could it possibly be?

'Don't you think it's wonderful?'

Eve nodded mechanically, taking in the basics. A floorboard had been lifted to show a space underneath. Eve remembered that Louisa had hidden her sketches of her sweetheart there. Her drawings were down there now, protected by a Perspex panel and lit from one side by an under-floor lamp. The bed next to it was covered with old-fashioned linen sheets and a quilt, pushed back as though the young Louisa had just leaped out of it.

It was effective, but in seconds, Eve's mind was far away again. Cammie was a daredevil. Ralph said skydiving had been too tame for her. She'd preferred to scale high buildings unofficially in the dead of night. What if *she'd* wanted to kill *Ralph*? Eve could imagine her being prepared to start a fire then leap from the balloon.

She walked over to look at the sketch under the floorboards. She could tell Moira knew something was up – or at least that she wasn't showing sufficient wonder and enthusiasm. 'What a clever idea!' she managed at last. Her voice sounded overly bright.

What was it Ralph had said? That Cammie had hinted she might tell him about her research, and that's what had made him leap on board at the last minute. Had she been tempting him to join her? Eve put a hand to her face, glad she was crouched down and Moira couldn't see her flush. It all made sense. She bet that's what Cammie had been doing. She could have burned the battery in the back garden of Lavender Cottage any time and planted it in the field, ready to be found later. It would make it look like some third party had sabotaged the flight. She could have created a tiny nick in the fuel line just before Ralph joined her. And she'd ushered the guy doing the safety checks out of the balloon. At the time it had seemed like bravado and a dislike of people fussing, but perhaps it had been more sinister.

Eve got up again, Moira clucking over her like a mother hen, cupping a hand around her elbow. Eve resisted the automatic urge to shake her off. 'Thank you.'

They went through to the next room, which contained memorabilia from Louisa and Seth's time in exile. Eve walked around, staring at each display, but her mind was still on

Cammie. Ralph had let her down badly at university – run out on her when she'd probably thought they had a future. And then, more recently, here he was again, flirting with her, kissing her, keeping his partner Erica well in the background. Erica said she believed in 'Don't ask, don't tell'. She knew Ralph was simply abusing his position to get information that might be crucial to her business plans. But had Cammie known about Erica? Or had she fallen for Ralph all over again, only to discover that he was using her? Eve's heart dragged at the thought. She was sure that's what had happened. Cammie had had a difficult life. Both parents were often absent, and it sounded as though she'd been closest to her father, who'd been killed. Soon after his death she'd come to Lovelace at a low ebb, grieving and alone, and had fallen for Peter but that relationship was never going to work. And then Peter had died and Cammie had grieved all over again. But afterwards, finally, things had seemed to be going right. Her university boyfriend was back and had realised the terrible mistake he'd made, running out on her.

Only it turned out he was just as false-hearted as he'd always been. Wooing Cammie for the secrets she could tell him, to benefit his wife of all people.

Cammie must have found him out. Maybe she'd got suspicious and followed him back to his digs, seen him with Erica. Perhaps she'd managed to work out Erica's business or overheard Ralph talking to Diana about buying the manor.

How it must have hurt... but to go from that to plotting his murder? All the same, Eve suspected that's what she'd done. Her plans had been ruined by the streamers which had landed in the balloon. They'd made Ralph look down and see the fire before Cammie had time to jump. Her focus had been entirely on the ground below, watching for her chance to leap. The shock of him escaping would have cost her precious seconds. Allowed the fire to spread. Become too unmanageable for her to control the craft and bring it down. It would have been the exact position she'd wanted Ralph in. Maybe she'd put the fire extinguisher somewhere inaccessible to hamper him. She'd intended for him to be the one whizzing high into the air as she landed safely, but instead it had been her.

42

As Eve wandered around the room, looking vaguely at a photograph of a barn where the runaway lovers were meant to have sheltered, her mind turned to proof that might back her theories. If the police found traces of battery acid by the scorch marks in Cammie's garden, that would be significant.

She wondered if Ralph had had any inkling that Cammie was responsible. Even if he had, he might have doubted his own instinct. It wouldn't be easy to accept, and then the CSIs had found the burned battery in the field, and the poisoned smoothie in Cammie's cottage. If he'd had any suspicions, she guessed he'd have decided he was wrong at that point.

Eve had come to a standstill in front of another display.

'Irene says the horsehair rug was stolen by Seth's half-brother Edwin when he ran off with the lovers,' Moira said. 'It was the only blanket they had between them, apparently. Imagine that!'

Eve had forgotten about Seth's half-brother, though now she remembered Diana saying he'd been forced to leave the manor or face repercussions.

At last, after walking through a room devoted to Louisa and

Seth's early married life, they came to the drawing room, which was laid out to reflect their time together once they were established at the manor. The photograph of Louisa and Seth in their later years sat on the mantelpiece.

'Well,' said Moira, 'this arrangement seems very much better to me. Much more atmospheric. Though of course you don't get to see dear Louisa's sketches of her young man up close any more. That's a pity.'

Through her jumbled thoughts about Cammie, Eve realised it was true. The position of them, displayed under the floorboards, conveyed the excitement and secrecy of the couple's relationship, but it lost something too.

Eve frowned, and used her phone to call up the copies Robin had sent of the photos the police had recovered from Cammie's computer. She remembered there were plenty of the Lovelace artefacts. A second later, she was peering at pictures of the sketches.

Louisa had been a good artist. The drawings brought her subject to life, giving an impression of a healthy young man with a cheeky smile and a slightly knowing look in his eye. He was instantly recognisable in each picture. Eve imagined Louisa had spent a lot of time gazing at him and she could see why.

Why had Sapphire robbed visitors of the chance to see that detail? Maybe she planned to put copies of the artworks somewhere more accessible in due course.

Eve enlarged the photo of the sketches with her forefinger and thumb, then looked back at the photograph of the older Louisa and Seth on the mantelpiece.

It was only then that she saw it. She shivered and the hairs on her scalp lifted.

There was no mistaking it. The pictures on her phone might only be drawings, but there were several of them and they all matched. In them, Seth Pickford had earlobes which were detached from the side of his head. But the Seth Pickford in the photograph's earlobes were attached.

The 'Seth Pickford' on the mantelpiece looked very much like the original, but it was a different man.

It felt as though Eve's blood had turned to ice. It had to be the missing piece of the puzzle. Cammie had discovered that Seth Pickford had disappeared and been quietly replaced by A.N. Other. It could explain the damaged loving cup she'd found in the moat. If Louisa and Seth had fallen out, maybe one of them had thrown it there in a moment of anger. But why was the letter opener significant? And what had happened to Seth?

Eve turned her mind back to the pictures. No one was likely to notice the discrepancy between them going forward. Previously, they'd been in the same room, but now they were at opposite ends of the house. Far safer for anyone trying to hide the truth. Next to no chance of a visitor spotting the anomaly, and no need to remove any of the pictures, which might lead to questions.

A feeling of heightened awareness and fear swept over her, as though a spider had scuttled across her skin. Her gut told her this was it. Something tiny, yet important enough to kill for. This had been the discovery Cammie had dangled in front of everyone's noses. 'Moira, did Irene say that it was Sapphire who rearranged everything?'

Moira looked at her oddly. 'Well, yes. It's much more her speciality than Sebastian's of course. You can't really expect a young man to—'

At that moment Eve heard a creak. Someone was approaching. Had they been listening outside? The door opened briskly, and Sapphire walked in. She was looking straight at Eve. 'Do you like what we've done?'

Eve's palms were clammy. 'It's much better – it tells a real story.' But it disguised the truth.

Sapphire smiled. 'Thank you.' She glanced at Moira. 'I

couldn't help overhearing what you said.' Eve was silently cursing herself for being so unguarded. 'I sounded out some visitors about new layouts.' She sighed. 'Diana wasn't keen. I feel terrible now for trying to push it, but I could see what a difference it would make. I'd already thought how romantic it would be to recreate Louisa's bedroom as it was. It was one of the visitors who suggested displaying the sketches where she'd hidden them, though I like to think I'd have come up with that too, given a bit more headspace. I know I can turn this place around.' She gave a small, sad smile. 'I just came to find you because I need to pop out to fetch some milk. Sebastian's here but he's tucked away in a meeting. You'll be all right to show yourselves out?'

Eve nodded. Was Sapphire being honest, or making excuses having seen the danger? If Eve was correct, and Cammie had died in an accident of her own making, then it made no odds that Sapphire had been absent that day. She could have planted the smoothie before she went. Eve watched through the mullioned window as she exited the manor and slipped into a blue Mondeo. There was no store within walking distance. She didn't seem concerned at leaving. That might mean she was innocent, but she'd left Sebastian in the house...

43

At last Eve stopped staring after Sapphire and became aware of the wider view outside. Next to where she'd been parked were an Alfa Romeo and a red Mercedes.

The second car set off something chiming in her memory. There'd been a Mercedes of the same colour parked outside Ralph Roscoe's rented cottage. Maybe Erica or Ralph was making one final attempt to talk Sebastian into selling. Eve had a feeling Sapphire would be devastated if he gave in. She wondered if it was the manor that she loved, not Sebastian. Perhaps putting up with his bad behaviour was a means to an end. He oughtn't to get away with it. He was so dishonest.

And then it came to her. A possibility she hadn't thought of. But which she shouldn't have missed, because people didn't always tell the truth.

Thoughts whizzed through her head at high speed, links forming, making her stomach plummet as though she'd just descended ten floors in a lift at high speed. The way Ralph Roscoe had constantly questioned Cammie about her research. He hadn't given up – just gone on about being kept in the dark. Had he protested too much?

She took a deep breath as Moira pointed out a diary Louisa Lovelace had kept. It was under glass. She peered unseeingly at the spidery writing. Her thoughts were all speculation, but what if Ralph had known about the discrepancy between the two pictures? He'd followed Cammie around, spent time volunteering at the manor. What if he'd seen the moment she made her discovery? Witnessed her casually sauntering from one picture to the other but known her well enough to see that she was onto something?

He'd have had a private look afterwards – scanning for what she'd seen – and at last, he'd have got it. After that he'd be desperate to make out he was still in the dark. But underneath he'd realise her knowledge threatened his and Erica's development.

The sale was already agreed. Ralph said the paperwork had been signed weeks back – they couldn't pull out without losing money. A vast sum, probably. But they'd sealed the deal with the promise of selling a magical location at inflated prices. The truth was very different.

The entire Lovelace legend, which would make the apartments they planned so desirable, was a myth. In reality, Louisa had lived out her life with another man, not Seth, and what's more, she'd lied about it. Rather than being associated with luck, long life and love – a place that was almost magical if you were superstitious – Lovelace would be linked with something cheap and unhappy. And the question remained: what had happened to Seth? He'd been gifted the manor jointly with Louisa, but it seemed he hadn't lived in it. Had he died? But if so, why hadn't Louisa made that public? More likely he'd walked out. Even the manor's ownership might be in question if he'd gone on to have children with a new partner.

And would anyone pay a premium for an apartment once the truth got out? The modern-day murders hadn't stuck to Lovelace. The press had focused on Cammie's cocaine and

Raven's fake identity, but a revelation that tore through the legend was different. Ralph and Erica had stood to lose a fortune. So one of them – Ralph, probably, given his relationship with Cammie – had planted the smoothie to kill her and protect their investment—

'What do you think?' Moira broke into her thoughts.

'Fascinating.'

For a moment, Eve shook her spiralling ideas away. It didn't make sense. Ralph and Erica had pots of cash. They could have ridden out this storm if Cammie had revealed the truth. But then more thoughts came to her. Just how well off were they really? They walked the walk big time, but what about that letter Eve had seen on a shelf in their rented cottage? *My dear Erica, based on past experience, Hector and I would love to come on board.* A private investor? So they weren't simply spending their own cash in the hope of a high return. And wasn't it a little last minute to be raising money? Were they having trouble convincing some of their contacts to join in? What if they'd got several already onboard with other schemes? Maybe they'd started to cut corners, using one investor's money to pay another.

And then Eve thought of the phone call she'd heard at their cottage and her icy body turned hot. *Oh no, again?* Erica had said as she'd answered. She'd sounded exasperated, but in an instant her tone had turned placatory. She'd apologised and said: *It shouldn't have happened.* After that, she'd talked about calling in the electrician they normally used and settling the bill their end. Then she'd rung off and muttered something about mothers, loudly, in an irate tone.

Eve had assumed she'd been providing her mom with organisational and financial support but now she thought about it, that made no sense. Eve had read about Erica's mother in that glossy magazine. She lived in a mansion with Erica's dad; they had their own staff.

Had Erica made that loud complaint to disguise the real reason for the call? Eve was starting to think so. What if... *Heck, yes, that was possible.* What if, far from being an extravagance, renting the tiny cottage in Wessingham was part of an economy drive? After all, they'd turned their noses up at Simon's rental, saying it was overpriced. What if they'd let their smart London home and the call had been from a tenant? They'd want to keep that very quiet. It was essential to carry on projecting wealth and success. They'd never get investors otherwise.

And if they were in dire straits – on the point of bankruptcy perhaps – that was a first-class motive for murder. Eve could see either of them choosing that option over financial ruin. Ralph was definitely ruthless. You only had to look at the way he'd treated Cammie.

And what about Diana? Ralph and Erica should have been safe to proceed with the purchase of Lovelace if Cammie's knowledge died with her.

But if the pair were in debt, they might have seen their chance to make more out of the deal. What if Ralph had faced Diana with what he knew? Threatened to reveal the truth if she didn't agree to reduce the sale price?

Eve bet Diana would have stood her ground and to heck with it. She'd had it up to here with the manor, and with Sebastian. But in refusing, she'd have become a target. Eve imagined Ralph had invented some plausible explanation for how he'd stumbled on the truth, but once the dust settled, Diana might guess Cammie had got there first. She'd realise Ralph had a motive for murder. And she'd been in a position to reveal the secret herself, too, and devalue the property. Ralph had said he'd discussed the sale with Diana the day she died.

And now, Ralph was downstairs.

He knew Sebastian had been dead against selling Lovelace, yet if Eve was right, here he was, in the house of the woman he'd murdered, trying to persuade him to change his mind. It was a heck of a risk. Roscoe must think there was a good chance Sebastian would agree. And if he was planning on sharing Cammie's discovery with him, he'd want him to let Lovelace go for a knock-down price too. What made him confident enough to try? In Sebastian's place, Eve would attempt to make it out of the house alive and call the police.

If he managed that, and proved Ralph's guilt, he'd be safe and Lovelace still his. The truth about Louisa and Seth would come out, but did that really matter?

She thought it through, her mind rushing over the details. Sebastian was selfish, ruthless and proud of his heritage. And it was his meal ticket too. His reputation in the modelling world was based on the magical aura provided by his great-grandfather – a romantic hero. If Seth had been jilted, Sebastian would be associated with failure and rejection in the world of unrealistic ideals he inhabited. He might try to prove he was descended from the man who'd replaced Seth, the guy who'd won the day. But it wasn't much of an improvement. Not ideal for any fashion brand.

Eve imagined his modelling career fading as people looked at him with new eyes. He'd be sitting at the manor struggling, just as Diana had been, without even the legend to help ticket sales.

Would that prospect convince him to sell Lovelace cut price in return for Ralph and Erica's silence? Eve imagined his decision would be finely balanced. He had more to lose than Diana, but it wasn't clear cut. Yet Ralph had come anyway, presumably to try to get his way. It suggested he was getting desperate. Was prepared to kill all over again if he'd miscalculated. The situation was volatile.

Eve needed to get out, and fast. 'Moira, I'm sorry, I've lost track of time. I must go.' She wanted to call the police. Suggest they check the garage at Roscoe's rented cottage. The evidence would be thin, but if there was an old canister of antifreeze that showed signs of recent use it might be enough to make them dig further.

'Of course, Eve. I thought you seemed rather distracted. You carry on. I'm just going to use the facilities and then I'll go myself. April will be wondering where I've got to.'

They left the drawing room and Moira trotted off in the direction of the cloakroom. Eve hesitated. It wasn't ideal, leaving her behind when Roscoe was in the building, but she didn't believe Moira was in danger. She wasn't a threat to anyone.

But as Eve hastened towards the entrance, a door off the hall opened and Ralph Roscoe appeared.

44

Roscoe was smiling, his shoulders relaxed – until he saw her, and irritation flashed across his face. Behind him, Sebastian appeared, his face ashen. Eve couldn't stop her thoughts. She was right; she was sure she was. She wondered if they'd met in Diana's old study, where Roscoe had probably gone to sign the paperwork relating to the sale. Heck, Diana had probably kept secret papers like that locked in her drawer. And that had been where the revolver was kept. He could easily have caught sight of it when he'd visited – and seen where the keys lived.

'What are you doing here?' Roscoe's question was abrupt.

'I came in with Moira, Irene Marston's stand-in, to look at Sapphire and Sebastian's new room layouts.' She shivered and tried to smile naturally but unless it was her paranoia, Roscoe knew there was something up. 'I gather Irene suggested it. Moira's just nipped to the loo.'

'And you're on your way out?' Sebastian sounded relieved and Roscoe glanced at him sharply.

At that moment her mobile rang. Automatically, she dragged it from her pocket.

DS Greg Boles flashed up on the screen. Of course, he was

returning her call. She glanced sideways at Roscoe and moved towards the door. He'd probably been interviewed by Greg. He'd know the name. If he'd seen the screen.

'Hello.' She was halfway across the hall, the phone to her ear, when he came at her from behind, gripping her wrist, his fist vice-like. In another moment, he had a knife to her throat.

Eve heard Sebastian gasp. Roscoe must have brought the knife in case he needed to use it on him.

'Cut the call and drop it,' Ralph said quietly.

Eve had no option but to comply. She did so and the phone crashed onto the tiles, the glowing screen going dark.

'Pick it up, Pickford.'

Sebastian complied.

'We're going through to the private bit of the house,' Ralph said, his voice low. 'And Pickford, you'll go ahead of us. Unless you want this nosy parker giving away your secret, of course.' He whispered in Eve's ear. 'Move slowly and carefully. Your friend will think you've gone.'

Sebastian had already dashed back through to the private rooms. There was no way he was going to fight for her. Roscoe had clearly talked him round to his way of thinking, and Sebastian was scared of him too. She could tell by the way he'd shrunk into himself the moment he'd seen the knife.

Eve could hardly walk, her legs were shaking so badly. All the air had gone from her lungs with the shock. Navigating the hall was almost impossible without getting cut by the blade that Roscoe held close.

What if Moira reappeared in time to see what was happening? Eve was terrified Roscoe would do something drastic, rather than risk losing control. But it didn't happen. Before long, Ralph had manoeuvred her through to the private quarters, closed the door and turned a key in the lock before pocketing it.

How long would Sapphire be? Would she go along with this

if she returned home? Eve doubted it, but she'd be in danger too, with two men determined to keep this secret.

'I wasn't sure if it was you or Erica,' Eve said. She'd done her utmost to keep her voice steady, but there was a shake to it.

'As Erica said, we set great store by don't ask, don't tell. She knew we were in trouble. I said I'd handle it.'

'So you've agreed to all this then, Sebastian?' Eve could tell he was terrified at the turn events had taken. As he walked ahead of her his body language said it all. His hands went up over his face, then twisted together as he turned to glance at her and Roscoe, his mouth hanging open. If she could just get him to see that it wasn't too late to pull back...

'I didn't know you'd come into it.' His voice was several degrees shakier than hers. Somehow it increased her confidence slightly. Roscoe seemed to sense it and pulled the knife closer. She felt it nick her skin.

She gasped, her voice jagged when she spoke, 'It's not too late, you know.'

'I'd say it's way too late,' Roscoe said. 'Pickford's already signed paperwork to sell me the manor despite knowing what I've done. If word gets out, he'd face criminal charges. You're going to help me, aren't you, Pickford? We both have skin in the game.'

'The police will trace my mobile. They'll know I disappeared here.'

'The base station will have them looking over a wide area. They won't be in time. If necessary, I think we'll pin your death on Josh Standish. These strong silent types are always volatile. He was trailing around after Cammie like a dog – jealous of me, I'll bet – and from what I hear he had good reason to hate Diana. The police will think you found him out.'

Fear dragged at Eve's insides. His plan might work, especially if Palmer looked into Josh's financial dealings and saw the payments for the plants and the overnight stays in the walled garden. He'd imagine Josh had killed Cammie, Raven and Diana to keep his secret and avoid the sack.

Eve had to keep Roscoe talking. Shock him into dropping his guard. But what could she do against two of them?

'Did you know Cammie intended to kill you in the balloon?' It was still a guess, but she needed ammunition. True or not, it could work.

But Roscoe's tone was calm. 'Yes. The instant I saw the fire I was convinced she'd lured me on board deliberately. She wouldn't have been scared. The method was right up her street. And she didn't react to the streamers. That was unnatural. She was staring at the ground. Watching for the exact moment to jump, I'm sure.' She felt him shake his head, it made the hand holding the knife move slightly. The sharp blade bit again. 'It's ironic really. Her attempts to lure me were pointless. I already knew her secret. But I went along with it anyway, for a laugh. One last adventure before she drank the poison I'd planted. Only it turned out she wanted me dead too.'

'She couldn't take your duplicity.'

'Seems not.'

'I can't believe you've dragged the Pickford family into this. Would it really be so bad if people knew Louisa Lovelace ended up with another man?'

Roscoe laughed suddenly. 'I should have realised you hadn't discovered the whole truth.'

45

In her panic, Eve tried to make sense of Roscoe's words. What
was it she didn't know about Louisa and Seth?

'It's far more scandalous than you realise,' Roscoe went on.
'Louisa Lovelace ended up with Seth's half-brother, Edwin.
And Seth didn't head off into the night to lick his wounds. They
killed him, using that rather attractive letter opener Cammie
found in the moat. I've always thought those things look lethal.
In case you're wondering, I do have proof.'

Of course, Eve and Robin had always wondered if the killer
had taken something extra from Lavender Cottage. 'What kind
of proof?'

'A diary of Louisa's, where she confessed how Edwin did
the deed. It was written near the end of her life, after he was
dead, and I guess the guilt was getting to her. She was weak as
well as duplicitous.

'It had been buried deep for years, in amongst boxes and
boxes of paperwork: decades of household bills, tax returns and
bank statements. Stuff that looked like nothing. Cammie was
clearly the first person to bother trawling through it all. I was

already on my guard by that point. I was with her when she noticed the discrepancy between the pictures. She acted casual, of course, but I knew her too well. I went back later and saw what she'd seen. After that, I kept close tabs on her. She pinched the diary from the archive material. I knew it was important when I saw her reading it here at the manor. She had no idea I was watching from the doorway. I managed to sneak a look for myself when she went for a break. The contents were ruinous for me, but I couldn't take it without her noticing. It had to wait until she was dead.'

'So that's why you didn't steal it when you planted the poison.'

'If I'd known she'd die on Sunday I could have gone ahead, but I thought she'd be back that evening and she'd guess I'd got it. I'd been in and out of her cottage and I'd been pushing for information on her research. But I did my groundwork then: spotted where she'd put it, in amongst all those books at her rental cottage. I didn't think the police would find it. It would be safe enough to pick it up later.'

'You sent Erica to steal it.' She'd worn her hair up when Eve visited. Maybe she'd let it down to change her appearance and help hide her face if she was spotted.

'We thought it would be best to mix it up a bit. I took care of the killings. But it wasn't just the diary we wanted. After the news of the loving cup broke, I was worried Cammie might have found other evidence. And so it proved. She had the murder weapon too.'

He sounded satisfied with their success. Eve's legs felt like jelly and hope drained out of her. There was no way she could talk Sebastian round; the secret was far too damaging for him to give it up.

She tried to steady her voice. 'What are you going to do? It won't work to kill me here. My blood will be everywhere.' She hated hearing her voice quake and she knew he'd have a neater plan. He'd brought the knife for Sebastian, to threaten him in case he stood his ground, but he wouldn't have used it to kill him either.

'You're going to have a drink, just like that cleaner did in Lavender Cottage. Then we'll put you in a cupboard until it's safe to move you. If the police come, Pickford and I can say you left and walked towards Josh's place. We'll bury your body on the land he tends. That might be best.'

Eve's throat was so dry. If she drank the poison, it would be too late. No antidote. No saving her. She had to take a risk – anything to avoid that fate.

They'd entered Diana's old study now and Roscoe steered her towards a briefcase he'd left next to a chair. 'Just as well I brought the poison with me in case Sebastian failed to see sense. I couldn't leave him alive to talk. We're going to crouch down now and you're going to get the bottle out. Then we're going to stand up slowly.'

The study was a north-facing room, panelled and dark, despite the May sunshine outside. Sebastian had left an Anglepoise desk lamp switched on and Eve could see Roscoe's reflection in the room's window ahead of her. She watched him as they descended into a crouch. He was so much taller than her. He'd be stronger. Sebastian stood further back as though distancing himself from proceedings, but he wouldn't intervene now.

How could Eve know when to act? When was her best chance? Roscoe wouldn't want her blood everywhere but Eve guessed he'd use the blade in an instant if it was the last resort. Eve would only get one chance. What if she simply refused to drink? But the results would be unpredictable. He might knock her out and pour the poison down her throat. He was bound to have thought it through; he'd have been prepared to tackle Sebastian in the same way.

As Eve reached for the sturdy plastic bottle her head felt

hot, her core chilled, her mind in turmoil. Would she get a better chance once they stood up again? But if Roscoe got her to drink straight from the bottle she might only have seconds left. He might not even let her stand up...

46

Eve didn't dare pause, even for a second. The timing was critical. She held her breath and swung the bottle up, focusing on Roscoe's eyes reflected in the window, ramming the bottle into her captor's face with all her might. Roscoe's hand jerked and the knife's blade grazed her, but she struck again, and the weapon fell to the floor.

Eve kicked it away, under a cabinet. Keeping hold of the bottle, she swung it round at Roscoe as she dashed towards the door. Thank goodness she'd taken him and Sebastian by surprise. It was only that which had saved her. She'd seen Sebastian start but shock made him slow to react. For a moment, Eve turned the way they'd come, then remembered the locked door, the key inside Roscoe's pocket. She swerved to change course, losing precious time.

Roscoe was on her heels and Eve's route to the bridge over the moat was cut off. She ploughed in the opposite direction instead, dashing through shady rooms with shafts of sunlight drifting through the windows, her breathing ragged. She could hear Roscoe close behind her, and a second set of pounding footfalls. Sebastian had picked up speed.

Something smashed behind her. One of them must have knocked an ornament off a side table. Roscoe, she thought. He must have been off balance, at least for a moment. He'd have blocked Sebastian's way. It might give Eve a crucial split second.

She could see the French windows leading out onto Diana's rose garden. Eve wasn't sure of her next move, but getting outside was imperative. She chucked the poison she still held to one side, lobbing it away from Roscoe's reach, then yanked a brass-bottomed lamp from its socket as she moved towards the windows, smashing at them as she went. The force broke the glass and pushed the floor-length windows outwards, the lock disengaging. Eve burst through to the open air, her lungs burning.

'Go round!' Roscoe was yelling.

Eve dashed around the screen that had given Diana privacy. There was no escape from Roscoe except via the water. If Sebastian managed to cut her off, she'd be sunk. Literally. It looked a long way down and the bank was steep but there was no choice. Eve jumped and felt the shock of the cold. She was gasping, and swallowing water. She went under and saw bubbles above her head. Water filled her nostrils, its chill catching her throat. She was choking, coughing. But the sight of the sun above brought her to her senses. She had to hang on. With all the effort she could muster she propelled herself towards the surface, spitting out water as she made it into the air.

Behind her she could hear Roscoe churning the moat's surface. He couldn't be any more used to the sudden cold than she was. Eve had to be the one that recovered first. She tried to remember front crawl. It ought to be automatic, but nothing was now. Her brain felt numb, just like her entire body.

She made it to the other side of the water, but Roscoe was perilously close. Eve felt the touch of his hand on her foot, then an attempt to grasp her ankle.

And how long would it be before Sebastian appeared? His heart hadn't been in it when Roscoe put a knife to her throat, but it was different now. Eve was a huge threat to him if she got free. Roscoe had locked the door to the hall, which might slow him down, but there would be a spare key. He and Diana must have had one each.

She kicked for all she was worth and grabbed handfuls of grass on the opposite bank, trying to get a purchase to haul herself out. It was so slippery. In desperation, Eve pulled her keys from her pocket and jabbed them into the bank. It gave her just enough purchase to get one foot onto the grass.

She pushed on up the slope with as much force as she could muster, dragging her other leg up behind her and flinging herself onto level ground. She was up in seconds, and running, but in a heartbeat came the crunch of Roscoe's footfalls, thudding after her. He'd made it out of the water too. And he was taller, his legs longer. Eve ran towards the front of the house, but she knew Roscoe would be on her in another minute. Out of the corner of her eye she saw Sebastian. He was hanging back, glad to let Roscoe get on with it.

Eve needed to find another way...

It was at that point that she spotted the manor's greenhouse. She switched direction and headed for it, flinging the door open and hurling herself inside. Grabbing one of the terracotta pots, she flung it behind her at Roscoe. It caught him on the arm, yet still he kept coming.

It was the next one which brought him down.

And a moment later, Eve saw Josh Standish approaching – looking from fallen Roscoe to motionless Sebastian. And in the background was Sapphire, getting out of her car.

47

The day after her narrow escape, Eve was baking scones at Monty's while Viv prepared some shortcakes with elderflower cream. Viv had wanted her to take the day off, but Eve was keen to keep busy. It was the quickest way to get back to normal. She'd told Viv exactly what had happened until the point when she'd knocked Roscoe to the ground.

'I'd say you could have saved yourself, even if Josh and Sapphire hadn't turned up,' Viv said as she sifted flour. 'It's almost a shame they stole your thunder.'

Eve put a hand to the scratches on her neck from the blade of Roscoe's knife. 'Thanks, but I'm happy to share the glory.' It hadn't taken Roscoe long to stagger to his feet, and even if she'd hit him again, she'd have had to bring Sebastian down too.

'So, what happened next?'

'Josh pushed Roscoe back to the floor while he was still groggy, and Sapphire rushed over to Sebastian. Then Josh chucked me his phone and I dialled 999.'

'Sebastian didn't try anything?'

Eve shook her head. 'He could tell the game was up. In any case, he was following Roscoe's lead. I could see how scared he was. He needed someone else to do his dirty work for him.' It was just as Heaven Jones had said.

'And you really think Cammie set out to kill Roscoe, just as he was planning to kill her?'

Eve nodded. 'His determination to protect his money-making plan sent her over the edge. She must have found out he was married and using her all along. He only got close to her because her research could affect his and Erica's investment and he was ready to kill to protect his interests. Nothing whatever can excuse what she tried to do, but she must have been devastated. And maybe she was on to him too.'

'How do you mean?'

'I wonder how much she knew about Erica, and about Roscoe's duplicity. If she realised they were buying the manor and that Roscoe had guessed her discovery, she might have reasoned he planned to kill her. Their development was in tatters unless they shut her up, yet they were still hanging around. Perhaps she decided she'd get in first.' She shook her head. 'Raven kept saying she and Cammie had a lot in common, and after a while I could see it. I should have realised it might make Cammie strike out.'

'How much do you think Roscoe knew?'

'Everything, by the sound of it. He admits he stuck to Cammie like glue once he realised Louisa had lived her life with two different men. That was bad enough, but the question of what happened to Seth had him exercised. Rightly, as it turns out.'

Viv shuddered. 'So the letter opener was the murder weapon. And what about the loving cup?'

'I presume Louisa took out her anger on it when she and Seth fell out, or it might have been Edwin, out of jealousy. I was always puzzled as to how it had become so battered. They must have chucked it in the moat, just like the letter opener, in case anyone spotted it and wondered who'd damaged it and why.'

Viv sighed. 'It's all so horrible. I really think you should sit down and have a cake.'

Eve had seen Robin soon after the police had interviewed her, the day of the stand-off with Roscoe, but it was Thursday evening before he was able to give her a full update on the case. She was sitting opposite him at his kitchen table on Dark Lane, with Gus at her feet, and a glass of chilled Pinot Grigio in front of her. Robin had laid on food too: the most delicious pasta dish she'd ever tasted, with sticky roasted tomatoes, garlic, parmesan and anchovies.

He reached to take her hand for a moment. 'You were right. They found traces of battery acid by the scorch marks on Cammie's paving.'

She'd been sure it was coming but sorrow still clutched at her insides. For it to have come to that...

'I'm sorry.'

She nodded. 'What news on the investigation into Roscoe?'

'The scientific support team found an ancient bottle of antifreeze in the garage at his rented cottage. It had been opened recently. Ironically, he'd rested it on a newspaper to avoid leaving fresh traces and giving himself away. The paper was dated the week before Cammie was killed, so he'd clearly been at it since then. The lab's matched it to the poison in the smoothie.'

Eve shivered. 'Has he confessed?'

'He's going no comment, but it's pointless. As well as the antifreeze, he kept Louisa Pickford's diary to use against Sebastian in case he ever crossed him. The evidence is stacking up. And when he decided to coerce Sebastian, he told him everything to drive home his advantage.'

'And Sebastian's talking?'

Robin's eyes met hers. 'They can hardly shut him up. He's

hoping he'll get off more lightly for cooperating. What's more, the team found the contract he'd signed for the sale of the manor. Roscoe would have got it for two hundred and fifty thousand.'

'Wow.'

'Whereas the previous paperwork – which the police found in Roscoe's cottage – named three million. Looking at the plans he and Erica had drawn up, they were expecting to convert the place into six apartments, selling for over two million each, on the back of the Lovelace legend. They stood to make a tidy profit.'

'And would they have spent it all on champagne, or were they in trouble?'

He topped up her wine as she took another mouthful of pasta. 'Deep, deep trouble. They've been using money from their investors to plug all sorts of holes and pay off other funders. It's fraud on a massive scale. You were right about their London house. It's let. They managed to hang on to his car to keep up appearances, but hers went back. The profits on Lovelace would have been enough to buy them more time, but I doubt they'd have escaped justice for long.'

It was horrific. Four people dead as a result of their greed. Eve thought through the implications. 'I guess their straitened circumstances explain the quality of cocaine they planted.'

'Could be. Its use is rife in the circles they mix in, from what I hear, but the price would definitely be a problem.'

'He must have thought it was worth it. It did what he wanted – got the press talking about Cammie and her celebrity lifestyle, rather than Lovelace. If he wanted to sell those apart-ments, he needed to do everything he could to preserve the manor's magical reputation.' She sighed. 'The more I think about it, the more I wonder if Raven was part of his carefully orchestrated plan too. Not just to take the rap for the murders, but to direct attention away from Lovelace again. She was such a colourful character, and her secret background was a gift for Roscoe. Before we could blink, the papers were down in Essex, pestering her parents. Her identity became the story, not Lovelace. I'll bet he knew. He'd wormed his way back into Cammie's affections; she probably told him. I think she was livid with Raven for hoodwinking Peter Pickford-Jones. I know her relationship with him was wholly wrong, but I'm sure she loved him.'

'You're probably right. And it's true, Roscoe was aware of Raven's real identity and her history with Cammie. He told Sebastian all about it, apparently, when he was explaining why he'd killed her. I guess he wanted Sebastian to know he'd stop at nothing.'

Eve shuddered. 'He certainly looked terrified when Roscoe decided he'd have to kill me.' The memories made Eve's chest feel tight. 'What about Erica?'

'She's up to her neck in it. Burgling Lavender Cottage, providing Roscoe with a false alibi, you name it, plus the financial fraud of course. They'll both go down for a long time.'

'That's something.'

'And Sebastian will be locked up too, for opting to cover up the murders rather than lose face and risk his modelling career.' His voice was barely controlled. 'And for not raising the alarm when Roscoe tried to kill you. He'll get years.'

Eve raised an eyebrow. 'I won't bother visiting.'

Robin's shoulders relaxed a fraction, and he gave a flicker of a smile.

'I wish I'd guessed about Seth Pickford's murder before Ralph let on, but what about my other hunches?'

He grinned now. 'Alarmingly accurate. Roscoe told Sebastian that Diana had turned down his offer to buy Lovelace at a reduced price in exchange for keeping quiet about Louisa and Edwin's crime. There was no pussyfooting around when it came to Sebastian. Roscoe wanted him to know what would happen if he repeated Diana's mistake. According to Sebastian, he told Diana he'd discovered the truth about Seth Pickford after Cammie's death. He implied Sebastian had killed her, and taunted her with that. But sooner or later, she'd probably have worked out Roscoe was guilty.'

'So he intercepted Diana and Raven and killed them both?'

Robin nodded. 'Sebastian says Diana took the call from Raven while Roscoe was there, so he knew where they'd be. Raven was killed as a scapegoat. Roscoe was livid she'd been found so quickly. He told Sebastian it left him in no mood to muck around. He threatened to kill him and frame him for the murders if he put up a fight.'

That would have had Sebastian eating out of his hand.

'Is there anything more on the murder of Seth Pickford?' Eve thought of his cheeky face in Louisa's drawings. It was so sad.

'Here. I've got a photograph of Louisa's diary confession.' He handed her his phone and she zoomed in on the tiny writing.

Reading the entry only made her feel worse. Louisa and Seth's relationship had gone downhill almost as soon as they'd left the manor. Beforehand they'd been swept along on hopes and dreams. After, they were hit with reality. Louisa said Seth had suddenly seemed like the source of all her hardships, and Edwin had been dashing, leading the way, keeping them from harm. Stealing when he needed to. Eve swallowed. 'It was Louisa and Edwin who returned to the manor, living as husband and wife. The villagers and servants never realised there'd been a switch. Seth and Edwin were very alike anyway, and it was a long time since anyone had seen them.

'Seth was left out in the cold – literally. Edwin didn't just walk off with his lover, he stole the roof from over his head. The manor had been gifted to Seth and Louisa, so he had a claim.

He was jealous and angry and one night he turned up, threatening to tell everyone what had happened.

'Louisa claims he and Edwin got into a row and Edwin snatched up the letter opener.' She shook her head. 'She clearly wanted to believe he'd killed his brother in the heat of the moment.' But deep down, Eve wondered. Edwin and Louisa had had a lot at stake. 'It's clear from this entry that she felt guilty, but she loved Edwin despite what he'd done. She helped him cover it up.'

No one would ever view her in the same way again.

She handed the phone back to Robin. 'I've got updates too, but mine are less dramatic. Moira says she's spoken to Irene' – no surprises there – 'and Sebastian's going ahead with the sale of the manor. I guess he'll want to make a fresh start when he comes out of jail. But now the news about Louisa Lovelace and Seth Pickford is out, the value's gone right down.'

Robin nodded. 'I'm not surprised.'

'Despite all that, the villagers want to buy the place.' She was impressed by their loyalty. 'The lower asking price means they're in with a chance of managing it too. They'll run it as a cooperative. Irene's putting in a lot, apparently, and Josh Standish is using some of his savings too. Irene's got Sapphire applying for grants. She's never been happy at Millingford Hall. If they manage the purchase, Irene wants her to take over as custodian. They'll give visitors its history, warts and all. And although the manor's murky past made it a bad investment as property, it'll draw in the crowds as a visitor attraction.'

Eve thought of Sapphire. She'd been in to visit, shaking and crying. It would take time to get over what Sebastian had done but running the manor would be an excellent focus. By the time she'd left, she'd been talking haltingly about her plans.

'Speaking of exhibits,' Robin said, 'Erica was the visitor who suggested Sapphire should move the photos and sketches of

Seth. Sapphire identified her. It's another indication that Erica was fully involved.'

He paused a moment. 'Eve, there's something I've got to say. It's been eating me up and I can't risk letting another day go by when life's so uncertain.' He paused and looked down for a moment but then his eyes met hers. 'I love you. You do know that, don't you?'

Eve felt tears prick her eyes and blinked them away. 'The feeling's mutual.'

As she leaned forwards, Gus shifted at her feet. A moment later he appeared and looked up at them, from one to the other. 'Don't worry, little mate,' Robin said, looking down. 'I love you too. Just not in quite the same way.'

Robin's declaration left Eve with a warm glow. Each time she thought of it, happy excitement bubbled inside her. It gave her the strength to draft her introduction to Cammie's obituary the following day.

It was the hardest piece she'd ever had to write, because of what she knew, and what would come out. The inquest into her death would colour everyone's thoughts.

Camilla Emily Harrington – historian and adventurer

Camilla (Cammie) Harrington, the charismatic TV historian, died in Suffolk at the age of thirty-six. Since her death, a man has been arrested on multiple charges, including an attempt on her life by poisoning.

Cammie's on-screen persona was known to millions. She was the effervescent presenter of many documentaries and renowned for her love of extreme sports, from skydiving to duelling and unorthodox climbing exploits. But behind her gregarious nature, she was troubled. Born to a hugely successful businesswoman and a famous racing driver, she spent little time with her parents growing up and seems almost to have been an afterthought.

Perhaps it was in Cammie's nature to pursue extreme activities, following in her father's footsteps. He died doing the sport he loved. But it seems she used them to blot out painful feelings, too. After a difficult break up with a boyfriend at university, she rushed to get herself onto a caving trip. By the time she returned, she behaved as though nothing had happened.

Cammie suffered one loss after another: first the university boyfriend who left her, then her father whom she adored, despite the distance between them. After that came the death of Peter Pickford-Jones, a man who'd welcomed her as a guest at Lovelace Manor five years ago, and finally she was disappointed in love once again, cruelly deceived by her university ex for a second time.

It's against this background that her actions must be viewed.

But although Cammie suffered, she had friends she held dear for life. She remained in regular contact with fellow history student, Phoebe Richmond, up until the last. She also looked out for others, rushing in if she felt an acquaintance was being badly treated.

To the end, Cammie was brave and entertaining, and loved by her viewers. The fact that she was deeply hurt can't be denied. When people draw conclusions about her final days, they will hopefully see the tragedy, not just the horror.

Eve sighed and blew her nose. She had to be cryptic at this stage, but some kind of context was right.

Gus spotted her mood and came to rest his head against her leg.

'Walk, do you think?' she said to him, and he rushed towards the door.

A LETTER FROM CLARE

Thank you so much for reading *Mystery at Lovelace Manor*. I do hope you had fun following the clues! If you'd like to keep up to date with all my latest releases, you can sign up at the following link. Your email address will never be shared, and you can unsubscribe at any time.

www.bookouture.com/clare-chase

The idea for this book came when I was browsing a website focused on unusual histories associated with stately homes. It turns out there are plenty of grand houses with scandals attached! I decided to come up with a history for my fictional setting, Lovelace Manor, and the story evolved from there.

If you have time, I'd love it if you were able to write a review of *Mystery at Lovelace Manor*. Feedback is really valuable, and it also makes a huge difference in helping new readers discover my books for the first time. Alternatively, if you'd like to contact me personally, you can reach me via my website, Facebook page, Twitter or Instagram. It's always great to hear from readers.

Again, thank you so much for deciding to spend some time reading *Mystery at Lovelace Manor*. I'm looking forward to sharing my next book with you very soon.

With all best wishes,
Clare x

KEEP IN TOUCH WITH CLARE

www.clarechase.com

facebook.com/ClareChaseAuthor

twitter.com/ClareChase_

instagram.com/clarechaseauthor

ACKNOWLEDGEMENTS

Much love and thanks as always to Charlie, George and Ros for the useful feedback on random ideas and the cheerleading! Love and thanks also to Mum and Dad, Phil and Jenny, David and Pat, Warty, Andrea, Jen, the Westfield gang, Margaret, Shelly, Mark, my Andrewes relations and a whole bunch of family and friends.

And as ever, importantly, I'm hugely grateful to my fantastic editor Ruth Tross for her brilliant and inspiring input. I'm also indebted to Noelle Holten for her amazing promo work and to Alex Holmes, Fraser Crichton and Liz Hatherell for their expert input. Sending thanks too to Tash Webber for her wonderful cover designs, as well as to Peta Nightingale, Kim Nash and everyone involved in editing, book production and sales at Bookouture. It's a privilege to be published and promoted by such a skilled and friendly team.

Thanks also to the wonderful Bookouture authors and other writers for their friendship and support. And a huge thank you to the hard-working and generous book bloggers and reviewers who take the time to pass on their thoughts about my work. I realise it's a massive job. I really do appreciate it.

And finally, but importantly, thanks to you, the reader, for buying or borrowing this book!

Manufactured by Amazon.ca
Bolton, ON

32138675R00173